CW01430620

THE DIGITAL APOCALYPSE

The Digital Apocalypse

David Groves

The Publisher's Apprentice
An imprint of Connor Court Publishing

Published in 2015 by Connor Court Publishing Pty Ltd

Copyright © David Groves 2015

ALL RIGHTS RESERVED. This book contains material protected under International
and Federal Copyright Laws and Treaties. Any unauthorised reprint or use of this material is prohibited. No part of this book may be reproduced or transmitted in any form or
by any means, electronic or mechanical, including photocopying, recording, or by any
information storage and retrieval system without express written permission from the
publisher.

Connor Court Publishing Pty Ltd
PO Box 224W
Ballarat VIC 3350
sales@connorcourt.com
www.connorcourt.com

ISBN: 978-1-925138-50-4 (pbk.)

This is a work of fiction. Names, characters, businesses, places, events and incidents
are either the products of the author's imagination or used in a fictitious manner. Any
resemblance to actual persons, living or dead, or actual events is purely coincidental.

Cover design by Maria Giordano,

Front Cover Photo: Colorful Aurora Borealis, Iceland, Taken from istockphoto, used
with permission.

Printed in Australia

Acknowledgements

The plot for *The Digital Apocalypse* was conceived after reading *Heaven and Earth* written by Ian Plimer and through discussions with Iain Groves and John Dunlop. I am indebted to my creative wife, Suzanne, for her typing, editing, extreme patience and 'humanising' the characters that I created. Without her assistance and encouragement, the book would not have been completed.

1

Bloody Hell, muttered Winston Frobisher to himself. My intuition was that there'd be a major crisis, but nothing like this. Unshaven and dishevelled, he emerged from his cellar in Hollingbury Cottage in the late afternoon and pulled back a curtain in the main living room. He looked out on a tranquil but eerie scene with no visible signs of activity: no villagers going about their business in St Mary's, no tourists out for a stroll, no boat sailing in the grey, choppy harbour, no fluffy white jet-streams of planes that normally filled the skies above the Isles of Scilly as they departed and returned to mainland England. It was if the world had paused or stopped altogether. Only the shrill, but somewhat plaintive, cries of the ubiquitous gulls piercing the otherwise quiet of the shoreline provided a sense of normality.

He thought back to his honeymoon so long ago, before they'd bought the cottage, when he and Laura had decided that the Scilly Isles would make a perfect safe haven, 'come the holocaust', as Laura had laughingly termed his weird predictions. Shaking his head at the thought of Laura, her beautiful blue eyes and wonderful warm smile, his eyes welled up as he tried to get a grip on his emotions.

He thought of life's stairway steadily climbing upwards punctuated by twists and turns, and choices of direction that could change one's destiny in a heartbeat. It could be compared to Nature, he thought: periods of calm suddenly disrupted by natural disasters, totally unexpected, just as no-one had predicted the events leading to his personal dilemma and certainly that of millions, even billions, of people like him throughout the world.

St Mary's normally had power delivered by underground cable from that connected to the UK national grid, but there had been no electricity since late morning. The ferry from Penzance was still in the harbour. The situation was unclear. Due to his sense of foreboding about world events more than a decade ago and his recent premonition of a crisis, Winston had a large emergency stock of firewood and canned food. He had installed a small generator when he and Laura first had the cottage and kept a drum or two of petrol to run it from time to time, but he decided to preserve these emergency supplies as long as possible.

After a snack of a sandwich and coffee brewed on an old primus he and Laura had bought years ago, he decided to go to bed to keep warm and conserve energy. A few minutes later his book slipped from his fingers and he fell into a fitful sleep, disturbed by his thoughts as he subconsciously relived the events that had brought him to this place on Tuesday 8th August 2017, a date that would go down in history. He dreamt of the good times of his relationship with Laura, his inner consciousness dreading to move forward to the times when everything had gone off the rails. Luckily, he had a long night to recollect the previous four decades of his life.

2

Winston was born in East Sussex Hospital on Eastern Road, close to the beachfront of Brighton, in 1978. His father, Neil Frobisher, was a business lawyer with an office just off Dyke Road, while his mother, Lavinia, was an English teacher at the prestigious Roedean School for girls close to their home at Telscombe Cliffs, an extension of Peacehaven to the west. They were consummate, rather fastidious professionals who had never intended to have children. But uncharacteristically, on an overnight stay in London for what turned out to be a particularly boozy party, Lavinia realising she had forgotten to pack her contraceptive pills threw all caution to the wind, resulting in pregnancy. As a fairly moral person she refused to consider abortion and so Winston was born, destined to become the only child in an academic professional environment.

The name Winston had been chosen because of Neil Frobisher's preoccupation with history, with his most treasured possession being a complete set of first edition *A History of the English-Speaking Peoples* by Winston Churchill with Churchill's signature on Book 1 *The Birth of Britain*. He had been reminded of this with its publication in magazine format in the early 1970s and its dramatisation as a series of plays in 1974 and 1975 close to the time of his child's birth, and hence the name Winston.

Britain is a treasure trove for archaeological finds, and Brighton has an incredibly long history of human occupation. So, it was no surprise that Neil joined the Brighton and Hove Archaeological Society to participate in their lectures and field excursions, something that would shape Winston's future interests and career path. Neil had marvelled at the evidence for early humans who hunted mammoths in the earliest Stone Age, some 200,000 years ago, preserved in an ancient shoreline carved into the famous chalk cliffs at Black Rock, near Brighton Marina. The group had also hiked up to the downs near Brighton Racecourse to view a late Stone Age enclosure of mounds and ditches dating back to 3500 BC, nearly 1000 years before the birth of the pyramids in Egypt, and visited similar sites near the Goldstone Soccer ground, the original home of Brighton and Hove Albion.

He also played golf on the downs at the Hollingbury Golf Course, the site of the spectacular Hollingbury Camp, originally a Celtic Iron Age encampment with massive circular earthworks, one of several hill-forts in east Sussex. The Romans had also left their mark, building a villa at Brighton in the 1st or 2nd century AD that was linked by road to the now charming village of Hassocks, formerly a Roman industrial centre, where Neil liked to have his Sunday lunch at the Friar's Oak. Following withdrawal of the Romans in the early 5th century, the Saxons settled in Brighton, with six burial sites discovered at the Seven Dials not far from Neil's office.

Through his field excursions, Neil learned that the first major settlement at Bristelmestune was after the Norman Conquest in 1066, with several grand mediaeval churches or portions of churches still surviving. He had been married in one of these, St Peters Church, near the town centre. He had made a point of visiting the oldest two elm trees in the world in the Preston Manor grounds, thought to be 870 years old, and marvelled at the fact that they had probably been planted in the reign of Henry II.

He had learned that this period of grandeur had lapsed as the settlement, now Brighthelmstone, became a fishing village. Its popularity only increased as interest was aroused in the medical benefits of seawater, including bathing. On his way to work, Neil passed many of the historic Georgian and Regency buildings that still survived from this growth period, particularly around the Steine, the most famous being the Royal Pavilion built by the Prince of Wales, later King George IV. The royal patronage drew many famous and stylish people to the town, now known as Brighton, which maintained its fashionable reputation until cheap travel drew Britons to holiday in warmer climes with sand, rather than pebble, beaches. Neil, as a resident, saw this as an advantage. He considered that the streets were busy enough without the hundreds of coaches and thousands of milling tourists that marred the pleasures of other historic locations around the world.

Once Winston was born, Neil planned how he would revisit some of his own excursions with his son and show him how the long history of Brighton had shaped its present status and culture. He also looked forward to excursions to other historic locations with castles, windmills and quaint museums along the southern downs of Sussex and Kent. The seeds of social history, so important in Winston's adult life, would be sown.

3

Once Winston was born, Neil and Lavinia resumed their normal busy professional lives in which there was little time for child minding. So, they hired a housewife with three older children of her own, who lived in an adjacent street, to look after Winston during the day and when they had meetings. Maureen Stuart effectively became Winston's Nanny. This arrangement suited both families and the company of other children gave Winston a good early start. Although Maureen's family included Winston in their everyday family life, he missed out on his own parents' attention, particularly his mother's.

When it was time for Winston to start school, it was decided that he should attend Telscombe Cliffs Primary School as Maureen's two daughters went there and it was within walking distance of their home. He had inherited a high IQ from his parents and excelled at his studies, although he was less adept at sport. Maureen's older son sometimes kicked a ball with him, but he was involved at high school and had sport practice and homework to do. Winston had never seen either of his parents take an interest in sport apart from his father's golf. During the early primary years, as Winston became a more interesting little person, Neil Frobisher regularly took him on historical rambles around Brighton on weekends, teaching him the rich history of the town. On other weekends, they went to the beach or to the Palace Pier for treats like candy floss, ice creams and Brighton rock. Lavinia sometimes joined them but, being an English teacher, was marking assignments on many weekends. These were happy days for the family, with Winston showing his academic talents and sharing his father's interests.

As Winston progressed through primary school, his superior academic prowess became more evident both to the staff and other children. His teachers increasingly asked questions that only he could answer. He was also chosen to read passages from the Bible or to make speeches when dignitaries visited the school, as his mother had taught him to speak with Roedean-style near-perfect diction. This caused jealousies to develop which resulted in bullying. His classmates started calling him 'Winnie' when they learned that Winston Churchill's name at home was Winnie. This evolved into 'The Pooh' after Winnie the Pooh and then Horse, Donkey or Ass after the whinnying sound made by saying the name Winnie. However hard he tried, he couldn't escape the bullying which escalated after Maureen's daughters left for high school, as they had tried to protect him from the worst bullies. Even when he tried to play soccer, the other boys ignored him and he was always last to be chosen for team games unless a teacher intervened. His father, who had himself been bullied at school because of his superior intellect, simply told him it would make a man of him.

So Winston spent the latter two years of primary school excelling at his studies but becoming more of a social outcast with increasingly obsessive behaviour as a consequence. He couldn't wait for weekends to go on excursions with his father, when his intelligence was appreciated and he could discuss more scholarly issues.

It was on one of these weekend excursions that Winston had his first experience of love and sex. He and his father had climbed up the earthwork rampart of Hollingbury Camp on a balmy summer afternoon and had commenced a walk around the perimeter, Neil explaining what a great site this was for a fort with its commanding views. On the inner side of the rampart there was a shallow grassy depression, only partly hidden from view by gorse bushes, with a completely naked man and woman lying on a coloured square-patterned travelling rug with their clothes piled up on its edge. The man was sprawled on top of the woman, heaving his body, and she was squealing: like a piglet he had seen on a farm visit, thought Winston, with a feeling of disgust. Neil quickly dragged him away to avoid embarrassing the couple.

"What were they doing?" asked Winston innocently while Neil thought desperately what to say.

"They are in love," he said finally "and want to have a baby."

"Is that how I was born?" asked Winston shocked.

"Not exactly like that, but yes that's how babies are started" said Neil. If that's love, I don't want anything to do with it thought Winston. He later considered that it was a critical point in his future views on love and sex.

When it was time to go to high school, Winston pleaded with his father not to send him as a boarder at Brighton College in Kemp Town. As Neil had gone to Varndean Grammar School, now Varndean High School and Sixth Form College, it was decided that Winston would study there with extra tuition from Lavinia in advanced English. Neil could drop him off on his way to the office, only a short deviation, and he could study in the library until Neil picked him up or he could catch buses to Telscombe Cliffs. Some days he simply walked the three kilometres to the town, visiting landmark buildings, walking through the Lanes, or wandering around Palace Pier. He was not bullied to the same extent as at primary school but still led a rather lonely, independent life with only a few inadequate friendships with others of his ilk. Neil recognised this and tried to make up for it with visits to Bramber Castle, the east Sussex windmills, and even as far afield as the medieval castles at Arundel, Hastings and the Cinq Ports. What Winston lacked in social experiences, he made up for with extended knowledge of the history of the British people, at least from a southern England perspective.

4

In 1996, Winston completed his A-levels with High Distinction, having by far the highest aggregate score at Varndean Sixth Form College. He received offers from several universities but decided to follow his father, the greatest influence in his life, into Cambridge University, where he gained entry to King's, his father's old college. An added attraction for Cambridge was the presence of Professor Rosamund McKitterick, who was rapidly becoming a world authority on ancient and medieval history after graduating with Honours from the University of Western Australia.

Predictably, Winston thrived in the academic environment, gaining High Distinctions throughout his BA and Honours studies in the Department of History, and later being awarded a postgraduate scholarship and completing his PhD in 2004 on *Social Change Induced by European Wars from the 11th to 19th Centuries in Britain*. While his academic life thrived, his social life was slow to take off. He was a solid, studious and serious young man in a new world where young women admired celebrities and sportsmen, and where muscles and tight abs were often more respected than brains. He failed to see why otherwise intelligent women liked men who were slaves to the fashion of the day, increasingly with stubbled chins, droopy jeans and baseball caps, with tattoos and body piercing becoming increasingly popular. We are taking on the worst of American culture, even in the elite University town of Cambridge, he thought to himself.

Winston was tall and quite good looking in a classic sort of way. He kept his dark hair cut short and parted and usually wore jeans with a sweater over a shirt, and always leather lace-up shoes. He was slightly short sighted and had tried contact lenses but preferred to wear glasses, not realising how they enhanced his attractive brown eyes and hesitant smile. He was kind, thoughtful and a good listener, qualities that women would have looked for in a partner at the time he was born but not so much at the turn of the century. He mixed with his fellow students on campus and, predictably, his was the shoulder that the girls would cry on when relationships went sour. He had listened to many sad stories of exploitation and seen the trauma that broken relationships could bring them, their friends and families.

He remembered one incident most vividly. Home on a weekend,

with his parents out at a function, he was having an ale and watching the late news on TV before going to bed. The newsreader was interrupted by a caption saying 'Breaking News', and the scene panned to a young woman standing on a cliff edge with her right hand held upright in a 'halt' gesture. Twenty metres away were a group of police, one of whom appeared to be speaking to her. It looked like Beachy Head, he thought and the girl looked familiar. Before he could hear what the situation that was unfolding was about, the phone rang.

"Winston Frobisher," he said as he anticipated the call would be for one of his parents.

"Sergeant Grover, Brighton Police here, sir," rasped a voice at the other end. "We have an incident at Beachy Head and a distressed young lady called Angela Langton says she will only speak to you. Are you her boyfriend or partner, sir?"

"No," Winston replied hurriedly, "she's just a friend I've known since school, but I do know she's in a really volatile relationship with some guy, which this may be about."

"A police car is on its way to you now," said the Sergeant, checking Winston's address. "Please respond and speak to her. Every time our negotiator moves towards her, she threatens to jump."

"Of course I'll help if I can, although I'm unsure of why she called me or what I can do to help." Winston answered as he grabbed his coat from the stand.

The police car arrived within minutes, and with siren blaring they reached Beachy Head in record time. Winston was relieved to see that Angela was still there. The negotiator approached him, introduced himself as Malcolm and asked, "Have you ever been in a situation like this before?"

"Of course not, this is stuff you see in TV dramas, not real life."

"Well it's highly irregular for us to use members of the public in this way, but we're at a total impasse here. Please approach slowly, speak reassuringly and try to seize on anything positive that you sense might distract her."

Winston followed orders and walked slowly towards the girl.
When he was a few metres away, she held up both hands to signal
him to stop.

"I'm sorry to do this to you," she said softly, tears streaming down
her cheeks, "but I've only ever confided in you about Kurt and so
only you can bear witness to what I have to do. He's abused my love.
He's hurt me physically and mentally, he's been unfaithful to me, and
I should hate him but I still love him. I'm torn apart. There's nowhere
left to go. I know my girlfriends confide in you," she sobbed. "Tell
them about this, warn them to choose more wisely than me. When
my Mum and Dad get back from France tell them that I love them
and don't want to hurt them, but all I see is a black world full of
despair."

"It doesn't have to be like that," said Winston in what he hoped
was a soothing tone. "You're an attractive and intelligent woman that
any man could love. Give yourself time and think of the better future
you deserve. Things'll look better in the light of day. Let me come
and get you."

"Have you ever been in love Winston?" she cried out hysterically.
"How can you know what it can do to you?" She put her arms out
towards him, and he saw a glimmer of hope. "I'm sorry" she cried,
then turned and plunged over the cliff top. The thing that haunted
him most was that she didn't utter a sound, the eerie stillness only
broken by the dull thud as she hit the beach below.

"Don't blame yourself for any of this" said Malcolm as a
policewoman brought them both a coffee. "You were kind and brave
to come when it was really none of your making. You did everything
expected of you. To be honest, I only agreed to my superior officer
getting you to intervene as a last resort when I realised I couldn't
talk her out of it and no one could get near her without endangering
their own life. She seemed to have an extreme case of 'battered wife
syndrome'. What I can't understand is the why the public display.
Why didn't she just jump alone and leave a note?"

"I think she wanted to repay Kurt with some of the torment she'd gone through and leave him with a sense of guilt. She loved and hated him at the same time. Frankly, having met him, I think he'll just move on and find other vulnerable women to exploit."

"But why did she ask for you?" asked Malcolm, intrigued "We've known each other since school" explained Winston wearily. "My mother taught her at Roedean, and felt sorry for her as her parents were always overseas, and left her alone with a sort of *au pair* lady. Angela said they were in France now," he added as an afterthought. "We could have been an item once but she fancied boys more rugged than me. So I became a friend and later a confidant when we met up at Cambridge. She was studying Commercial Law. She cried on my shoulder a lot, so I knew the bad relationship she was in. I think her last act was an unselfish attempt to warn her friends of the dangers of modern relationships" he went on as Malcolm nodded. "I know she felt wretched for several months when one of her friends got in a punt, set it off its moorings, took an overdose and was found dead by early-morning rowers. I don't know the details but I think it was a similar situation to hers."

"Yes" said Malcolm "love's often described as temporary madness, and people do crazy things in its name. We see it all the time in the force. It's often short term and one can get over it, but it doesn't seem so at the time for many. It's such a waste of a young life."

"It's been the same throughout history" added Winston. "It's had its triumphs, but has caused the downfall of empires, the abdication of kings, and even the deaths of celebrities in recent times."

The Sergeant made a police car available to take Winston home, and feeling very upset, he waited for Neil and Lavinia to come in before going to bed. The whole experience had saddened and unsettled him and he needed to share it with his parents before he could feel any semblance of normality before trying to sleep.

During these weekend breaks Winston and Neil still liked to visit the historical sites together or take rambles on the local downs to place like Ditchling, Stanmer and Lewes, with the inevitable discussions over pints in the local pubs. Winston realised that his father somewhat envied him his chance to be an academic historian, and was living some of his fantasies through his own achievements. Every time they met, Neil would encourage Winston to further his studies with the aim to become a lecturer and eventually a professor at a British university. He imagined the Frobisher name on learned articles in international journals or on text books that he could proudly display in his Brighton office.

The more Winston thought about it, the more he considered it to be the logical course for his life. Where else could he go with his Arts degrees: into the diplomatic service or a government office somewhere? He certainly didn't want to end up like a Mr Chipps in a school where children often had little interest in history, and the curriculum didn't allow for it as it once had. History was his life, and his father would support him and be proud of him. It was the obvious choice, but he knew there were precious few positions available in Britain and he may have to wait several years to get his chance.

5

At about the time that Winston was completing his PhD research and commencing writing his thesis, Maria Gomez was studying first-year history at New York University. Mid-afternoon on August 14, 2003, she was on her way to visit a sick friend in the NYU Largone Medical Center, and entered the elevator to go to the 10th floor. It started to rise, stopped abruptly and the lights suddenly went out. There were groans of frustration from the occupants, some of whom were Center employees and others who had dropped in to see patients after their early shifts. Frustration turned to fear and then to panic as they realised their danger. Although the youngest there, Maria was used to command structure after living most of her life with her Army Colonel father. She asked if anyone had a torch and one young intern obliged with his pen light.

"See if you can press the emergency button" she said. "We're safe if we have enough oxygen. There should be an emergency trapdoor in the roof of the elevator car. Maybe we can release it and keep a supply of fresh air." The intern managed to release the trapdoor and the group sighed with relief as the fresh air made its way into the car. He tried the emergency button again but there was no response on the intercom.

"This can't be an isolated incident," one of the nurses volunteered, "Security would have called or got help by now." It had been a full seven minutes since the elevator had stopped.

"What do you think is happening?" asked Maria.

"I guess we've suffered a power cut," she answered with a wry smile. "The Center has its own emergency power generator. We learned about it during emergency drill."

"It kicks in for critical equipment in operating theatres and ICU wards" added the intern. "I'm sure that at least some elevators are on the system and we'll be rescued in time."

"I suppose we'll just have to sit tight then," said Maria. "No point in climbing out the trap-door like they do in movies."

"No" declared the intern, "We could be crushed if the power came back on and the elevator moves." So they sat tight and shared a bottle of water that the nurse had with her.

After what seemed an eternity, the lights came on and the elevator descended slowly to the ground floor. The doors opened and the group jostled to get out. One young woman started to cry and was comforted by others. The men gave each other high fives: as if they had saved the day themselves, thought Maria disdainfully. They emerged into the fading sunlight to find gridlocked traffic around the Center. Someone told Maria that power was off in the whole of New

York, the subway was closed, no traffic lights were operating, and only those with bikes, mainly couriers and such, could negotiate the roads. Resigned and with all hope of visiting her sick friend dashed, Maria accepted that she would have to walk several miles back to her apartment. She was glad she carried pepper spray as she walked through the crowds who displayed emotions from frustration to anger, some with intent on taking out that anger on others.

Relieved, she made it to her dark apartment. There was no news as the TV stations were down and she had no battery driven radio. Even her cell needed charging. Luckily she had some scented candles which she lit. Deciding to conserve her torch batteries as long as possible in case the power stayed off for more than twenty four hours, she made herself a sandwich and opened a coke. She decided to go to bed and read by candlelight for a while before the effects of the long walk home caught up with her. There was really nothing else to do.

By morning, the power had been restored and she could get the news. The power outage had affected over fifty five million people in northwest USA and neighbouring Ontario. She didn't really understand what had happened to cause it, but one station suggested it was a computer software bug in the alarm system in the First Energy Company's control room in Ohio. Apparently, a failure in the system there caused a cascading effect, after power lines came into contact with overgrown trees. New York itself had been plunged into chaos in a very short time. The news was full of the contrasts between the good and bad behaviour of the population. Some had been heroic in helping others less mobile than themselves to reach safety or in volunteering to help overstretched emergency crews. On the other side of the coin, burglars had taken advantage of the blackout, looters had ransacked shops, and some women had been attacked and even raped on their long way home from the city. Surprisingly, there had been only six reported deaths due to the outage, the most unfortunate being a man who climbed seventeen flights of stairs to get to his apartment and then died of a heart attack.

Maria's father had often gone on and on about the dangers of living in a totally serviced society where each part of the population was reliant on services provided by others without the discipline they demanded in the army. He told her that if one essential service went down, everything could fall like dominoes, a phrase she had picked up from the news cast. This experience had taught her what he meant. If the outage had gone on for longer, days or weeks even, public road transport would cease as the gas pumps wouldn't operate, shops couldn't open, water couldn't be pumped, and so on. She thought that New York City would be like a concrete shell with its vital organs decaying.

Being a history student, she researched if there had been similar major outages in the past. She was surprised that an outage affecting an even larger population had occurred in southern Brazil in 1999 and another in Montreal in 1998. She thought that when she reached the stage of choosing a research topic later in academic life, she would study the historical evolution from a simple Stone Age existence built on self-sustainability through hunter-gathering, through more complex Bronze and Iron Age and medieval village life, where trading became important, to the Industrial Revolution and its evolution to the present day. She could see herself writing a thesis on the dangers of a totally serviced society where most of the population relied on technology without understanding how it operated. She thought how thrilled her father would be when she outlined her plans and told him that his seemingly boring tirades suddenly made sense.

6

Back in England having realised he would complete his PhD in November 2004, Winston knew he would need to apply for postdoctoral fellowships if he was to become a University lecturer in the future. The normal progression to a lectureship was via one or more postdoctoral positions that led to papers in prestigious journals that, in turn, attracted international attention and established ones credibility in the field. Winston had already been co-author on two papers with his thesis supervisor and a minor author on two multi-author papers resulting from archaeological digs for which he had done volunteer work and made significant discoveries. So, he prepared his CV and, inclusive of a compelling reference from his postgraduate supervisor, sent it off with applications to advertised positions and, on speculation, to other universities with strong history departments. He knew that things moved slowly in the academic world, but he still hoped that he would receive at least one offer of interview well before the new academic year commenced in September 2005.

He nervously checked his mail every day and, predictably as an obsessive sort of character, asked the college porter at least twice a day if he was sure there was nothing for him. A month went by without a single reply and Winston started to worry. He chided himself for having an over inflated opinion of himself, thinking there were very few positions and that he had better start thinking of an alternative career. All these thoughts went through his head each night and he awoke with them in the morning. He also worried about the onset of depression as he had seen the suicidal effects in his undergraduate years.

Then, out of the blue, he received a letter from the University of Exeter marked 'Private and Confidential'. He was surprised as he had only written a letter *on spec* there, as no postdoctoral positions had been advertised. Winston did the British thing and made himself a cup of tea to calm his nerves and, after a few minutes of contemplation, he slit open the envelope and read the letter. He was completely taken aback at its contents, then disbelief turned to joy as the impact of the offer hit home. He was being offered a lectureship without going through the hoops of postdoctoral experience. As he read, he could not believe his good fortune. His thesis had been examined by the Professor at the University of Exeter who had ranked it *cum laude*, one of the very best he had examined. The Professor, as Head of Department wished to introduce new undergraduate and post graduate courses in what he termed 'Social History', emphasising the impact of historical events on social change for the normal population, with an emphasis on understanding modern social behaviour in terms of past history.

He explained that he wanted to develop the opposite of the principle of Uniformitarianism used in the geological sciences. There the present is the key to the past in terms of understanding processes that formed ancient rocks in early Earth history in a millions to billions of years framework. He wanted courses to emphasise that, in terms of human history in the past few millennia, the historical past is the key to understanding the present and, hopefully, should help society not to repeat the mistakes of the past. He had become increasingly concerned about the lack of knowledge of even Britain's history by the average school leaver in the past two decades. As he explained in the letter, he considered the current obsession with 'now', current global celebrities, sports stars and fashion, was producing a generation with little appreciation of their heritage and was curbing their ability to reason in a rational way. Winston, from his own experience, could not agree more, and was increasingly thrilled to be able to make a difference, even if initially only to a limited group in the population. In his imagination, he saw a future TV program that synthesised the individual *Time Team* discoveries and integrated them into a series on *The Evolution of the British Race* from the early Stone Age to the present. It was a thrilling ambition to be involved in such a project, which he could adapt to explain the lessons from the rise and fall of civilisations and empires. He wanted to help the Western World, particularly the USA, understand that all the signs of poor culture, greed, reliance on technology not brainpower, a global economy moving out of control, and a population following cults like sheep, signalled the end of their dominance. Personally, he predicted twenty to thirty years before it started to collapse, probably first in the weaker economies of Europe. He smiled wryly to himself as he thought he might be getting ahead of himself.

He wrote a formal letter of acceptance of the position which commenced in late July in order to develop courses for the Autumn Term in Late September. He anticipated that he would be asked to travel to Exeter to be introduced to the staff after the Christmas break. He now had an important decision to make in terms of the next few months, so he turned to his father for advice. Neil Frobisher, being a realist, knew that this may be the last opportunity to spend what was colloquially known as 'quality time' with his son as he realised that Winston would become totally absorbed in his new academic environment. So, he asked Winston to come home and work for him over the winter months, reorganising and updating his client files, digitising important older documents, and doing any time-consuming research required by clients that did not require a law degree.

So, Winston spent a happy Christmas at home, enjoying the relatively mild weather compared to most of Britain due to the proximity of the sea. He formed the strongest bond of his life so far with his parents who were both proud of his achievements which had exceeded their expectations.

7

Wednesday 19th January started in the ordinary way but turned out to be a turning point in Winston's life. He had always loved the theatre and enjoyed the Theatre Royal in Brighton with its rich history and impressive internal architecture. So, when his parents offered to buy him a ticket to *The Lion King* at the Lyceum Theatre in the west end of London, he jumped at the chance. He had loved the Disney film as a child at the cinema and was thrilled to be able to see the stage version. He had never been to the Lyceum, although he knew that the site dated from the 17th Century and, like the Theatre Royal, had originally been built in the 18th Century, although the present theatre dated from 1904.

He travelled by train to London and arrived early at the Lyceum to have a snack and then look around to absorb its rich history. After eating at a popular steak house nearby, he became so absorbed in the atmosphere both outside the theatre and in the lounge, that he was surprised to hear the final bell, warning that the production was about to start. He walked rapidly to his row and found that his seat was just one from the aisle. The elegantly dressed young woman seated in the aisle seat rose to let him pass and, as she did so, half turned towards him. He stopped in his tracks, transfixed. His mind was registering her beautiful bright blue eyes and fine cheekbone structure reminiscent of the stars of old Hollywood movies that he'd seen as a child.

"Is something wrong?" she asked softly.

"No, no" he spluttered, now highly embarrassed, "I thought for a moment that we'd met before" he lied, trying to regain his composure.

"Yes, you look familiar too," she also lied realising his predicament as a bright flush spread over his face. "Perhaps we could have a drink at interval and investigate where that might have been."

Blushing profusely, Winston sat down next to this goddess and whispered that he would be delighted to do so. Although he was fascinated by the show, particularly the clever depiction of the form and characters of the African animals, Winston kept glancing surreptitiously at her hoping she wouldn't notice. However, as a woman, she was totally aware of his interest in her though he barely moved his head, and was at the same time flattered and somewhat surprised at the immediate consternation she had caused to this seemingly well mannered, well dressed and rather handsome young man.

At the interval they introduced themselves, she as Laura Wright, and Winston quickly went to fetch them each a glass of wine from the crowded bar, at which most theatregoers had pre-ordered drinks. By the time he returned, it was almost time to resume their seats, but they promptly established the remarkable coincidence that they were both from the Brighton area and that they were both returning by train after the show. They happily agreed to share a taxi to Victoria Station and travel together to Brighton. Laura recognised a feeling of security envelop her as she talked to Winston. He oozed dependability and sincerity and had not tried on the corny pick-up lines she detested so much. He's civilised, she thought to herself. I can't miss this chance, he though privately.

As they came out of the theatre, it was very cold and, as there were only three trains between 11pm and the last train at midnight, they decided to go straight to Victoria and get a coffee there if anything at the station was still open. On the journey home they found that they had a great deal in common. Laura was an only child from a well-educated and fairly wealthy family. Her father owned several bookshops in east Sussex and they lived in a luxurious five-floor Regency townhouse in Portland Place in Kemp Town, with ocean views from the upper levels.

"We rattle around in all the space," she grinned. She had been educated at Roedean, explaining Winston's first impression that she spoke like his mother, and he wondered if she had taught her as she explained that she had gone to the University of Sussex, near Falmer, to do her BA.

"It has a very good reputation" she explained "and it allowed me to be near my mother who was suffering from depression at the time and needed my support."

"Is she alright now?" Winston asked solicitously.

"Oh yes, it was just a matter of getting the medication right, but it took most of my degree years before her condition stabilised."

"So what do you do now?" enquired Winston.

"Oh, I'm a librarian in the Jubilee Library. I guess with my upbringing I was destined to love books and the Library is close to home, which is very convenient as I have a whole floor to myself."

Winston was desperate to find out about boyfriends as it was as if she filled all his senses, like a sudden madness. He didn't want to do anything that might offend her, so he simply asked,

"What about social life?" It seemed unbelievable to him that such a gorgeous and cultured woman should be going to the theatre alone, not really aware of his own parallel situation.

"Well, I have some close friends and we quite often go out for a meal or just a drink, occasionally to the cinema or theatre. Before you ask, I have no boyfriend. Not because I'm not asked out, just because I choose not to." Winston's heart dropped a beat or two and he plucked up courage to ask, "Why not, with your looks you must have so many to choose from." He noticed that she actually blushed at the compliment which had caught her unaware despite the fact that she could clearly see his attraction to her.

"Most of the men I meet are self-centred and opinionated," she said with some feeling. "They think that muscles and tattoos replace brains and manners, and that dressing down is a way to attract attention. My girlfriends dress up for an evening date, only to be picked up by a scruffy male with his brain in his pants. And all the decent men are snapped up!" she blurted, realising that she had got carried away. Clean shaven, tattoo free and well-dressed, Winston exulted in this diatribe.

"It's interesting," he said, "I spend my life wondering why these otherwise intelligent women are attracted to those sorts of guys, and having them cry on my shoulder when it all goes wrong. A problem with modern society," he went on "is that it's difficult to meet potential partners outside of a bar, nightclub or dating agency. The social networks of the past seem to have all but disappeared."

"It looks as though we've a lot in common" commented Laura. We're probably both conservative souls out of equilibrium with modern society. Social outcasts if you like. But I don't intend to conform and lower my standards."

"Would you consider lowering your standards enough to allow me to take you to the theatre or cinema one evening if I promise to dress for the occasion and be on time?" Winston asked cheekily, realising they were approaching Brighton Station.

"Only if dinner is included and you tell me more about your life and ambitions," she said quietly, realising that she was making a commitment to an almost complete stranger. She noticed that Winston sighed with relief and then glowed with pleasure, and she imagined that he was a bit smitten, and smiled, surprisingly pleased with herself.

Winston suggested that they share a taxi so that he knew exactly where to pick her up for their date and they exchanged phone numbers and email addresses to keep in touch. Otherwise they travelled in silence, each reluctant to break the mood. Winston wanted desperately to hold her hand and kiss her goodnight but restrained from the impulse. He wanted to do nothing that would give her a poor impression of him. He had never been in love, but thought that the sensations he was experiencing must represent it. They arrived at Portland Square and he gallantly got out of the cab and opened her door. As she kissed him on the cheek, he felt a burning sensation on his skin.

"Goodnight," he stuttered "I'll call you and arrange our evening very soon."

He watched her climb the steps to the front door and gave the driver his address in Telscombe Cliffs.

"Lucky man" said the driver with a grin. Winston smiled to himself thinking, you will never know how lucky I feel. How one day can change your life. From the plains to the Acropolis, he mused, realising that only a historian would understand. I've found HER and I mustn't let go whatever it takes.

8

Winston spent the next day mooning around and feeling absolutely useless. Neil thought he was sick, so sent him home from the office. On the way, Winston bought *The Argus*, the local newspaper, to check whether there was anything on at the weekend to which he could invite Laura. He simply had to see her again to get rid of his restlessness. The *Argus* confirmed what he had gleaned from his Google search that it was still the Pantomime season in the theatres and that only second-rate movies were showing at the cinemas. That evening, he plucked up courage and phoned her.

"Oh what a pleasure to hear you" she said, much to his relief, "What are you up to?" He didn't dare share his thoughts that all he was doing was thinking of her.

"Nothing much," he replied after a short hesitation, "just checking up on what was on in Brighton that I could take you to this weekend if you're free."

"I have to work on Saturday as I'm on roster" she said as his heart sank, "but I'm free on Sunday and would love to meet you again" and his pulse beat faster.

"There's nothing much on at the theatre or similar" he explained. "Is there something that you'd really like to do instead?" She thought for a while as he waited expectantly.

"Why don't you pick me up here" she finally replied. "Let's walk from the sea front to the Pier and have lunch at the Palm Court Fish Restaurant. I haven't been on the Pier for ages, but I loved the smell and atmosphere when I was little, and my friends tell me that the seafood is great at the Palm Court. Then we can decide where to go from there."

"That's fantastic" replied Winston who had loved trying to tip coins over the edge into a collection tray in the amusement area with his father when he was younger. So they agreed that he should pick Laura up at 11.00 on the Sunday. As he hung up, he felt like pinching himself to make sure it was real.

As an obsessive character, Winston worried for the next two days about what he should wear, what he would say and what he shouldn't say or do. He felt totally disoriented now that he had met HER as he liked to think of Laura. He was so calm and sensible with the women who used to sound off to him about their relationships and he suddenly realised why. Losing HER now would be a disaster. He thought he would do everything to keep her interest without being pushy and he realised he needed to curb his tendency to speak with his 'inner voice', as his mother called it, so as not to appear insensitive.

After what seemed like an eternity, Sunday finally dawned. It was near-freezing in the morning but sunny with a forecast of 48°F for the afternoon. First hurdle over, he thought as he surveyed himself in the mirror: green polo-necked sweater, light brown jacket, casual dark grey chinos, black leather shoes and the inevitable umbrella for the unpredictable British weather. He arrived punctually at Portland Place and knocked on the door. She opened it straight away, making him wonder if she was anxious to see him or didn't want her parents to meet him. She looked stunningly casual, her long blond hair hanging loosely over a fashionable light blue, three-quarter length coat with dark blue denim designer jeans and long black boots.

"You look lovely," he blurted out, looking again at her deep blue eyes and high cheek bones framed by the blond tresses.

"You don't look too bad yourself" she replied, surprised again by his boyish yet appealing candour.

They walked down to the promenade along Marine Parade and descended a level to Madeira Drive, with its attractive arches and colonnades, to walk to the Pier alongside the deserted pebble beach lacking the colourful deck chairs of the summer months. The day was a delight for Winston. Laura took his arm as they wandered around the Pier. Several attractions were closed for winter, but the domed amusement centre was open, and they played a few slot machines with some unexpected success, before Winston showed her how he used to run round the glass cases where he tried to dislodge coins into the trays below, checking those trays for coins that fell under their own weight after a player had left. This happened often, he explained, so he collected the coins and then fed them back down the shute to try and dislodge more. Again, she was amused by his boyish enthusiasm which she perceived was a defence mechanism against his natural reserve and shyness.

Over a lunch of traditional fish and chips and a glass of French white wine, they chatted intimately, discovering more about each other's families, childhoods, University lives, interests and professional ambitions. Each was surprised at how similar their upbringings had been and how both their interests had been shaped by interaction with their fathers: she in literature and he in history. Neither had mentioned special relationships with the other sex nor past or present lovers, boyfriends or girlfriends. Winston was reluctant to discuss it as he was sure that Laura must have a boyfriend at least, although she had said not on the train and had gone out with him on her one day off. It was she who asked the question.

"What about girlfriends? An attractive, intelligent man like you must have women chasing you all the time!" He paused before replying, as it was Catch 22 whichever way he answered, but decided to be honest.

"Afraid not" he said "I don't seem to be the sort today's girls fall for. They like me as a sort of brother figure to offload to. Anyway I haven't yet met anyone before that I could fall for." He realised he had used the word 'before' and blushed. Laura had clearly picked up on the significance of his use of 'before' and saw him squirm.

"As I said on the train, I'm the same," she said softly reaching across to touch his hand. "I like the company of my friends but it makes me a bit of a loner in the romance department most of the time. It's not that I don't meet people but I find that if they buy you a drink or spend the evening in your company flattering you, then it's expected that you go to bed with them. No intelligent conversation, no romance, no Mr Darcys." She stopped her diatribe, realising that she was extending her private thoughts to someone she had only just met.

"You can see I'm a fan of Jane Austen and the Brontés," she continued, not admitting that she often watched videos of movies based on those novels with a box of tissues for company.

"Does this mean I'm acceptable?" smiled Winston, pleased that his intuition that this was HER in every way. She nodded and smiled at his old-fashioned ways. Here was someone that suited her, whom she could really like and even love.

"Let me pay the bill," said Winston, "and perhaps we could continue our adventure this afternoon." She agreed and took his arm as they headed for the Lanes where it was possible to wander around away from the wind which was now blustering, sending whitecaps scudding over the darkening waters of the English Channel. They wandered around, looking at the antique and other small shops that lined The Lanes, popping into The Little Teacup café for afternoon tea to stave off the increasing cold. As Laura had not mentioned going home, and they had both had lunch, Winston thought a restaurant dinner inappropriate. Instead he suggested a drink and bar snack in the nearby The Cricketers. There, they continued to talk of their experiences and current lives. Eventually, the conversation arrived at his future professional plans and Winston explained about the lectureship in Exeter and his invitation to move there in mid-year.

"So, you'll be leaving Brighton in a few months," she said, with Winston searching for signals of sadness in her voice. "Looks like I'll stay here unless something else comes up as I have a great job and I don't want to be more than a couple of hours train ride from my mother who is still a bit vulnerable," she continued.

"Look," said Winston hopefully "this has been a wonderful day for me. Yours is the most pleasant company I've experienced for as long as I can remember. While I'm still in Brighton, could we meet like this every weekend and I'll take you on rambles around Brighton to show you Stone, Bronze and Iron Age sites, plus evidence of

Roman and Saxon occupation here. I promise it will be scenic and interesting, not filled with academic gobbledegook." She laughed as he went on, "We could also hire or borrow a car and visit historical sites with lovely villages and pubs in Arundal and Hastings or nearer home at Bramber or Ditchling. What do you think?"

"That would be great" she said, giving him one of her exquisite smiles. "I'm free on Wednesday night. Why don't we meet and make a plan of where we'll go, weather permitting," she added wryly. "Let's be informal and meet at Sutherland Arms pub near Brighton College. It was a favourite of my father when he was young and is old fashioned and cosy."

"Fantastic" said Winston. "It's a date."

"Now you'll have to take me home" she said, "I'm at the Library early tomorrow helping with referencing some of our older volumes."

Winston took her to the nearby taxi rank and then on to Portland Place where he told the taxi driver to wait while he escorted her to the door.

"You said earlier at the pub that this has been a wonderful day for you," she said rather wistfully. "It's also been the best day I've had in ages. Please don't disappoint me. Meet me here again at 6.00pm on Wednesday or call if there are problems." With that she touched his arm, and kissed him gently on the lips. To Winston, the sensation was electric, like tasting honey and smouldering embers at the same time.

"Once more" he murmured. She obliged with the same delicious effect, turned and went inside. Winston spent the rest of the taxi ride in a daze reflecting on the ecstatic sensation a simple kiss could produce and vowing not to let Laura slip through his fingers. His senses told him to back off the physical attraction and concentrate on romance to keep her interest. It was going to be a long few days till Wednesday came around and he saw her again.

9

Over the next four weeks, Winston and Laura spent each Sunday together, alternating between local walks around Brighton and visits to villages in east Sussex. After the second week, they also started to have dinner together each Wednesday, sometimes in a restaurant or sometimes a pub. She now held his arm or his hand, if it wasn't too cold outside, and her goodnight kisses were more and more lingering and smouldering, so that his whole body ached for her. However, he made no move to take things further, following his intuition that this may spoil the relationship. He was now convinced that they were an item and that no-one else was lurking in the shadows to usurp him. They never grew bored with each other's company. She seemed enchanted by his historical tours and he by the novels that she introduced to him.

On their trip to Arundel on 20th February, she surprised him by saying that her father had invited him to dinner at their house on the following Wednesday, if he was available. When Wednesday evening arrived, Laura ushered him into the house and introduced him to her mother and father, Jeremy and Penelope. Winston could immediately see that Laura had inherited her good looks from Penelope. They seemed to be pleased to meet him and made him feel very welcome. Winston was impressed with the beautifully furnished hall and sitting room. The hall was decorated with Regency wallpaper and was big enough to comfortably house a small suite of what appeared to be Queen Anne chairs and a settee. The sitting room was like a sunburst with lemon hues on the walls, the colours which were also picked out in the curtains and furniture upholstery. There were several prints of scenes by Constable and above the fireplace was a superb reproduction of Monet's *San Giorgio Maggiore at Dusk*, which added perfectly to the delightful ambience.

During the meal, Jeremy proposed a toast to Winston for making Laura so vibrant, with renewed interest in everything around her.

Laura was somewhat taken aback by her father's forthright manner, although she knew in her heart that what he said was true, that new possibilities had been awakened. They clinked glasses and relaxed. A little later, Jeremy asked if it would be a major imposition for Winston to organise a Sunday minitrip to as many historical sites around Brighton as possible in a day, for the whole family. He explained that Laura was full of chatter about Brighton's history and he was intrigued to see for himself.

"I'd be delighted" said Winston "shall we make it this Sunday or the next? Perhaps I could ask my father to come along as well as he is the real expert who taught me all I know about local history."

So it was agreed that they would all ramble around Brighton, visiting sites in chronological order from the early Stone Age at Black Rock to the Iron Age at Hollingbury Camp on Sunday week if Neil Frobisher was available. Winston phoned his father who was delighted to accept and suggested dinner afterwards so that his wife could meet everyone. She remembered Laura very well for her excellent manners and academic ability and was interested to meet her family.

On the Sunday before this family gathering, there was sleeting rain and drizzle with gloomy grey skies, and choppy uninviting seas.

"Why don't we just catch a bus along the cliffs to Eastbourne and sit out the weather in a snug pub there? We could have some scampi and chips and a glass of wine or two" suggested Winston. Over the wine next to an open fire, Laura snuggled close to him.

"My family are very impressed with you" she started. "To be honest, I spent so much time with my girlfriends that I think they were starting to suspect that I was a lesbian, something they would find hard to face in their conservative world." She chuckled at the thought. "Seriously, I have so enjoyed your company that I don't know how I'll face returning to my life before I met you when you head off to Exeter." He thought he saw the trace of a tear in those deep blue pools, and decided impulsively to risk everything.

"I can't even imagine life without you now that I've finally found you" he said softly. "Would you consider marrying me and coming with me?" His heart stopped as he waited for a reaction in this make-or-break moment that he had thought of but not imagined to precipitate so soon. It was only a few weeks since they'd met. She gave him a dazzling smile and he could see there was moisture in her eyes.

"Only if you provide me with a romantic proposal, Mr Darcy" she replied. To her delight, and the surprise of the patrons around them, Winston went down on one knee, took her hand and asked, "Will you do me the honour of marrying me and becoming my wife Miss Elizabeth Bennett. It would give me the greatest pleasure of my life."

"Passingly romantic" she quipped. "Yes of course I will."

Those watching this enactment started to cheer and clap, a sound that grew more raucous once Laura turned round and gave Winston such a passionate kiss that he simply sizzled and turned bright red. The crowd around them were ecstatic at his embarrassment and the bartender brought over two glasses of champagne for them to celebrate.

Once the noise had died down and they were alone again, Laura said quietly, "I hope I didn't force you into that proposal with my remark about Exeter."

"I think I've been in love with you since that moment in the theatre" he said gently. "I've been looking for you all my adult life. I'm glad you said what you did. I was too frightened to ruin our relationship by asking you although I've wanted to all along. You are everything I've ever dreamed of my darling Laura."

The weather had cleared somewhat, so they went back to Portland Place. Winston thought that she might invite him in, but she said, "Let's meet on Wednesday, to make absolutely sure this is what we want to do. We can tell our parents on Sunday on our excursion and have a celebratory dinner after that." She kissed him passionately, holding her body so close that he could feel her form against him, despite the winter clothes.

"Until Wednesday" she said softly as she went inside.

Wednesday came and they met in a new Indian restaurant in Kemp Town within walking distance of Laura's home. Their relationship had clearly changed. Laura now held his hand continuously unless eating, and they snuggled together, kissing each other's lips, noses, ears and necks, oblivious to those around them. Winston had never been happier. Laura was the one who interrupted their reverie, pulling herself upright and putting on a serious face.

"It seems your proposal was not a rash one and you're really serious about marrying me. And I you, my darling, darling Winston. So we really have to agree on how we go forward from here. My desire for you is overwhelming and I know from our close encounters that you feel the same." She blinked and blushed. "But I want to feel like Elizabeth Bennett or Elinor Dashwood on their wedding nights, full of hope and anticipation, not prior knowledge. I know virginity is not a virtue in the modern world, but I'm old fashioned, probably living in my book dream-world" she added.

"I love you for that" murmured Winston, thinking that a pair of virgins must be as rare as hen's teeth. "If we get married before going to Exeter, there's not long to wait, so expectancy it is, as long as your expectations are not too great," he chuckled and she smiled, something he treasured no matter how often she did so. Secretly he thought he must seek some lovemaking advice from some friends with experience. Somehow, he couldn't imagine his parents having sex, and was loathe to ask his father. "There's just one other thing" said Laura. "I don't want to sound like a dictator, at least not before we're married" she smiled widely, "but, if you're going to buy an engagement ring, could we make it an antique one, something like my grandmother would have worn for her engagement. And no hand-me-downs from your own grandmother" she added, mischievously. "As long as you don't want a million pound one previously worn by Cleopatra or Queen Victoria." he replied in kind. "Seriously, if you can get time off on Saturday, we could go to those jewellery shops in

The Lanes and find one. I can mortgage my soul to buy it."

"That would be lovely," she acquiesced. "We could then make an announcement to both families on Sunday and seal it with the ring. I'm so excited, I can't wait for the weekend." The embrace at her door that evening exceeded all previous ones in passion and longevity. Winston simply floated home.

As agreed, they met on Saturday afternoon, while Laura looked for her perfect ring. There were some spectacular rings on display, but most of the prices were spectacular too, and she realised that economy was important as Winston did not yet have a job. Finally, she chose a halo-style cushion-cut diamond with a raised half-karat diamond surrounded by twenty small deep blue sapphires, to match her eyes, in a fourteen karat white gold ring. Relieved, Winston had enough money in his bank account to pay for it, but he would have to ask his father for a loan against his lectureship after the announcement on Sunday. A quick meal, ride home, and a passionate embrace ended a perfect day, leaving time for Winston to finalise details for tomorrow's historic ramble with his father. They decided on only the most spectacular sites in historical order with a booked lunch in the traditional Swan Inn across the footbridge from historic Falmer village which had been there since the Norman Conquest.

10

Sunday morning dawned a clear day with a wintery sun. As agreed, the Frobishers and Wrights met at a cafe near the Marina at Black Rock for coffee at 8.30a.m. to make the most of the day. After introductions were made and Penelope had asked them to call her Penny, Neil and Winston first showed them the earliest Stone Age shoreline at Black Rock, pointing out that significant sea-level change was not human-induced in the past. They then drove off in their two cars and parked at Brighton Racecourse to see the late Stone Age mounds and ditches with wonderful views of Brighton and the coast from the rolling downs.

"They certainly chose the sites with the most attractive views" said Jeremy.

"And the best places to defend in times of trouble" added Neil.

Satisfied with their morning excursion, they drove to the Swan Inn at Falmer for a ploughman's lunch and a pint of ale or glass of wine. Neil was glad he'd booked as the inn was now buzzing with patrons. They had their lunch with desultory conversation about Brighton's history, the weather and the current political situation. When they had almost finished their meal, Winston announced that he had something important to say.

"To cut a long story short" he began "Laura has agreed to marry me and we would like to seal our engagement in your presence with your approval." Neil almost choked on his beer and smiled hugely while Jeremy kissed Laura and shook Winston's hand.

"Thank God for that" exclaimed Penny. "All we've heard for the past month is Winston this and Winston that and Laura wandering round like a lovesick puppy."

"Agreed," joined in Lavinia. "I thought it was non-Christian to worship a goddess these days." Amid the blushes and congratulations Winston produced the ring and slipped it on her finger so that she could show them.

"Was that your grandmother's?" asked Penny, and they both burst into a fit of giggles.

"Private joke" laughed Winston. "Well we'd better get going and we can talk about our plans tonight at dinner." As they were in the area, they visited Falmer Village with its mediaeval pond, which Laura had never seen despite studying at the nearby University of Sussex.

That afternoon, the couples walked hand in hand around the raised Iron Age Hollingbury Camp, now covered by gorse bushes, and surrounded by the golf links.

"I'm amazed that we didn't even know this existed" said Jeremy, now intrigued by Brighton's rich history. "Now we're about to become family, let's do other trips like this from time to time."

"Can I ask a question?" said Penny. When we visit these forts, we just see mounds and ditches, never real rock walls. We don't see the grand old stone buildings or the bleak houses that dominate Laura's novels set in the moors."

"That's because the South Downs are made of chalk which crumbles away with time: the reason you're not allowed to walk too close to the cliffs" Winston explained. "The only hard building stones are small blocks of flint that the Stone Age people used as tools and arrowheads. So East Sussex has 'long barns' where flints are bound together with mortar, whereas the North has large stately homes made from blocks of sandstone that formed in a great basin beneath the sea that covered the whole of northern Europe." He paused. "Sorry for the lecture but this is something that's interested me since I was a boy, and once I get started it's hard for me to stop. If you see a photo or picture of an old stone house or even a stone wall, you can tell which part of England it came from if you know your geology."

"Interesting" commented Penny who was genuinely impressed. "Perhaps we could add an historic architectural tour of England to our future excursions."

"Don't forget Scotland and the red sandstones of Glasgow," started Winston, but Laura put her hand up to signal enough. Over dinner, they toasted the engagement and the future. The discussion came around to Winston and Laura's future plans.

"Neither of us believes in long engagements nor living together before marriage" said Laura. "We know it's old fashioned and that our friends will think we're crazy, but that's how it is. So, we want to marry before July, so we can go to Exeter together and start our new life" she continued. "But of course with frequent visits to see all of you" she added hurriedly.

"Where do you intend to marry?" asked Jeremy.

"If possible we'd like to follow in the family tradition and get married at St Peters, although we know the schedule there will be tight as it's such a popular venue."

"Leave it to your father and I" said Neil. "We have a lot of friends in high places, including the church in Brighton. What about trying for late April to early May when the weather will be improved. Better for the honeymoon," he added.

So it was left at that. A long kiss out of the view of their parents and their first family get-together was over. Each was glad it had gone so well and that their parents had genuinely enjoyed each other's company. Laura and Winston learned later that their fathers had agreed to meet for a coffee the next day and had started lobbying for a suitable wedding slot. By the next weekend, Saturday 7th May had been set as the wedding day and Laura and Winston asked to draw up a list of invited guests and decide on a honeymoon venue to be paid for by their parents.

At their regular Wednesday evening meeting, they drew up a list of potential wedding guests. As they both had small families, with few close relatives and few really close friends, their list came down to 28 guests apart from their parents. When Laura arrived home, Jeremy immediately suggested that the reception be held at Portland Place as it would avoid hiring a venue.

"We could have the reception catered here," he said. "Now once you're married where will you live before you go to Exeter?"

We haven't really thought that far ahead," she replied. "I know that Winston has been offered a small University flat for rent once he starts in Exeter, and we'll go there to begin with, while we get settled at least."

"Just an idea, but you have the third floor to yourself" he went on, "Why not adapt it into something more like an apartment. You already have a bathroom attached to your bedroom which is big enough to have a larger desk in it, and the spare room would make a cosy little sitting room. You could stay there when you come back to visit," he went on artfully, as he would miss her terribly.

"I'll ask Winston, but I'm sure he'll agree. It's such a sensible solution and I'm sure his parents won't be jealous as they are both so busy with their careers."

"You'd better think about your honeymoon as well" he said. "It'll be the start of spring and things will be booked out very quickly. You don't want to miss out." Laura nodded and resolved to raise it with Winston the next day. She was already planning to find somewhere romantic where no one else would think to go.

On Saturday, they visited various travel agencies in Brighton looking for their honeymoon destination. Laura suggested that they stay in Britain as she was sure that Winston would be invited to conferences all over the world once he got established. Winston thought they might go to the south west of England and that he could drop into Exeter University for a couple of days to check out his program for the following academic year. He also suggested that they could look for a librarian's position in the University or elsewhere for Laura. They had already decided that they both wanted careers and that they would not have children until Winston, at least, had established himself and they could travel together while they were still young.

Just by chance, they noticed a brochure for the Isles of Scilly with cottages for rent. They were remote, romantic and relaxing according to the brochure, with ferry access from Penzance in Cornwall to St Mary's, a spectacular journey according to the reviews, and the possibility of return to Exeter by a Skybus airlink. The travel agent checked bookings and luckily found one cottage still available from 3rd to 17th May.

"They are normally booked out on a weekly schedule Friday to Friday," he explained, "and this was a very recent cancellation. There are hotel rooms and B and Bs available" he added.

"No, please book the cottage and we'll pay a deposit to make sure we get it" said Winston.

Once decided, they looked at a schedule. The wedding was on

Saturday 7th May and the first ferry to St Mary's was on Monday 9th May at 9.00am.

"If the reception is at home, we could spend our first night together in our new apartment upstairs" said Laura. "Don't worry, the walls are very thick and they won't hear a thing," she laughed. "If we take the train from Victoria to Penzance and stay the night, then we could catch the ferry early on Monday."

"OK and on our way back let's take the Skybus to Exeter on the Friday," Winston went on, "spend the weekend there to get our bearing and then a look at the flat, at least from the outside and visit the University on Monday and Tuesday." They looked up hotels in Penzance and decided on Lombard House, a romantic early 18th century building near the Ferry terminal and not far from the Railway Station. It had all panned out well, with the icing on the cake being that their parents, as promised, footed the bill, surprised that their children had taken such an inexpensive option.

11

The weeks leading up to the wedding were uneventful. Laura's girlfriends had a hen's night with a male stripper brought in to embarrass her, although, much to her friend's surprise, she played up to him.

"Practice for THE event" she quipped to the laughter of her friends. Winston had a stag's night, being dumped in Lewes in his underpants at 2.00 a.m. and picked up by police soon after. Luckily, the weather was improving as spring finally arrived.

As predicted, their wedding at St Peters was a quiet and short affair, as they had been fitted into a busy schedule at short notice, thanks to Jeremy. Laura looked beautiful in traditional white on the arm of her father. Winston stood at the altar, with his best man, a student colleague from King's College. He pinched himself to be sure that he wasn't dreaming as he watched her arrive with her bridesmaid. They exchanged vows and rings, kissed and it was all over, months of dating and planning over in a heartbeat. They stood outside the beautiful grounds with the church as a backdrop for wedding photos by a professional photographer and the family.

Jeremy and Penny had done a wonderful job of decorating their ground-floor room for the reception. To Laura's great surprise, her father, through his book business had produced coloured posters of Elizabeth Bennett and Mr Darcy, Jane Eyre and Marianne Dashwood, as portrayed in various movies, on the wall behind the bench holding the wedding cake. Laura hugged him with tears and laughter intermingled. Food was eaten, drinks were drunk, toasts were made and speeches concluded. The parents made endless jokes and references to having the only children in England that lived as if they were in the previous century. Secretly, they were thrilled by this old-fashioned love affair and by the high principles of their children in a world where courtesy, manners and respect for others was rapidly declining.

After many hugs and kisses from family and friends, it was time to climb the stairs to their apartment of the next few months. Winston was exceptionally excited and nervous at the same time, trying to remember the advice given to him by his friends. He moved towards her, kissing her lips and neck and blowing gently in her ear. He slowly removed her clothes, kissing her exposed creamy white skin as he did so. He could see that she was aroused as her breasts jutted out with taut fine nipples. He pushed her down gently, while undressing himself. Whispering to trust him he massaged her body, working his hands up her legs and then stroking her warm moist cleft protected by fine blond hair. She moaned languorously, the volume increasing until she climaxed, shuddering and calling out his name. Gently, he entered her slowly, feeling slight resistance and then a slight release of pressure as she gasped momentarily. It was all too much for the pent-up emotion he had held back for weeks, and he climaxed rapidly.

"I'm sorry," he said, "I wanted to make it unhurried and special."

"It was special" she murmured, kissing his ear. "I'm pleased you wanted me so much. Relax and we'll do it more slowly this time." Winston remembered that they did more than once before falling asleep, exhausted by all the emotion and lovemaking of this special day.

They woke to the sound of an alarm, set the night before. They had their own kettle, toaster and microwave upstairs, so Winston made Laura coffee and toast in bed.

"We'd better finish packing" he said "and head for the station. It'll take us several hours to get to Penzance and I'm looking forward to another evening with you in our romantic hotel."

The hotel in Penzance did not disappoint them after a lazy day luxuriating in the first class seats courtesy of their parents. Neither had been to Devon or Cornwall before and both were impressed by the countryside and the towns they had passed. That evening, they lay in a historic room in an old-fashioned bed exploring each other's bodies and senses until exhaustion finally set in. In the morning, they reluctantly crept downstairs for breakfast before heading to the ferry. The waiter, who to their surprise was Irish, asked for their order. When they both asked for a full English breakfast, he asked if they were catching the ferry as he had overheard snatches of their conversation. Laura asked why he was interested.

"Because it's a touch windy today" he replied, "and I'm thinking you might be needing your seasick pills."

Once they got out of the harbour, they were glad they had heeded the waiter's advice. They had read the tourist guide and had taken seasick pills but there was quite a swell with waves cascading into the bow of the ferry and fine spumes of sea water spraying the ship. Their breakfasts seemed to churn in their stomachs, nausea crept over them, so they couldn't fully appreciate the beauty of their surroundings as the ferry passed several islands, some with ancient buildings on the cliffs, before they docked in St Mary's. Remarkably, they were not actually sick, something that Laura described as their first joint triumph against adversity. Winston pointed out the near lack of trees on the island and what he took to be granite knolls and tors from his rudimentary knowledge of geology.

They were both taken with the beauty of the harbour with its myriad of small colourful yachts and motor boats, and the town with its largely stone houses nestled in a sandy isthmus between two low granite hills. They were transported to their stone cottage in Old Town, just a few minutes' walk from the main settlement at Hugh Town, noticing the neat shrubberies and gardens with daffodils breaking through for spring. Having settled in, they went out to buy necessary provisions before trying out the bed and making love. The next days were spent walking the nearby fields and beaches with their amazing differences between high and low tide, hiring bikes to explore the rest of the island, and taking half day cruises to nearby islands, enjoying the seabirds and lighthouses along the way. They noticed the weather was milder than even in Brighton, with little temperature difference between day and night, but could imagine from the vegetation that it must be very stormy in the winter. Winston, of course, was interested in the long history of the island, with evidence of Stone Age to Bronze Age occupation at Bant's Cairn, with its entrance grave, and both Stone Age and Iron Age settlement at Halangry Village. They realised that most of the other landmarks like Harry's Walls, the Garrison and Star Castle, Giants Castle and Telegraph Tower were all fortifications dating from the 16th to 19th Centuries, in part due to the fear of Elizabeth I concerning another Spanish invasion after the Armada of 1588 and in part due to the Napoleonic wars. Some of the old cannons were still preserved around the town. As Winston became captivated by the history of the island, Laura visited the library in Church Street to look at the large collection of books that detailed that history and other features of the Isles. It was fascinating for them both.

In the evenings, they alternated between cooking for themselves and dining out at the surprising number of restaurants, some with spectacular views of the harbour or beaches. They were both falling in love with the Isles of Scilly and their honeymoon was over far too quickly.

"I'd love to come back here for holidays and to live when we retire" said Laura on their last evening.

"I've thought of it too" mused Winston "but the cottages cost about five hundred thousand pounds to buy and we'd need a miracle to afford that on our salaries."

On the Friday afternoon, they flew by Skybus to Exeter, seeing the Isles of Scilly from a totally different aspect from the air. Their impression that this was destined to become a special place for them was heightened.

12

Arriving in Exeter, they made their way to the Georgian St Olaves Hotel, chosen, of course by Winston, for its historical significance. They were enchanted by its lovely walled garden and by its stately spiral staircase inside. They were even more enchanted by their bedroom, rapidly removing their clothes before diving into the bed. I love her and lust after her at the same time, thought Winston, before being brought back to Earth by her urgent signals of passion.

They woke late on Saturday to have a light breakfast and explore the town, and look at possible places to live when they returned in July. Winston had researched Exeter's history which had a long pre-history before it became the most south-western Roman settlement in Britain. They walked the remnants of Roman walls, inspected the Scenic Clock Tower, and the ruins of the Norman Rougemont Castle, where Laura was delighted to find that the local repertory company at the Northcott Theatre presented Shakespearean plays in the summer.

"It would be nice to live in a nearby village" said Laura, so they visited Ide, just southwest of Exeter on the Sunday. It was a wonderful English village, cut off from reality by the highway, but there were few rentals and sale prices were very high. Luckily, they had a University flat in Exeter for two months after Winston began his lectureship, and they agreed to see where Laura might find a position before getting too worried about where to live. The weekend was an extension of their honeymoon, and they were still bewitched with their romantic journey.

On Monday morning, they went to the University, Winston to introduce himself and ask for potential positions for Laura. He had noticed that the University had an Accommodation Office, and thought Laura could ask their advice about the flat and also future rental apartments, although he suspected they mostly dealt with student needs. The day further emphasised that the Gods were smiling on their relationship. Not only was Winston pleased with what he saw in the Department, but the central Library had two vacancies in the next academic year. The University was keen to accommodate its academic staff, so Laura was to have an interview the next day. A champagne dinner was in order.

As they travelled back to Paddington on Wednesday, they discussed their continuing good fortune. Laura had been tentatively offered a position in the library provided the present incumbent didn't change her mind about moving abroad with her husband. They had also found an apartment which they liked, within walking distance of the University and which would become vacant a month after they moved to Exeter. They were grateful to have the flat for a buffer and it looked as if Winston could more than pay for the rent if he took some tutorials outside normal hours. They were met at Brighton Station by both sets of parents who took them to a country pub near Lewes where they interrogated them mercilessly all evening on their honeymoon and experiences in Exeter. Exhausted but happy, they repeated their lovemaking of their wedding night in their temporary apartment in the Wright household.

The weeks until their departure to Exeter in July passed quickly and pleasantly. Laura worked until they left as Winston prepared the courses for his first Term. They alternated their weekends between excursions alone and together with their parents. So far everything was going to plan.

13

Winston and Laura travelled to Exeter to begin the next phase of their journey together after a tearful farewell from Penny and Jeremy and Neil and Lavinia. They reflected that their only children had left the nest, and would only return occasionally as they built their new lives.

At about the same time, Adam Lampton, a second year medical student at London University, was acting as a volunteer to assist his father Andre with his work with *Médecins sans Frontièrs* in Africa. They visited refugee camps in, or on the borders of, Sudan, Somalia, Kenya and Burundi where refugees from drought, pestilence and/or conflict came to get food, water, shelter or medical care. Adam found the plight of the refugees pitiful. Their few possessions had to be left behind as they abandoned their homes, with women often raped on their way to the camps. The children stared up at the doctors and staff with wide, dark brown trusting eyes that would melt the heart of anyone there to witness. You could not be a compassionate human being without trying to save them, but for what future he wondered.

Adam was a young man with head over heart tendencies. Despite his unconventional behaviour bordering on Eccentric Personality Disorder, Adam had been popular at school. He had the ability to persuade others to join in the activities he chose, and his dark good looks and engaging smile coupled with a tall, lean frame added to his persuasive powers. His teachers realised that he had the ability to analyse issues and see 'the big picture'. They recognised that he was able to think in a holistic and logical way, attributes that he, himself hoped would allow him to succeed at medical school and become a doctor like his father or a medical researcher, which was his own preference. His parents had always been concerned about Adam's eccentric ways, but his mother, Angela, in particular had worked hard to ensure that he developed friendships and was a hardworking and focussed student. Quite early on in his childhood she noticed that he had very short periods of a few seconds when he seemed to blank out and be unaware of his surroundings. Her GP had diagnosed that it was a mild form of 'petite mal' and not to be too concerned, but it heightened her desire for him to have a normal, happy childhood. She regretted that she was unable to have more children as she believed a sibling or two would have helped keep him grounded. Andre, his father, believed that in view of these traits, it would be good experience for Adam to join him in Africa during the long summer breaks, as it would encourage him to be more attuned to the needs and opinions of others.

However, the more Adam saw the endless procession of refugees, the more he wondered at the futility of it all. He pondered what would have happened in the days before mass media and global communication. Darwin's theory of survival of the fittest would have applied, he argued to himself. The population would have been reduced through natural causes during times of drought or war and come to equilibrium with its environment, as happens in the animal kingdom at large. His feelings were strongly divided. Having seen the people themselves, he felt a humane obligation to save them. At the same time, he knew that the survivors would have more children, such that over-population would be an even greater issue during the next crises. He thought that there would come a time when aid would have no impact at all and there would be major humanitarian disasters with millions, not just thousands, of casualties in Africa. He pondered that the same would occur wherever millions of people live on flood plains such as the Ganges where so-called hundred year flooding events would cause devastation with the following one a total disaster. He thought that it would be the same with coastal dwellers in earthquake zones where thousands to millions of people would die during inevitable super-tsunamis.

Like many before him, he came to the conclusion that the Earth's population had outgrown the habitable niches on the planet with dire consequences in terms of extinction of other species, and periodic failure of food and water supplies or natural disasters in some of those over-populated corners. He could not discuss this with his father, who was humanitarian first and foremost and politically correct in everything he did. However, he felt it required a solution before it became too late as the human population approached totally unsustainable levels and self-destruction.

With the French inspiration of the *Médecins sans Frontièrs* in front of him, Adam decided, towards the end of his third year of study at the Medical School, that he would form a group which would attract other intellectuals to discuss these issues honestly, without rancour, and to try to seek a solution. Being an egocentric but highly persuasive character, it didn't take long for Adam to attract like-minders to his group which subsequently became known as *Vers Une Terra Verde* (Towards a Green Earth). The formation of this group was to have a more far-reaching effect on the world than even he could have imagined at this time.

14

The next three years passed quickly for Laura and Winston in Exeter. They were as Winston described them, essentially uneventful, steady years, the straight sections of his staircase of life. Winston progressively changed and expanded his courses as he assessed the relative interest of his student classes. With lecture notes increasingly being required to be presented in a digital form on the University website for student access, he noticed that the number of students attending lectures was falling as they felt there was no necessity to attend every one. From his own experiences, he felt that it was the interaction with his lecturers that had taught him the most important lessons for his future career, not the factual data in lecture notes. His mentors had stressed over and over again that if you wished to solve a problem, you needed to view it in perspective at the appropriate scale. If you looked at too small a scale, you would not solve it as you were too close to it.

Secretly, he felt this was the problem of most modern governments. They devolved responsibilities into discrete departments, who competed for prestige and budget, and there was no-one at the top who could see the interconnections. For example, he thought, concentrating on full employment could lessen crime and stress-induced illnesses and suicides, reducing the stress on police and hospital systems, while paying back cost through an increase in the number of taxpayers. It was over-simplistic, but it was a new way of looking at problems, not fixing them with an individual 'band aid' approach. He had also been taught to challenge conventional wisdom: to 'disbelieve if you can', as one of his mentors had put it. He introduced this concept into his lectures, as he realised that the students liked to be involved in debate, not just sit back listening to their lecturers drone on.

So, he discussed subjects which were controversial and kept his students entertained as well as informed. His Social History classes were the best attended at the University. In these early days, he emphasised the repetitive nature of the rise and fall of civilisations and empires, with leaders failing to learn from history and repeating the mistakes of the past, leading to cycles of the demise of one power and the ascendency of another, commonly after a period of instability when so-called barbarians roamed the world. He emphasised the impact that religion had on European conflicts and European and African and Asian civilisations. His estimate was that conflicts between religions, or at least using religions as an excuse, and persecution of religious groups, was the single most important cause of death throughout post-Stone Age history. "The current problem with Islamic extremists is just an extension of the mediaeval crusades," he would say. He also stressed the importance of natural resources in conflict using examples from modern history: Hitler turning east to secure oil supplies; the Japanese bombing of Pearl Harbour so that they could procure oilfields in the southwest Pacific; the US invading Iraq to liberate oil supplies in Kuwait. "The names of historical periods like the Stone, Bronze and Iron Ages, reflect the importance of resources," he would say. "Today we are living in the Petroleum or Cement Age, and the Nuclear Age is at hand." It was too early to address Climate Change or Global Warming, but it was on his list of things to think about.

His lecture series concluded with an assessment of the future based on the past. He emphasised all the symptoms in the Western economy and culture that were leading to imminent decline, while those in China were indicative of the rise of a new superpower, renewing its glorious past in the days of Confucius when it was the cultural centre of the world. This, of course, had the desired effect on the students, who vigorously defended their life styles, social behaviour, and cultural and political beliefs. Students wanted to hear 'The Stirrer' and see the line of large wooden spoons hung on his office wall as trophies from various student nights. Winston had found his niche in academic life.

Laura was a pleasant and hard-working addition to the library staff, and was sought out by students because she was attractive, attentive and very well informed. She was always amused when students queried her on what Winston really thought and how best to approach him to be their supervisor. She realised that she had reached a plateau in life while Winston was still progressing. Inequality and resultant jealousy could ruin our relationship, she thought, so she decided to study towards a Master of Arts as a first step towards her further education. She discussed it with Winston who told her to 'go for it' and to research something she was passionate about, so as to achieve and enjoy at the same time. It was inevitable that she would choose *Changing Perceptions and Impacts of the Bronte and Austen Novels from the 19th to 21st Centuries* as her thesis topic. She soon became embroiled in it.

During the week, they had little time to themselves, but they made a point of having excursions every other weekend to enjoy the interesting places in Devon and Cornwall. By now, Winston had a small car which made it easier to get to start off points for their jaunts. They hiked on Dartmoor and Bodmin Moor, walked the coastline near Exmouth, Torquay, Plymouth, Falmouth and Boscastle, and visited historic sites such as Tintagel, a site strongly linked to King Arthur's birth. On other weekends, they enjoyed the theatre or cinema, entertaining or being entertained by colleagues, and exploring Exeter and its surrounds. Every six weeks or so, they returned to Brighton, and their apartment in the Wright household. Neil would organise family outings either on Saturday on their way to Brighton or Sunday on their way back to Exeter, with lunch at picturesque villages.

Each summer, they spent a week in St Mary's, never tiring of the island and vowing to buy a cottage there as a sanctuary for the future, if and when they could afford it on their University salaries.

The only sadness experienced was through domestic problems of some of their colleagues and friends. Both Winston and Laura were good listeners and viewed as a totally contented and committed couple by those they knew. So others came to them to air their woes. They could only listen and provide perspective, because most problems were irresolvable. Among themselves they discussed why people who had so much going for them should be so unhappy in their relationships. They decided that modern life had become very complex. In the eras leading up to the two great wars the man was normally the provider, with the woman having responsibility for the home and family. Positions were clear, with women seldom having the resources to leave unhappy situations. Children were also taught that qualities such as honour, stoicism, heroism and consideration were important, and these as well as a good work ethic should be upheld as the 'British Way.' With the growing equality of the sexes and liberation of women through readily available contraception, Winston and Laura considered that responsibilities had become less clear, each partner had their own resources, and societal pressures had eased in terms of divorce or separation. Partners who were unhappy with their relationships or sex lives could more easily seek solace elsewhere.

"In many cases sex has replaced love" said Laura. "We've become more obsessed with physical pleasure than with spiritual satisfaction."

"Agreed," said Winston. "It's great that we have both, and you don't know what a poor lover I am by previous experience."

"You're a great lover, but you know there are women and men too who have to put up with violent partners and bullying. At least these days it's easier to get out of that sort of relationship. Thank goodness you're so gorgeous" Laura chuckled as she bit his ear. Winston laughed as he reflected that he had her total love. He was glad that he had waited to find HER and thought that if he'd experimented with love and sex earlier in life, he may have ended up like some of the friends who seemed constantly at odds with their lot. As it was, he had everything he desired in life and just hoped it stayed that way.

Life in Exeter, as elsewhere in Devon and Cornwall, was generally peaceful, with little of the ethnic tensions that were progressively enveloping the larger, more multicultural cities in England. An exception that caught Winston's attention was an attack on the Islamic Centre near Truro, a cultural centre for probably less than a hundred Muslims who lived in southwest England. In June, 2008, an

Islamophobic attack involved right-wing graffiti, pig's heads nailed to the door, and a fire bomb attempt. It was suggested that this was linked to retaliation for the 2005 bomb attacks in central London and subsequent foiled terrorist attacks. It was decried by government authorities and Christian churches, but reflected an undercurrent of hatred, even in this otherwise peaceful society. Winston resolved to upgrade his lecture notes on the futility of religious prejudice and hatred when members of each religion held similar broad beliefs and social values. The devil was only in the detail.

He argued in his notes and lectures that those outside a particular religion, or non-believers of any mainstream religion, couldn't understand why Protestants and Catholics had fought for centuries when they were all Christians, and that there were still tensions today in northern Ireland. "It's the same with Muslims" he would argue, "for those outside the religion, which emphasises peace, it is hard to imagine why Sunis and Shiites persecute each other when, to most people in the western world, their differences in beliefs appear trivial. In much of the western world, people are becoming atheists or embracing evangelical creationist religious groups or groups like the Scientologists that appear more relevant to their modern lives, even if many of their scientific beliefs are out of kilter with established scientific data." His students liked these religious debates because, living in southwest England, they had not been subjected to any major religious prejudice or conflict in modern times and they could remain impartial. Issues like climate change, the global economy, and the role of women and sport in modern society provoked much more passionate debate.

15

Laura and Winston decided to take the train on their visit back to Brighton in August 2008, and they were met at Paddington by the Frobishers who were very excited and dying to share their news with Winston and Laura before travelling on to Tunbridge Wells for lunch with the Wrights.

"Do you remember Mark Jones from the Archaeological Society?" asked Neil as he drove them slowly out of a crowded London. "He came on some of the trips I took you on when you were a nipper."

"I think so" replied Winston, a little unsure, "wasn't his wife a teacher like Mum?"

"Yes you're right" said Neil. "Well, he's always been interested in the history of South America, but never been there. He particularly wanted to visit Machu Picchu, but it was quite expensive. Apparently the main tourist season is in the dry season from April to October, and it's very popular in July and August because of the summer holidays in Europe. But he managed to get a very good off-season deal for a tour in November that examines the Inca civilisation in Peru at places like Machu Picchu and Lake Titicaca and the Mayan civilisation in Mexico on the Yucatan Peninsula. There were other trips to Mayan sites in Honduras, Guatemala and Belize, but Mark preferred what he considered to be more stable Mexico."

"So are you telling me that you're going with them?" Winston interrupted, suddenly realising what this was about.

"Yes" piped up Lavinia excitedly. "We're off to Mexico and then on to Peru. Neil's partner will look after the business and Roedean have given me the time off in lieu of some of my Long Service Leave. We're always working, so it's a thrill to get away overseas, particularly to somewhere warmer and escape the cold here."

"That's fantastic" said Winston, "you both deserve a break. It could be like a second honeymoon."

"I wouldn't go that far." Lavinia made a sweeping motion with her hand as if to tell Neil not to get any ideas.

"We're with the Jones's until the end of the tour," said Neil, then when they come home we stay on in Lima for a few days at the end. Your father, Laura, has kindly agreed to check on the house once a week to make sure everything is OK. We'll text you and perhaps we can Skype you around lunchtime Exeter time on pre-arranged days while we're having early breakfast. I think the time difference is about six hours."

In mid-November, the Frobishers and Jones departed, with farewells from all involved at Heathrow airport. Over the next two weeks, Winston and Laura had somewhat interrupted Skype conversations with the Frobishers, due to poor reception. It was obvious that they had an absolute ball at Chichin Itsa, with its Pyramid Kukukan, and Dzibitchaian being the Mayan highlights in Mexico, and Machu Picchu the out-and-out standout Inca highlight in Peru.

"You can see it all on travel programs on TV" said Neil, "but it doesn't prepare you for the grandeur and architectural majesty and scale when you're up close on the ground." Their only problem, it seemed, was an attack of what Lavinia described as the 'Bombay Belly' despite being on the wrong continent.

The day after they arrived in Lima, they Skyped Winston.

"We're not very comfortable here" explained Neil. "People keep accosting us on the street and we feel a bit unsafe. So we've decided to go to Iquito for a couple of days. I've always dreamed of seeing the Amazon since my father read to me about it when I was young, scaring me with stories of piranha fish and Amazon Indians with poison arrows. There was a picture of an anaconda swallowing a whole animal which I looked at with dreaded delight. Anyway it's the wet season, but we can still get a feel for the jungle. Your mother's a bit nervous but I'm sure we'll be fine. We'll Skype when we get back to Lima. We're looking forward to seeing you when we get home. We really miss you and Laura. Please give her our love."

When Neil and Lavinia arrived in Iquito and had settled into their hotel, the Victoria Regia, Neil thought it would be a good idea to hire a small boat or canoe on the following day to experience what it might have been like before the advent of civilisation and tourism in Iquito. Next morning, on the advice of the hotel concierge, they took a twenty minute motor rickshaw ride to Bellavish Nanay and hired a small boat with an outboard motor. The proprietor said they could just navigate the river or visit the nearby tourist villages of Padre Cocha and San Andrés if they felt more adventurous. He assured Lavinia there were no piranhas in the river when she asked him nervously. They had just cast off into the river when Lavinia noticed they had no lifejackets.

"Nothing can happen," assured Neil "the river is high but not fast flowing, and we're both strong swimmers if we did have trouble. We've lived near rough seas all our lives." Lavinia was not convinced but he seemed so happy and boyish, she decided not to spoil his fun by protesting. About twenty minutes later, it started to rain heavily and visibility suddenly became poor. Neil now nervous himself, immediately turned the boat around to head back to the jetty where they had hired the boat.

"What's that sound?" called Lavinia, alarmed.

"It sounds like a motor boat coming up fast," yelled Neil, "Let's hope he sees us. Brace yourself in case he doesn't." As he spoke a sleek motorboat appeared out of the rain, pulling a water-skier behind. The pilot was turning towards the skier and yelling something at him, when the motorboat ploughed into the Frobisher's boat, the impact knocking them unconscious before they hit the water. The skier was thrown over the top of the two boats, hitting the water head first, the motorboat careering out of control into the river bank, pulling him with it.

Two days later, Winston was getting a little concerned that his parents hadn't contacted him as promised. He texted but both their phones seemed out of range as there was no response. On returning to the apartment, the landline rang. That will be them, he thought, feeling relief. He was surprised when a rather cultured voice asked,

"Am I speaking with Winston Frobisher?"

"Yes" he replied, "Who is this?"

"My name is Jacinta from the British Embassy in Lima, calling on behalf of the Ambassador. Do you have someone with you?" Winston replied in the negative and she went on slowly, "I'm afraid I have some bad news for you. Both your parents have been killed in a boating accident on the Nanay River at Iquito. They were involved in a bad collision that killed both them and a water-skier who was being towed by the other boat. Both the Ambassador and I are sorry for your loss," she said, using the words Winston recognised as those accepted as official condolences worldwide. Winston sat down, stunned by the suddenness of it all. He tried to gather himself together to see what must be done.

"What do I have to do from here?" he asked, trying to keep his dismay under control and his wits about him.

"It's a little unclear as you have some options which I'll explain" said Jacinta. "You have to remember this is Peru not England. The pilot of the motorboat survived the accident and has given a full account which totally exonerates your parents from any blame."

"But what happened?" Winston couldn't imagine what his parents had been doing. Jacinta told him what had happened explaining that the sudden heavy rain had affected the visibility and that they had crashed. She went on.

"We believe that the local coroner has issued death certificates without performing autopsies as no foul play was involved."

"I'm grateful for that. What follows now?" asked Winston.

"We can arrange for the bodies of your parents to be flown to Lima if you authorise it" she said gently. "We can act as guarantors of payment, but the bill will have to be paid by you or from your parents' estate. We can also arrange for your parents to be sent to the UK, but this may be difficult and it would be preferable if you could come to Lima and make formal identification for our records and the Peruvian authorities before proceeding from there. For cost and convenience, most of our subjects in this position have the bodies cremated in Lima and take the ashes home for a formal farewell with family and friends in the UK, unless you prefer they be buried in the UK. We can help you organise a cremation if you wish."

"Let me discuss this with my wife before I make a final decision. Can you give me your direct phone number or email?" He wrote the details down and continued, "Thank you for all your help. You've been very kind in a difficult situation."

He sat back in his favourite armchair, grabbed the family photo off the sideboard and cried, sobbing for the senseless loss of life and for the realisation that his close family now revolved around Laura and the Wrights. No more tramps across the downs or lunches in historic pubs with his father and no more hugs from his mother which had grown more frequent since his marriage. A little later Laura came home to find him uncharacteristically slumped in the armchair with a half-empty whisky bottle on the table and a glass in his hand. She knew instinctively that something was very wrong. Winston had visited the doctor earlier that week and her first thought was that he'd been notified of cancer or worse. Winston saw her consternation and read her thoughts as usual.

"Sit down," he said "and no, there's nothing wrong with me. I'm not sick or anything like that."

"Well what then?" she sighed in trepidation. He told her about his parents as gently as he could. She too had grown to love them as part of her family, and a flood of tears rolled down her cheeks. He put his arm around her and they cried together, as one spirit, as in everything they did together.

"Take me to bed," she said unexpectedly. "I just want to forget this awfulness for a moment, then we can make plans after dinner."

Later that evening, Winston phoned the Embassy in Lima, calculating that it was early afternoon there. Having been put through to Jacinta, he asked her when the bodies of his parents would arrive in Lima. She told him that they would have them in the city morgue within the next two days and asked him what he had decided to do.

"I'm doubling up my lectures over the next week" he explained, having phoned the Head of Department a little while earlier. "I think we'll have a cremation but I just have to check with our solicitor. I can get a flight on Sunday and be at the Embassy on Monday morning if that's OK."

"That's really good. We'll see you then and don't worry, we can help you organise things. Will you be alone or with your wife?"

"Alone, I'm afraid, it's difficult for us both to have time off now, but we both hope to come in the future. My parents loved Machu Picchu and Lake Titicaca and we want to see for ourselves."

16

On Monday, after a long, but uneventful, British Airways flight from Heathrow, via Madrid, Winston arrived at the British Embassy. Jetlagged, tired, despondent and a little disoriented he was surprised at how close the Lima city centre was to the azure-blue Pacific Ocean. He spent the day in somewhat of a haze going first to the morgue to formally identify his parents who looked quite peaceful in death, and then to the crematorium to finalise details for their cremation the next day. He had checked with his father's partner in their law firm about a will and his father's wishes. The partner, David Hughes, indicated that the wills could not be read until the death certificates were to hand, but that there was no indication in either about a burial. A check through Jeremy Wright at St Peter's indicated that the Frobisher's had not reserved a burial plot in the diocese. So Winston felt justified in arranging a cremation on foreign soil. He thought he would keep their ashes with him until he decided on a permanent home and that maybe he would later scatter them at one of the historical sites his father had loved.

The cremation complete and the ashes collected, Winston embarked on the long flight back to Heathrow after visiting the Embassy once more to thank Jacinta for all her trouble. She was delighted with the flowers he brought her, and told him how nice it was to be recognised for her work as so often members of the embassy staff were taken for granted or criticised. She gave him a traditional South American hug before saying goodbye.

He took a taxi to Paddington and then the train to Exeter where Laura rushed into his arms on the platform.

"I really missed you" she whispered in his tingling ear. "It was so lonely without you."

"And I without you, my darling Laura" he answered gently "even if the South American women were really hot." He grinned and she laughed at his attempt to stir her up. As they drove home, she explained that her parents had suggested that, on the weekend after the one immediately coming up, they could organise a 'wake' for Neil and Lavinia with just a few close friends. They felt that this could substitute for a funeral and allow people to pay their last respects if Winston brought their ashes along. Her dad would again hold it in their house if this was acceptable, which it clearly was from Winston's nod of affirmation.

"If we go on Friday evening," he said, "I can pop into my father's law firm on Saturday and pick up the wills now I have the death certificates. I guess that they've left their estate to me, but I have no idea what it comprises. They may have mortgages and debts that I'm unaware of. We'll just have to see what life brings next weekend."

So having decided to go by train this time, in order to relax, they arrived at Paddington about 10.00 p.m. on the Friday night, stayed at the nearby small Brunei Hotel on Praed Street, just down from the station, and then travelled via Victoria to Brighton the next morning. Jeremy Wright was there to meet them and took them the short journey to David Hughes at the law office off Dyke Road. David had coffee and biscuits ready for them, checked the death certificates, and handed Winston the wills. It was as Winston had anticipated. Each had left their entire estate to the other, and then to him in the event of both their deaths. David realised that this was a sensitive issue, so he raised it after asking that Jeremy give them a few moments privacy.

"I've checked what I can for you, as your father had a copy of all his documents in the office and gave me Power of Attorney to access them should anything happen to him. Your father and mother had no mortgage on the Telscombe Cliffs house. My guess is that, as a detached house in a great location, it would be valued at around two hundred and fifty thousand pounds. They also had an investment account with Barclays, with a current value of about four hundred thousand pounds designed for their retirement. Neil was also a foundation partner of this law practice" went on David "and his estate is entitled to about a hundred and fifty thousand pounds in terms of current assets. So, I guess that by the time you've paid off any debts and outstanding expenses related to their deaths in Peru, as they did have insurance, you will inherit around seven hundred and fifty to eight hundred thousand pounds. Both Winston and Laura gasped at this amount. They never imagined the Frobishers were so wealthy, although Winston realised that much of it was property not cash.

"There is one other thing" went on David. "About a year ago, Neil gave me this letter to give you in the event that anything happened to him and Lavinia. I guess you should open it now or privately if you wish." Winston took the letter, hesitated for a moment, then opened the envelope. Inside was a short handwritten note that said:

Dearest Son,

Lavinia and I did not plan your birth but you and now Laura have been the greatest blessings of our lives. Do not feel sorry for us when you read this. We've had a wonderfully fulfilled life and all good things must end, unfortunately. Please use our estate to buy your cottage on St Mary's. It would give us so much pleasure for you to remember us every time you stay there. If you read this before the funeral, please take our ashes with you. We will live on through you and Laura and your children.

Your loving father,

Neil Frobisher.

Winston tried to hold back his tears in front of David Hughes, but they flooded out when Laura, who had been looking over his shoulder, was crying unashamedly as she sobbed, "We are so lucky to have such wonderful parents." Even David Hughes had to turn away, pretending that he had gone to let Jeremy Wright back into the room.

The 'wake' at Portland Place was everything that Winston could have hoped for. The Wrights had put on a wonderful spread with beer, wine and spirits in abundance. Tudor music played in the background while a series of images of family historical visits combined with images from the Archaeological Society and Roedean School, put together by Penny, rolled over on the large TV screen. Guests mainly from the Archaeological Society and Roedean, Telscombe Cliffs and Neil's law firm, came to Winston and Laura, in turn, to offer condolences and touch the urns carrying the Frobisher' ashes.

"At least these are ashes the Australians will never get," said one cricketing fanatic among the guests. At the end of the evening, everyone was in an alcoholic haze from the incessant toasts to various facets of the Frobisher's lives, many of them humorous incidents not known to Winston. Jeremy insisted that guests leave their cars and take taxis home.

"Or we'll be toasting your ashes next week" he joked. Finally everyone had gone.

"You did them proud" said Winston, a lump in his throat. "I can't tell you how grateful I am that they got such a touching farewell. It's a pity that we only realise just how wonderful they were when they are gone."

"I hope you get your cottage in St Mary's" said Penny gently, "and they can rest in peace there."

"And that you invite us to the ceremony" added Jeremy. With that, Winston and Laura went to bed, for once too exhausted to even make love.

"At least they were farewelled in style," murmured Winston.

"Yes, you've done your very best. I'm proud of you" whispered Laura as she dozed off into a fitful sleep full of fond memories of the past few years, interspersed with some worrying visions of problems to come.

17

On returning to Exeter, Winston phoned David Hughes to give him Power of Attorney to formally wind up his parents' estate and transfer funds to his joint account with Laura. He also asked if he would act on their behalf to put the Telscombe Cliffs house on the market for sale once he and Laura had visited in two weeks time to salvage memorabilia and furniture that they might like for their cottage on St Mary's, if and when they could purchase it. He had already retrieved the treasured set of Winston Churchill's Histories to remind him of his father each time he opened them. He and Laura needed to go through their things and mark what was for sale and what could be given to Oxfam. David had a friend in Real Estate in Brighton whom he said was willing to help if Winston would trust David to put it in his hands. Winston then phoned the list of Estate Agents who dealt with properties on the Scilly Isles. They all pointed out that there were always houses, apartments and businesses for sale but old cottages only came up once in a while. Winston, using his title of Dr Frobisher to try and pull some strings, asked them to let him know if something came up, and said that he could make a quick decision and pay cash if necessary.

The next few months were busy. Over Christmas, they managed to retrieve the items they desired from Telscombe Cliffs and put them in storage before putting the house up for immediate sale, while employing a neighbour to keep the garden in good order. Christmas and New Year were happy times, if somewhat subdued, at Portland Place, and Winston and Laura visited old haunts, sometimes in a melancholy mood as they remembered times with Neil as a guide. By March the estate was finalised and by May they had sold the Telscombe Cliffs house, and they now had almost eight hundred thousand pounds in the bank. It wasn't until late June that they got a call from Kate, an estate agent in St Mary's, to tell them that an old resident had died and her cottage was coming up for sale. On Saturday morning they took a flight from Exeter to the island, saw the stone cottage with its small walled garden, agreed to the price and organised a deposit via internet banking, all in about six hours.

"My God!" said Winston, "I never imagined that I would part with a lifetime's savings in less than half a day. My father will be smiling down on me, realising how out of character that was. The only other impulsive thing I've ever done is propose to you."

"I can't believe we did that either," said Laura as they embraced each other with the pleasure of knowing that their dream was coming true if the sale went through. "And we got the lovely old furniture as well, although the grandson has the right to anything he wants from the interior. I doubt that he'll want anything substantial, living in Spain as he does."

The next day after returning to Exeter, they enjoyed a celebratory lunch at the historic Poachers Inn in Ide village and discussed the future.

"What do we do next?" asked Laura, "assuming of course that the sale goes through."

"Well I think we should work towards setting up the cottage as a sanctuary for the future as well as a retreat for now," answered Winston. "You know the misgivings I have about the future with conflicts starting to escalate or break out in new parts of the Middle East and Africa, and increasing threats of global terrorism. There's always increasing violence in our society. As we've become what I consider to be 'Americanised', we've taken on their propensity for undisciplined behaviour. Even their TV dramas are dominated by crime shows with escalating violence. Have I ever told you that about a quarter of all known prisoners in the world are in American jails?"

"Only a million times," laughed Laura "and keep your voice down, you're having lunch, not haranguing a bunch of eager young students in a lecture theatre." She always enjoyed the fact that he reacted to her criticism, and was always slightly affronted. She guessed it was because it didn't happen often.

"Well, do you want me to go on or not?" he whispered in reply. She mouthed "OK," and he laughed, realising he was rapidly becoming a testy British academic with an intolerance to criticism.

"I think we should plan to become self-sufficient over there," he went on. "Dependent on any planning regulations, of course, I think we should build an extra underground water tank to take rainwater from the roof and that we should dig a cellar to store canned food and fuel and, importantly a wine supply. It would serve as a great resource in normal times and a nuclear shelter for the worst possible scenario. What do you think?" Laura thought he was going a bit over the top, but was prepared to let him ramble on for the moment.

"If we're going that far," she replied thoughtfully, "we should buy a petrol-driven generator for emergency power. That's always important and how about investigating the possibility of growing fruit like apples and pears, which should suit the climate, and have a vegetable patch. We can ask the locals what grows best there. Flowers obviously flourish on the island."

"Great ideas," gushed Winston, "this is really exciting. What about some berry bushes as well. You remember Simon O'Connor from the faculty; well he and his wife have a holiday cottage in the west of Ireland where they grow wonderful raspberries. They bring them home here and freeze them. They should thrive in a similar climate, although we'd have to plan for the wind when we plant."

"You're making it all sound as if we're buying into a mediaeval village," laughed Laura, "with your talk of subsistence and crops. Now what shall we call our new cottage, provided we are allowed and it isn't a historic site."

"I thought about that," mused Winston. "I know I'm being a bit self-centred but we wouldn't have the cottage if it wasn't for my parents. The first real association with my dad I remember is our visit to Hollingbury Camp, so I thought Hollingbury Cottage might be a good name." Laura reached across the table, took his hands and kissed him.

"That's why I love you," she said quietly. "You are so thoughtful about everything. I love the sentiment and the name. If it can't be Bronte House, then Hollingbury Cottage it is!"

"Now we have a home in St Mary's, what about our situation in Exeter? We have enough money left over to buy an apartment or small house."

"I think we should just continue renting our apartment. We essentially get it free through your tutorials and it'll probably be expensive to make building extensions to our cottage. It'll also be expensive to travel to and from the island. Why don't we just concentrate on the cottage for now." Laura nodded wisely as she spoke.

"Agreed," said Winston, "but what about starting a family?" He squeezed her thigh provocatively beneath the table, and she blushed.

"Again, I think we should wait a bit longer, at least until we've completed the cottage refurbishments. It would be very difficult to cart a baby across to St Mary's and then get work done there. Besides I'd like to finish my MA first."

"OK," agreed Winston. "Let's leave it until we're organised and ready. We're still young," he said, patting his first grey hairs, an inheritance from his father. "Let's live while we can." They toasted each other and the acquisition of their cottage, then drove home and spent the evening in bed.

18

In Winston's terminology, the next two years were 'steady' years that passed quickly as he and Laura were constantly busy or on the move. They worked hard in Exeter, and spent all long weekends and holiday periods at Hollingbury Cottage, carrying out their renovations and additions, planting fruit trees and vegetables, and finalising interior furniture from a mixture of that originally in the cottage and that from Telscombe Cliffs. They got to know some of the locals, particularly the storekeepers, tradesmen and restaurant owners, as they tried to keep up the romance between them with dinners overlooking the beach or historic sites, between all the hard work and travelling back and forth.

Their friends and associates from the university thought they were crazy spending all their spare time on the Isles of Scilly: 'silly' jokes were common and they suffered quietly.

"You could be holidaying in the South of France, Majorca or Acapulco, like us," they'd say, "instead of wasting your youth with hard work." Winston and Laura tried to explain that it gave them a sense of achievement while building something solid for the future, but to no avail. Winston secretly reflected that he and Laura didn't really belong in their generation probably because of their upbringing and in part their own old-school personalities. He believed life was for a purpose not simply for entertainment.

"You'll be fighting to be the ones to join us come the holocaust," was a favourite retort, to which their friends would simply laugh.

By the early spring of 2011, the cottage was essentially complete and they decided to ask Laura's parents over for a visit at Easter. Although Winston and Laura often flew across to save time, they all experienced the ferry trip, with Penny in particular vowing to return by air, although she soon forgot her nausea as they approached St Mary's. They both loved the sights of the island rising out of the choppy seas, just as Winston and Laura had done six years before. They had a most memorable long weekend, with walks to historic sites and along the beach, long boozy lunches and even longer relaxed dinners, the first of which was to toast the completion of all course work for Laura's MA: now only the thesis to be written before submission. The only downside Winston and Laura decided, giggling about it, was restriction on lovemaking as sound carried through the rather confined space in the cottage. The conversation always came back to the happy days in Brighton when the Frobishers were still alive.

"You aren't really gone, till those that love you stop talking about you," murmured Winston to the small ash-filled jars on the ledge above the fire place. He and Laura were still deciding on a more permanent resting place.

While they were finalising the cottage, Winston was enhancing his reputation as a fine teacher and inspiring speaker. He had been quite rapidly promoted to Senior Lecturer on the basis of his teaching skills, and had been an invited speaker to conferences in the UK and Europe. Laura had gone along where work and study permitted, and they had used these times as real holiday breaks away from the hard work in Exeter and St Mary's. On several of these trips, academic colleagues had strongly advised him to increase his research profile in order to reach Reader and eventually Professor status. Winston realised that, with a heavy teaching load, he would need a postdoctoral fellow, who could carry out research full-time, to achieve this. Without much hope of success, but using several prominent international researchers as co-investigators, he applied as principal investigator for a grant from The Arts and Humanities Research Council (AHRC) to research *The Current Economic and Social Position of the Western World on the Evolutionary Curve of Civilisations and Empires: A Historical Perspective*, that included a post-doc position. His concept was to examine where the western world now stood in terms of the rise and fall of the Greek, Roman, Ottoman and British empires and the civilisations they brought to their areas of influence. After Easter, to his surprise but delight, he learned that he had been given the AHRC grant on the premise that he could appoint someone of acceptably high calibre to the post-doc position. So, taking his colleagues' advice, he advertised internationally in journals such as *Nature*, and several globally read newspapers, renowned for their pages of advertisements for academic positions. He also emailed copies of application forms to History Departments in North America, Europe and Australia, the most likely sources of post-docs with an intimate knowledge of the western world.

19

In New York, continually motivated by her experiences in the 2003 power outage, Maria Gomez had completed her PhD, the first person in the family to do so. Her parents were so proud to introduce her as Dr Maria to their friends, much to her embarrassment. As her research involved the modern period as well as the past, Maria was an avid reader of news articles, so she picked up the advertisement for the post-doc at Exeter in both the *New York Times* and *Washington Post*. She thought that the advertisement could have been written specifically for her and that it was something she could kick ass on. She knew that she had always been highly ambitious, and immediately saw this as a means to expand her research horizons, work diligently, write papers, make an international impact and become a respected academic herself. Her future seemed to loom before her in a flash and she realised that this could be the turning point and that she had to go for it. She considered that Exeter was a bit small after New York, but rationalised that she could do any serious partying in London which wasn't too far away by train. She was certain that it wouldn't be as bad as getting across New York in traffic.

She sought the advice of her primary supervisor on how to best make her application, wrote it, edited it, rewrote it, re-edited it and, finally with a sigh of inevitability, sent it off both as an email attachment and an express letter, just to be sure, and sat back nervously to wait.

In Exeter, Winston received the applications through the University office. If this was for an academic position, a strict procedure of appointing a selection panel to narrow down the top three to four candidates, formal interviews, and presentation by those candidates would have to be followed. In this case, it was his grant and his decision, although he would need to justify it in writing for the University records in case there was a 'miscarriage of justice' with a complaint from an unsuccessful applicant: an extremely rare occurrence. On the basis of the qualities of the applications, he rapidly narrowed down the list to three applicants. Some of the PhDs applying seemed to lack basic English skills and Winston thought that they needed remedial English courses. He wondered how they had got through University to such a high level without any sense of strict grammar, or understanding of how to present information in a logical hierarchical order: probably because they don't read Bronte novels, he laughed to himself thinking to share this thought with Laura later.

His choices were two men, one an Australian and the other a Scot, and an American woman. She appeared outstanding with High Distinctions throughout her undergraduate years, a Distinction or *cum laude* for her PhD thesis and several co-authored papers published prior to the award of PhD: a similar academic history to his own. Although he was not a fan of modern American culture, she was clearly the standout choice. To be fair, he phoned the referees of all three applicants, and again she appeared the best. Words used constantly to describe her included 'dedicated', 'efficient', 'persistent', 'effective' and 'passionate', with phrases like: will write seminal papers; has the rare ability to meet deadlines; always ahead of the game; best student I've ever had; passionate in everything she does; and simply awesome student. He was impressed, if a little surprised at the excessive use of passionate to describe her talents. He thought that the Americans had a different way of looking at things to the British, and that this candidate appeared to be a bit obsessive like himself. At least we always get the job done, he thought.

Rather than use some of his rather meagre funding on plane and rail fares and hotel accommodation, he decided on an interview via Skype. Maria was rather nervous, unsure what to wear or how to behave fronted by an Englishman. She judged by comparisons between Hollywood and British movies and American and British TV that the English were less obsessed by beauty and celebrity and more interested in character. Like Winston, she had watched programs like *Time Team* on TV and thought how eccentric to outright weird the archaeologists appeared. She pondered on how uncool they seemed, with baseball caps, tank-tops or top-brand T-shirts replaced by sweaty old hats and strange woollen jumpers on guys with hairstyles from the seventies if they had hair at all. She wondered why she enjoyed it so much in spite of the almost unintelligible English some of them spoke.

Having considered all this, she decided to wear a modest blouse and skirt with a simple silver necklace and to remove her nose stud. The small tattoo on her left shoulder would not be visible and she would limit her makeup. She ignored the advice of friends to wear glasses with plain glass that might make her look studious, although she had noticed that some politicians did this. She would project an image of an earnest, conservative young woman keen to come to England to work with the renowned Dr Winston Frobisher.

She need not have worried because they hit it off straight away. Winston was struck at how exactly the opposite of Laura she appeared, with her dark hair and brown eyes, although she had the same passionate, unfathomable depths in her eyes. He thought his associates would think him unprofessional, politically-incorrect or even sexist if they could read his initial thoughts. In turn, her immediate impression of him was a rather handsome, certainly distinguished and well-spoken guy with a delicious accent like in the old black-and-white movies. Very desirable, she thought.

On a professional level, he asked her why she was interested in social history, and was intrigued when she said that the day in 2003 had changed her perspective on life. As they chatted, Winston could see that they shared many common opinions about where the modern world stood in a historical context, but had a different perspective on the level of decline in the modern world. He reflected that Americans in general were more optimistic than the British who tended to think that the decline was due to 'Americanisation' of more conservative global societies, who still had good manners and more discipline, whereas to Americans it was the framework that they had been brought up with.

As the interview drew to a close, Winston decided that she would be a welcome addition to the group in Exeter. He considered she could bring a younger, less conservative, American viewpoint to their research and also help address the imbalance between males and females in the academic workforce that University administrators were always banging on about. He would have no problems justifying her selection in terms of academic results, co-authored papers and femininity with the university administration. His largely politically incorrect student group would also welcome an attractive American woman giving tutorials. However, he would have to talk to Laura about it before finally deciding. She always had a common-sense attitude and could see problems to which he might be oblivious.

"If we do decide to appoint you as the post doc on this project when could you join us?" asked Winston.

Essentially right away," she replied, 'dependent on the paperwork that might be needed for a US citizen to work in the UK. I have a valid passport and no commitments here, apart from family."

"If you give me your mobile number, or is it cell in the US, I'll call you within forty-eight hours and let you know the verdict."

Laura looked through the application and looked up Maria's webpage which she guessed she would have, although Winston had not thought of it.

"She looks great on paper," she said finally "and has experience in all the right fields. I think you have to appoint her, but my intuition tells me she will be a feisty customer and that repetitive use of the word 'passionate' to describe her concerns me deep down. Perhaps she'll cause some problems, but I think you should appoint her. Qualifications are more solid than women's intuition and you really liked talking to her."

So Winston called Maria, sent off the formal offer, and received a formal acceptance, all within ten days. Dr Maria Gomez was now part of the Social History group.

20

In London, Adam Lampton was just completing his studies at King's College London Medical School, specialising in Immunology, Infection and Inflammatory Disease in his courses. He had joined his father Andre in *Médecins sans Frontiers* in Africa for a few weeks on each long vacation, not because he had a philosophical commitment to their cause, but mainly to retain his father's respect and, more importantly, trust. During his student years he had formed *Vers Une Terra Verde*, seemingly to provide a platform for debates on sustaining a green Earth, renewable energy sources, the impact of humans of global pollution, climate change and animal conservation. He had even succeeded in obtaining help in locating meeting rooms from the Green Party of England and Wales and funding from both of them and the Australian Greens, because his public website displayed similar sentiments to those defining their policies of a cleaner, more sustainable Earth, and they were keen to have his site accessible as an external link to their own. He had secreted these funds in a bank account for future use. Neither group, of course, had any inkling that there was anything sinister in *Vers Une Terra Verde*.

During this time, Adam organised talks by prominent British and visiting environmentalists and experts on renewable energy, climate change, human demographics and population control. The membership of *Vers Une Terra Verde* grew rapidly as many in the current generation were tired of what they viewed as self-interested politicians with no coherent politics damaging the British economy and social structure. Although Adam did not know Winston, he would have shared his views that the world needed strong leaders such as Churchill or John F. Kennedy, but conceded how difficult this was in a world dominated by media interrogation and the power of minority groups and where democratic principles had gone off the rails. The majority of the population seldom got what they wanted, he thought to himself.

As the popularity of the society grew, Adam sought to identify what he termed 'like souls', with similar beliefs on the problem of an escalating world population, to join his inner sanctum, the power group of the society. He had read widely on the subject of eugenics, essentially genetic screening to promulgate Darwinian principles of 'survival of the fittest' among humans, which had been popular in many countries prior to the excesses of the Nazis in World War II. Negative eugenics had been termed genocide, and eugenics had become politically incorrect in the current era. However, he believed that there was a growing need to re-examine eugenic principles as the population exploded, and he needed to find others who felt the same. As his experience grew, he defined several criteria to help decide whether a member was suitable or not to join the inner sanctum. In terms of family, he concentrated on people who had been orphaned or fostered as children, those without siblings or with a history of family child abuse. In terms of religion, he favoured atheists or those from minority persecuted sects.

An arrest during demonstrations against globalisation or in anti-government rallies was considered a positive asset provided they were no longer being monitored by the authorities. In short, he was looking for those most likely to think in a logical way, unshackled by popular psychological thought, embrace the eugenic concept and likely to put the general good above family interests. In self-denial of his own growing fanaticism, and increasingly frequent hallucinations in which he was seduced into believing that he was the one chosen to provide the world with cleansing to produce a sustainable Earth, he deluded himself that he was not seeking out fanatics or those who could be influenced to become them.

One of the first to be welcomed to the inner sanctum was a classic Aryan blonde from Berlin, an only child who was studying for an MA in London. Helga Dietrich's great grandfather was a member of the Nazi Party prior to World War II, and his son, her grandfather was proud of the fact that the family had a close relationship to that of Albert Speer, Hitler's long-time Deputy. Her grandfather had insisted that, when old enough to understand, she read his first- edition copy of Hitler's *Mein Kampf* because he considered there were many concepts there that still applied in the late twentieth century. She told Adam that the book was very poorly written and rather boring, she was surprised by his hatred of the Jews and other ethnic minorities, and was shocked by the 'holocaust' which was orchestrated under his leadership.

"He was a fanatic who was blinded by a vision and failed to see reality and the consequences for the German peoples, or at least that's my view," she said. "However there are some parts of his rambling philosophical arguments that I do think make sense. His comments that the Aryan race, particularly Germans, are superior, at least in work ethic and determination, has, in fact, been born out of their rapid re-emergence after two defeats in the World Wars and their present position as arguable the most stable economy in Europe today. Even the East Germans had the most successful economy in the communist block under the Soviets, and emerged as a major sporting nation at the Olympics and World Cup Soccer."

"You're right," agreed Adam. "I've also thought the same. The

Germans have an incredible work ethic and resilience. It just needs to be harnessed in the right way. You mentioned some parts of his philosophy in your opening remarks. What are the other parts you think still apply?"

"It was his eugenic insight that destruction of the weak and sick is, in the long term, more humane than their protection," she went on, striking an immediate accord with Adam's views. "He saw a purpose in eliminating what he termed 'the weak' in order to provide space and purity for 'the strong' in the community. He seemed to recognise the problem of over-population and the fact that humans are the only animals who do not follow the Darwinian principle of survival of the fittest." Adam nodded in affirmation.

"Yes he was a realist in that sense," he added.

"However, he flouted his own philosophy with his ethnic cleansing of strong and weak indiscriminately," she went on. "The Jews are as hard-working and clever as we Germans. They have always been at the heart of the global financial systems and have for a long time dominated the Hollywood film industry. Not that it's always something to be proud of these days." She grimaced as she said the latter, having a dislike for what she considered 'sausage-factory' movies with repetitive themes and excessive violence and sex: junk fodder for the masses in her opinion.

Adam was delighted by these sentiments and she soon became his second-in-command as well as his lover. With her long blonde hair, high cheekbones, blue eyes, stunning figure and high intelligence, he viewed her as the definitive woman, both inside and outside the bedroom.

Her feminine insights and uncanny judgement of the sincerity and potential loyalty of others made her invaluable in Adam's search for his inner sanctum of the fifteen or so compatriots he calculated he would need to promulgate his mission. In general, their expertise was not relevant for his purpose with the exception of one person. He calculated he would need someone with experience in controlled explosions, such as were carried out in underground mines. He knew that it might take several months to years to recruit the appropriate group, but he considered this to be a reasonable time frame for his complex operation.

The first thing was to convince his father that he did not want to carry out an internship and then join his father's medical practice. He would prefer, he said, to enter the medical research field dealing with disease control, which would be appropriate due to his background of medical studies.

Four months later, partly through his father's influence and partly through his outstanding academic results, he was given a position as Medical Research Assistant, with a probationary period of twelve months in which to assess his ability and reliability. The position was at a secret location in North London. He could not take up the position until he had signed an Official Secrets Act document to swear that he would not reveal the real purpose nor the location of the research facility to any other person, including family. His employment was recorded as with Allergy Pharmaceuticals whose name adorned a small plaque to the right of the main entrance. He gathered from his interview that secrecy was required for any government medical-research laboratory complexes due to the constant disruption caused by Civil Liberty, Animal Rights and other protestors in the local community and also the constant threat of terrorism. 'No knowledge is best knowledge' he was told. Security was a top priority and it was mandatory that he first attend a three day course dealing solely with biosafety and security. Once he started he would undergo a period of supervision with specific training in handling pathogenic and potentially lethal agents. He couldn't wait to begin, elated at the idea of a 'cloak and dagger' position and the challenges of bringing his plan to fruition.

Meanwhile, he increasingly experienced hallucinations where he could see that population reduction was the ultimate Green way forward to save the Earth. Charles Darwin espousing his 'survival of the fittest' philosophy was a frequent vision. Through an unconscious selection process, he was increasingly able to isolate in his visions an image of a conservative somewhat austere, bearded 19th Century gentleman resembling the likeness of Darwin that he had viewed on the web. What he could not control were the occasional flashes of bright lights in front of his eyes which appeared like fireworks but had no associated noise.

It was fortunate that he was able to compartmentalise his various activities so that the visions were rarely present during his work, the Green Earth group activities, or his relationship with Helga. She regarded him affectionately as being a bit eccentric. However their bond was strong as they had similar beliefs and enjoyed a good sex life. Adam also encouraged her in her studies and he became a good sounding board for her to expand her ideas. It was only during his obsessive planning that he imagined the images in his visions encouraging him, convincing him that he would become the Earth's saviour.

21

Another two years went by in a 'steady' way for Winston and Laura. She expected to complete her MA by early 2012 and was now talking about starting a family. Maria Gomez' appearance in Exeter had accelerated Winston's research and they had a number of papers in preparation or submitted to international journals. They were both enthusiastic and productive and fed off each other's energy in terms of co-operative research.

Laura was a little sceptical about Maria's motives. She saw how Maria gazed at Winston. Like a spider waiting to pounce, she thought. Maria was always suggesting they had discussions over cappuccinos in a local café or even over a drink in one of the local pubs after work.

Laura raised her concerns with Winston, but he seemed oblivious to Maria's attentions, simply considering them part of their close and very productive working relationship.

"Besides, she seems to have lots of male admirers to keep her happy" said Winston nonchalantly. "I think you're imagining all this. Still, I'm happy about it, because it shows you still don't want to lose me, even after all these years. I love you as much as I've always done and have eyes for no-one else, even if they are very attractive," he added, teasing her. She dismissed the remark with a flippant wave of her hand and kissed him passionately on the lips, with the inevitable consequence. Laura considered that she was in no danger of losing him at this stage, but vowed to keep an eye on Maria.

Winston's lecture courses were going well. There was particular interest in his lectures concerning the role of religion in conflicts as tensions in the Middle East increased, with major civil unrest to civil wars erupting in Tunisia, Libya, Egypt, Iran and Syria, other unrest appearing in Bahrain, Yemen and Jordan, and sectarian violence in Iraq and Pakistan resulting in hundreds of deaths through suicide and car bombings, sometimes against worshippers in mosques who held, to his view, essentially similar beliefs. At his students' request, he expanded his notes on the website.

His students were also intrigued by climate change. Some had noted that the initial concept of human-induced global warming seemed to have been replaced by the term climate change, with emphasis on an increase in extreme weather events. The news seemed to emphasise one day that this was the hottest day or month for a decade or a century and the next point out that there were record snow falls in eastern USA or Japan, all being ascribed to human-induced climate change. Some noted that several of Europe's airports had long closures due to extreme snow and ice conditions. Others had read that scientists were concerned about sea level rise of one to three metres in the next hundred years, while TV shows on the history of Europe were discussing sea level changes of over a hundred metres affecting the lives of Stone Age men. Most were confused by what appeared to be conflicting information of the relative impacts of Nature and Man on climate change. Some of the more sceptical students considered that the emergence of Climate Change Ministers in western governments was another capitalist ploy to gather more revenue via a carbon tax or various carbon-trading schemes, which went into government coffers rather than into developing alternative energy systems that did not release carbon dioxide into the atmosphere. There seemed to be a consensus that wind, tidal and/or solar power could not replace fossil fuels because they were not available in sufficient quantities throughout the planet, and, where present, were energy-efficient transient rather than continuous sources. Many argued that nuclear energy was the answer, initially nuclear fission and then the much safer nuclear fusion, but there was protest against this throughout the world.

So, a delegation of students came to Winston to ask if he could put Climate Change into a historical concept so that they could better understand the various evidence and arguments that were becoming a daily discussion point.

"Ok, I'll try," said Winston, "but you must understand that this can only be a debate. There is such a widespread belief in human-induced climate change by governments worldwide that it has become a major source of research funding. Climate change sceptics are seen as pariahs by funding agencies and as liabilities by most universities who rely on research funding for their existence. That's why there are so many papers presenting evidence for, and so few arguing against it. I'll provide some background at geological to historical time scales and then we can have an open debate on the subject at one or two of the tutorial sessions."

In his lectures and notes, he divided his discussions into the historical past, measures in hundreds to thousands of years, as it affected human activity, and the geological past, measured in millions of years as it affected the climate of the planet since its inception.

First he presented the evidence for recent rise in CO_2 emissions and discussed the predicted scale of global warming due to the 'greenhouse effect', which experts suggested would cause changes of several degrees Celsius in the next century and a rise in sea level of about one to three metres in the same period. He pointed out that the sea level rise was minor in terms of changes in the historical past. Until about ten thousand years ago, before the end of the most recent Ice Age, Britain was part of continental Europe and most of Scotland, Ireland and northern England were under ice sheets, probably leading to the ultimate extinction of the mammoths. The English Channel, which has saved Britain from invasion several times in the past thousand years, only existed when the sea level rose about a hundred metres globally. The low sea level fifty thousand years ago allowed Australian Aborigines to migrate into Australia via land bridges from Asia via what are now South East Pacific Islands and Papua-New Guinea. Once the sea level rose, such migrations would have been impossible, although there have been other, approximately one to ten metre sea level changes since then, visible as wave-cut platforms throughout the world.

He also pointed out that global temperatures had fluctuated during the present interglacial period. For example he wrote in his notes, the River Thames has frozen solid forty times in the last millennium with a mediaeval period referred to as that 'Little Ice Age' with frost festivals held in London to celebrate these marvels of Nature. Before this Greenland was green, and farmed by the ancestors of the Vikings. He pointed out that some believed that these temperature variations were due to solar flare or sunspot activity rather than variations in carbon dioxide in the atmosphere, because correlations go back way beyond the Industrial Revolution.

He drew attention to the larger, longer time-scale, geological and astronomical framework, and that the Earth is not a static completely spherical object at a constant distance from the Sun and the planets in our galaxy. Instead, it is a planet wobbling through the solar system on a dynamic journey through the variably energetic galaxy, he argued. This produces cyclical changes, the largest cycle being around 145 million years, and the shortest group of five cycles between 210 and 11 years. The longer of these produce the so-called 'hundred year events' that result in massive flooding or long-lived droughts, he went on, and the shorter of these produce the alternate periods of high and low rainfall, the normal drought-to-flood cycles that dominate colonial poetry and novels in countries like Australia: 'a land of droughts and flooding rains' according to Dorothea McKellar, for example.

There is solid geological evidence that there have been ice ages throughout geological time, Winston's notes declared. There were three periods when the Earth was like a giant snowball with most, if not, all continents covered in ice. Geologists sceptical of human-induced climate change, point out that the coldest period in the past half billion years was about 450 million years ago, about three times the 145 five million year cycle, when there was a 'Snowball Earth'. Some experts suggest that the atmosphere contained CO_2 levels about ten times those of the present atmosphere, and hence argue about global warming through infinitesimal increases in CO_2. Others suggest that the ice ages were caused by draw down of CO_2, leading to global cooling.

His students, who had largely accepted human-induced climate change as a fact, were so interested at these perspectives that they discussed them with other students. So, when Winston came to give his tutorial and set out rules of engagement for a student debate, the room was overflowing with interested onlookers, and the tutorial had to be moved to a larger lecture theatre.

"So, having read the background précis provided on the website and the critical references I gave, I suggest that we debate the following issues among others you might propose," Winston pontificated, thrilled that this had attracted so much interest, but realising that he could not jeopardise the economic interests of the University.

"What about the following questions which I've put on the web for possible adaptation?" he flew in each question in a Power Point Presentation on a screen, and read each aloud as it appeared.

1. *Is human-induced climate change a proven theory or an incompletely tested hypothesis that needs more careful scientific research?*

2. *Do humans subconsciously wish to prove that they can no longer just harness the forces of Nature, they can also influence them by their activities?*

"I suggest you look at the five-part BBC TV series *Catastrophe*, hosted by Tony Robinson of *Time Team* fame, to really comprehend the power of Nature."

3. *Do governments really believe that there are viable alternative energy sources and provide incentives and funding to develop them, or are carbon taxes and trading schemes just another capitalistic way to fill government coffers?*

4. *What impact will global warming have at world scale? Will it only affect coastal communities due to sea level rise or will it have wider consequences?*

5. *What would be the consequences to humans if the opposite occurred and we had global cooling, with ice sheets advancing, Himalayan snow not melting to feed some major rivers on the Indian subcontinent etc.? What would be the consequences of resulting human migrations towards the tropics?*

6. *Should we view any human-induced climate change in the context of higher-order problems such as unsustainable growth in the human population with reduction in the support square for each individual? Is human-induced climate change, if it exists, just one symptom of a population out of equilibrium with Nature, with resulting unsustainable pollution of all kinds, and communities increasingly living in disaster-prone niches such as tsunami-endangered coastlines, earthquake zones, flood plains and de-vegetated hill-slopes vulnerable to massive landslides apart from being vulnerable to super-volcano eruptions or asteroid strikes?*

7. *Is the concept of human-induced climate change just the tip of the iceberg of evidence telling us that overpopulation is the major problem facing the human race and that governments should be following the example of the Chinese in trying to restrict it, and that influential groups like the Catholic Church should respond to it in a common sense, not traditional, way?*

8. *Would the world have sustained the current population of six billion people without the utopian climatic conditions of the past century or so?*

He paused, and an excited chatter broke out across the lecture room. Winston realised he had opened a can of worms but he hoped that it would stimulate thought and debate. Most of all he hoped it would encourage the students to learn to challenge conventional wisdom. If you could challenge and accept, you had a good foundation for belief, he thought. If you challenge and the concept fails the test, you had the foundation of a new hypothesis to test until it was generally accepted as a theory. This is the essence of scientific and historical research he reflected, feeling very pleased with himself. He laughed, as he believed that Laura would say that he was a self-satisfied, pontificating academic who was up himself.

As anticipated, these questions provoked heated debate among students and some of the other staff who wanted to share their perspectives from their academic specialities with Winston. His popularity as a stimulating lecturer grew, attendances at his courses were at an all-time high, and he was happy with his progress, always wary of going too far in terms of climate change to protect University interests. Laura noticed that Maria's open admiration for Winston had increased, but that he seemed oblivious of it, and that to her knowledge, and a lack of any gossip, nothing had happened between them. Winston still seemed devoted to Laura and sought her wisdom on everything he attempted to introduce into his lectures and research.

In London, Adam Lampton interviewed one of Winston's students, who was visiting family in Notting Hill, for membership of *Vers Une Terra Verde*. The student said that his inspiration to join had come from debates in Exeter and showed Adam the website. Adam was very interested and thought that both he and Winston had reached a similar conclusion through different perspectives. He imagined that they probably had totally divergent views on how to redress the problem. Academic versus pragmatic, he thought.

22

By early 2013, Winston had made an international reputation for himself, Laura had successfully submitted her MA thesis with her supervisor predicting a Distinction, and their cottage was finished and its garden flourishing. Winston accepted invitations to be a speaker at conferences and conventions at times and in places where Laura could accompany him. She, in turn, made sure that he did not travel alone with Maria to exotic locales where he may succumb to temptation, which she felt that Maria would provide given the chance. He also travelled more and more to London to sit on committees, and if convenient, Laura would go too, particularly if they could engineer a long weekend and visit her parents in Brighton. Jeremy was still as fit as ever but Penny was increasingly suffering from panic attacks that seemed to relate to anxiety about the progressively more violent and drug- and drink- filled world portrayed on the news and in the media. Her doctor had diagnosed her heart palpitations, sudden sweating and nausea as metathesiophobia, or fear of change, and was attempting to help her with various therapies, while suggesting she try to stay in her comfort zone and not read or view confronting information.

Laura was now making noises that it was time to have a family and went off the pill, but however hard they tried, after three months she had not become pregnant.

"Relax," was their family doctor's advice "you are probably over anxious and trying too hard. Just keep to your old routines but without contraception."

Winston was increasingly interested in his courses on religion and conflict as civil war erupted in Syria, and further unrest started to appear in Egypt and elsewhere, sectarian bombings claimed increasing numbers of victims in Iraq and Pakistan, and repression of women, and even violence against them, appeared to be escalating on the Indian subcontinent. Success in the war in Afghanistan had been limited, and the western allies were progressively withdrawing with the Taliban still highly active. Winston wondered what it all achieved?' History is full of such conflict led by zealous leaders that destroy the lives of millions of peace loving people, and for what: momentary power at best! Why don't we ever learn from past mistakes? He asked himself over and over again.

Britain itself had been lulled into a false sense of security concerning the impact of the War on Terror on its own shores. There were reports that terrorist plots had been averted by the British Intelligence Agencies such as Counter Terrorism Command and the Special Branches of individual police services, with intelligence provided by MI-5 and MI-6, if required. It appeared unlikely that the shocking attacks in London in 2005 would be repeated. Then, out of the blue, on May 22, there was a horrific murder of an off-duty British soldier, who was hacked to death by machete on the streets of London in front of shocked witnesses who heard the perpetrator call out "Allahu Akbar" after the killing. There were graphic images in media coverage of a young man with his hands covered in the blood of his victim standing defiant, apparently proud of his deeds in the cause of Islam. His alleged accomplice was also a British national but of Nigerian decent. This brought back memories of another Nigerian who attempted to blow up a Detroit-bound plane with explosives concealed in his underwear on Christmas Day, 2009, and who also called out "Allahu Akbar" or "God is great!" several times during his sentencing hearing. His action probably cost the west billions of dollars in the extra security for screening liquids carried by passengers following the incident.

Britain was shocked by what the population viewed as the senseless killing of one of them simply going about their business. It created fear of what might come next, because the new enemy, the terrorist, could be home-grown, no longer necessarily some foreigner from outside their country. The difficulty of detection was multiplied many fold. The Americans had already learned this from the widely publicised Boston Marathon bombings a month earlier on April 15.

Winston viewed this dispassionately as one of the few, inevitable negative aspects of multiculturalism in global cities, and decided to discuss these events with his students in future courses, stressing the difference between the terms multinational and multicultural, which seemed to be treated as the same in many media discussions.

23

As Christmas approached, it was evident from long-range weather forecasts that storms were likely through the Scilly Isles, the ferry would not run, and flights would be intermittent and bumpy. For these reasons, combined with Laura's concern for Penny's health, Winston and Laura decided to spend their Christmas break with her parents in Brighton, having been invited to do so repeatedly. Jeremy Wright had gone to the trouble of booking them all tickets to see *War Horse* at the New London Theatre in Drury Lane on 27 December, and surprised them with first-class rail tickets for all the family from St Pancras International to Paris under the English Channel on New Year's Eve. He had booked an old-fashioned hotel, the Passey Eiffel, so that they were close to the celebrations around the Champs-Elysees and within walking distance of the Eiffel Tower that evening. Winston and Laura were overwhelmed by his hospitality and generosity and were looking forward to the exciting break.

Over dinner at Portland Place the night they arrived, Laura produced a bottle of champagne and announced to her parents: "I've got two surprises for you. First I've finally got confirmation that my MA thesis was passed with Distinction, and I've brought you a leather-bound copy in gratitude for your help and encouragement. I hope you like the acknowledgements inside." She passed it around, and they hugged her and told her how proud they were and that she had been overgenerous in her acknowledgement that they had steered her along the literary path from childhood.

"We didn't have to at all," said Jeremy "you devoured books before you could even read. We were both exhausted from the pleading cries of 'just one more chapter' or 'just one more page before I go to sleep,' every night of the week."

"I knew about the MA already piped up Winston, but what's the other surprise. Don't tell me you've been awarded a gold medal or Nobel Prize for your research?" he said jokingly.

"Well, I deserve a gold medal for listening to your pontifications all day and night," she smiled, "and carrying your baby for you too."

She sat back and enjoyed the joyful moment that Winston realised that he was to become a father after what he thought was his failure for her to conceive and her parents' realisation that they would soon enter the realm of grandparents. They all gushed and started to give her advice to look after herself, all speaking over each other with a rush in their excitement, until Penny asked the inevitable question of how far gone she was.

"I'm about two months pregnant" she said, and "no, I'm not going to find out the baby's sex. It's more natural and romantic to be surprised at the birth."

"If it's a boy I expect we'll have to call him Jeremy Neil Darcy Frobisher," said Winston jokingly.

"What a great idea" piped up Jeremy pleased that Winston had put him first, "but I hope he's artistic and not a sportsman. With a name like that, he'll be ragged at school." Winston's own memories flooded back, and he thought that, as parents, naming a child was a great responsibility. In retrospect, it was a wonderful Christmas and New Year. The 'War Horse' was an amazing production, and reminded Winston and Laura of that first romantic meeting in the Lyceum Theatre not far away. Paris was a magnificent adventure. None of the family had been by train under the English Channel before and thoroughly enjoyed the Eurostar service. On New Year's Eve, they took a taxi to the Champs-Elysees to visit the spectacular, seemingly endless Winter Markets, with throngs of Parisians and visitors alike milling around the Avenue. On return to their hotel, they saw a smaller Winter Market, looking like a fairy land with a skating rink and an old-fashioned carousel at Trocadero, just a few hundred yards from their Passey Eiffel Hotel. From there, they could enjoy some hot sausage and mulled wine and view the spectacular light show around the Eiffel Tower as midnight arrived. They had all seen fireworks displays in England at midnight, but this show took their breath away.

On New Year's Day, they reluctantly returned to London and parted ways, the Wrights to Brighton and the Frobishers to Exeter. Jeremy had to re-open his book stores, Winston had to attend meetings, and Laura had a library stock-take to attend to.

24

In early March 2014, as the weather was improving marginally, Winston had to attend a quarterly committee meeting in London on Monday afternoon. Normally, he and Laura would go together on Saturday morning, see a show or visit a gallery on the weekend, and return by late afternoon train on Monday evening. On this occasion, Laura insisted that he go alone as she was rather nauseous from morning sickness and was not keen on the train journey nor driving up, and Winston wanted to catch up with colleagues on the Monday night to plan a conference in Scotland in 2015.

As a consequence, he had Laura drop him off early on Monday morning so that his train arrived on time to get him across London for his 2pm meeting after lunch.

"I'll drop the car home and walk as we usually do" she said, and she kissed him goodbye. "I need to keep up the exercise to stop becoming fat." Winston laughed as he could not imagine Laura being anything but perfect.

"I'll be home before lunch on Tuesday" he said, "I'll pop home to drop my overnight bag off and then come round to the library and take you for a quick lunch. I love you." She smiled, waved and left him to find his platform, feeling sad that he had to go alone, but relieved that Maria was not on the same committee. She worries me somehow she thought, and then forgot all about it.

Winston had an uneventful day with a successful committee meeting and a most enjoyable dinner with his close colleagues from several London universities who were planning the conference on Celtic culture in Edinburgh the following year. He was so absorbed in the discussions, and was getting rather tipsy on the beer and then wine that flowed at dinner, that it was after 11pm when he glanced at his watch. With dismay he realised that it was too late to call Laura to see if she was OK. She'll have gone to bed long ago, he thought. He decided to call it a night and farewelled his colleagues, before going upstairs to his room where he collapsed into bed, falling asleep almost immediately. When he woke the next morning he was mortified to realise he had not set his alarm and was running late. He now had less than an hour to get up, shower, and hail a taxi to Paddington to catch the train that he had prepaid as a return ticket. He made it with a few minutes to spare, found his seat, and phoned Laura on their landline, practising his apology in his mind. There was no answer. Hell, he thought, of course she's already gone to work. He tried her mobile and was not too surprised when he got the standard reply that the person he called was currently unavailable, as he knew Laura turned off her phone when on duty at the library with its 'Silence' policy. He imagined he would get the 'rounds of the kitchen', remembering fondly that it was on one of his father's favourite expressions.

He thought he would pick up some flowers from the station and take them to the library as an apology. He knew Laura would like the romantic gesture in front of the staff. Keeping up my Mr Darcy persona, he chuckled to himself as he realised he was speaking out loud. Winston arrived at the station, hurriedly bought the most expensive bunch of flowers he could see, grabbed a taxi and headed for their apartment. Their car was still there, so he concluded that Laura must have walked to work as usual. He opened the door and was immediately aware that the apartment was colder than usual. Checking the windows to see if Laura had left one open, he noticed that there was no obvious evidence that she had been there overnight. He had cleaned up, put the dishes away and cleared out the rubbish before leaving on Monday morning and nothing seemed to have upset that tidiness since. Perhaps she was sick and stayed overnight with a friend, thought Winston hopefully.

It was only a few minutes walk to the library, so, now somewhat concerned, he walked briskly clutching his bunch of flowers, with petals falling to the ground as he pumped his arms. Arriving at the library, he asked the receptionist if she could tell him where Laura was working.

"Oh," she replied, "she didn't come in this morning. We all assumed that she was sick as she'd told us all about the expected baby."

"Was she here yesterday, on Monday," asked Winston, now thoroughly alarmed. "Did you see her go home in the evening?"

"She was here all day," was the reply "and she was still here when I left, looking up something for a student who came in just as she was about to go home."

"I don't think she was home last night. Would it be OK if I checked with the other library staff to see if they might know anything about where she might be?" he asked persuasively.

"Of course, as far as I'm concerned, but you'd better check with the boss as she's a stickler for protocol, doing things by the book, so to speak. I hope it's all OK. We all love Laura here."

Winston checked with the boss and staff but no-one remembered seeing Laura leave the library, although two of the volunteer assistants remembered that she was still there servicing a student enquiry when they left.

"Was the student a regular at the library?" asked Winston now suspicious about this.

"Oh yes, he was in all the time. Nice looking guy who tried to chat me up one day," said the younger woman, who Winston guessed was about nineteen.

"Did he try to chat up Laura?" asked Winston, looking for a reaction.

"Of course not, she's an old lady and a staff member. He wouldn't dare" she said with certainty, unaware at the raised eyebrows at the mention of old lady.

"Could you point him out to me if it became necessary?" asked Winston to which he got an affirmative nod. He thought quickly about his options, now extremely concerned. He went into the lobby and phoned Laura's parents in Brighton to ask if they had heard from Laura recently and Penny told him they hadn't heard from her for more than a week.

"Just checking that she hasn't made an arrangement I've forgotten about" said Winston, not wishing to cause alarm that might aggravate her condition. He checked all her friends whose names he had in his mobile phone directory, but no-one had seen nor heard from her since Monday afternoon. He was now convinced that she had disappeared and that something was drastically wrong. He was about to call 999, when he remembered that he had seen another number used for missing persons on one of the TV programs. He quickly checked by Googling *Missing Persons UK* and found the number was 101, so he dialled.

"Good afternoon, Constable Sarah Miles, Officer on Duty speaking. How can I help you?" was the polite enquiry.

"My name is Dr Winston Frobisher," he said using his title as it often earned greater respect. "I'd like to report my wife Laura Frobisher as missing. I'm really concerned that she's come to harm, and that we need to act quickly to find her. Can I please be put through to a senior detective?"

"I'm sorry but I'm obliged by operational response procedure to ask you several questions in order to access whether we rank your wife as Absent or Missing before following protocols" explained the constable.

"But I know my wife and she would not simply be missing of her own volition," answered Winston, in an agitated and frustrated voice.

"You must understand that we've about 400,000 missing persons calls a year, many of whom are people who've visited friends, had an accident in another neighbourhood, suffered temporary memory loss, or some other non-suspicious incident," she explained patiently. "We simply don't have the resources in terms of manpower to thoroughly investigate every concern. We are already stretched to cope with all the modern problems relating to drink and drug abuse and unprovoked and domestic violence. I can sense you're an intelligent man, Dr Frobisher, and can understand our situation. I have to follow protocols set out for me and enter your answers into our data files."

"OK" said Winston, realising that what she said must be true, "ask your questions and then something can be done to find Laura."

"Look", concluded the constable after Winston had answered what seemed the interminable standard questions, becoming more and more agitated and frustrated as he did so, "this is a difficult case to characterise. There is no evidence that your wife was under any threat, is likely to self-harm, or cause a problem to others. This would normally be referred to as Absent in our definitions. However, her absence is out of character which could place her in the Missing category despite the lack of indications of threat and hence potential criminal activity. Please email me several recent photographs of your wife. I'll then register your wife as Missing on the Police National Computer. This means that every police station in the UK will be alerted to her disappearance and even international law enforcement officers can access the details. I'll specifically alert all police stations in southern England of the case."

"Is that all that'll be done?" asked Winston, now highly disturbed.

"I suggest that we give it 24 hours and then review the situation at that time. She may turn up in the meantime, as most missing persons do."

"But she may be out there somewhere, alone, afraid and in harm's way," yelled Winston. "Is this all you can do?"

"As I tried to explain earlier" she said, trying to mollify him without success, "we just don't have the manpower to initiate a major investigation, with examining CCTV tapes, door knocking etc., unless we're sure that the person is genuinely missing and/or a crime has been committed. I promise you some action if she is not back in 24 hours. Meanwhile, the report and photos will alert all nearby police stations to be on the lookout for her."

Winston realised that she was just doing her job and had probably been more sympathetic to him than she needed to be. The last thing he should do was antagonise her, so he concluded: "Thank you Constable Miles. You've been very professional and kind to explain the protocols to me. I'll follow up with my own investigations so I'm in a better position to assist the enquiry in 24 hours time. I'm absolutely sure that Laura will not re-appear by herself overnight."

25

Feeling an overwhelming sense of panic, Winston first went home to select the photos of Laura and email them as requested. As he hadn't eaten since the night before he went to a nearby café and ordered a two-shot long black and an apple Danish. He needed caffeine and sugar to sharpen his senses. As he sat drinking the coffee, a sudden thought occurred to him. He remembered that one of the senior librarians had a daughter in her 30s who had married a senior police officer. Perhaps he could help or at lease offer some professional advice. He had decided not to go to the police station as it would seem as if he was complaining about Constable Miles and he didn't want to antagonise her.

He sought out Mrs Tapsell and explained the situation to her, asking if her son-in-law might speak to him. He explained about the protocols and asked her to be tactful. She agreed to call her daughter and ask her if she would call her husband, although she knew he was always busy.

"He's always complaining about escalating violence and stupidity on the streets and in pubs and clubs among the current generation" she said. "He says the police simply don't have the resources to deal with it," she went on, re-iterating what Constable Miles had told him earlier. She took his mobile number and promised to do her best.

"Laura is such a wonderful person," she concluded, "you should be very proud of her. I hope with all my heart she hasn't come to any harm." Winston couldn't settle. He paced around the campus uncertain of what he could do. Mind over emotion, he kept on telling himself, realising it was applicable when you told someone else but not when the trouble came to you. His normally logical mind was not functioning properly. It was late afternoon before his mobile rang.

"Hello, Dr Frobisher?" A pleasant voice with a deep authoritative timbre, queried.

"Yes," replied Winton feeling sick.

"This is Detective Inspector Rex" the voice said. "You can call me D.I. Rex and not Inspector Rex or Detective Dog like my colleagues," he laughed to try to put Winston at ease. "I presume you've seen the TV series with the intelligent German shepherd. I'm ragged about it all the time. Now about your problem. My wife's filled me in on your situation and I fully understand your anxiety. I must tell you straight away that it is not within my power to order an investigation involving physical activities of police officers. We simply don't have the resources to respond to every missing person enquiry. At best, I would be reprimanded and at worst suspended for doing so. However, from what my mother-in-law told my wife, there seems to be a genuine cause for concern for her safety."

"That's right," butted in Winston, "it's totally out of character for her to go missing like this and she's pregnant and vulnerable."

"This is what I suggest you do to speed up the investigation that should be set in motion about 20 hours from now. It's what we'd do in the initial stage of an investigation anyway. Can you jot these points down?" Winston said that he would text them into the memo pad of his iPhone and D.I Rex proceeded to give him details of what he might do.

"Contact University Security and ask them to check their CCTV tapes for the period around the time your wife was last seen. We can then be sure she left the University. Print out copies of a map from Google or similar that shows your normal route home. I presume that you normally go home together. Check to see if there are any CCTV cameras along the route. I've had a quick look through our records and I can't see any along any obvious route, but there may be overzealous residents along the way." He paused so that Winston could get it all down. "Knock on neighbours' doors and check if they may have seen your wife or anything that may have been abnormal or suspicious on Monday or before. Record the names of potential witnesses to speed up our enquiries. Ask everyone if there are residents in the street or nearby who are busybodies; usually old ladies who peer out behind curtains, or are seeking out gossip. These will be the 'Miss Marples,' as we term them, of the neighbourhood. If anything unusual has happened, they will probably know and will be useful witnesses. Notify all friends and relatives to call you immediately if they hear from your wife."

"I've already done that" Winston uttered despairingly.

"Good, now there are a couple of other things you can do. Check your wife's or joint bank accounts and credit cards to see if any withdrawals are made and where. This will help locate her or anyone who has stolen her cards. Also get the library staff to identify the student that your wife was talking to at 5pm on Monday as soon as he comes in and get his details. He may have been the last person to see her before she went missing and could be a person of interest in an enquiry. As I said, you'll be effectively doing our job and saving the 24 hour delay required in this case. Good luck and I hope all this turns out to be unnecessary when your wife turns up with amnesia or similar. Note that our discussion was off the record and shouldn't be mentioned officially."

"Thank you, so much," replied Winston, having made extensive notes for reference, "you can be assured of my discretion. I didn't know what to do with myself, and now I feel as if I've a mission to fulfil. I'll do my best to get all this information by tomorrow afternoon." Being Winston, he followed through in a logical way. The security guards on duty promised to check the CCTV tapes at the library and the exit from the University that Laura would have used. They had her photo on the University website and would check the clothes she wore on Monday from earlier CCTV in the library. They agreed to record relevant times for later police investigation, if required, and to let Winston know as soon as possible.

Then he went doorknocking with the help of a couple of Laura's special friends who volunteered to help. People were suspicious so they developed a routine of saying, "No, we're not Mormons nor

Seventh Day Adventists and we're not serving you with a summons," with a smile and chuckle. This put the residents at ease and they could ask their questions. It seemed no-one had seen Laura walk up the street, which was, perhaps, not surprising considering it was dark at 5pm and everyone was inside preparing dinner or watching TV. Most people they talked to, however, said that old Mrs Winter at the end of the street was the local 'old biddy' as they put it, and was generally the source of gossip about the goings-on in the neighbourhood. 'A one-woman Neighbourhood Watch' as one resident called her.

While Kate, one of Laura's friends continued doorknocking, Winston asked the other, Anita, to question Mrs Winter while he looked forlorn in the background, as he felt this was a good strategy to promote any gossip that might be relevant. As it turned out, the old lady, a widow for more than a decade, was very lonely, and welcomed their company and their interest in her observations. It seemed that D.I. Rex's comments were on the button, as she was quick to tell them that her favourite TV shows were *Marple* and *Poirot*. With her permed hair, glasses, cardigan and knitting needles by her armchair, she even looked like Miss Marple as portrayed on the BBC.

"Sit down and I'll make a nice cup of tea and butter some scones," she said, "best to be cosy if were having a chat." Winston, perched on a sofa, looked around the living room which appeared like something from the pre-war period with several photos of a rather handsome man in uniform on the mantelpiece. Can't be World War II, he thought, she's not that old. As if reading his thoughts, she said, "Korea, killed in his first term of duty, God rest his soul. Now, what do you want to know?" After they explained the circumstances, she sipped her tea from its fine china cup and frowned.

"Now let me see, Monday was very quiet in the street except for the rubbish collections and that handsome young man visiting Mrs Sexton at number 8 as he does every Monday."

"No strangers in the street?" prompted Anita.

"Now I come to think of it, there were two men there in the

afternoon. It was getting dark, so I didn't get a good look and, anyway, they were wearing those hoodie things that all the teenagers wear these days. Makes you scared to go outside because they all look like thugs and murderers," she reflected.

"Anything distinctive about them?" prompted Anita again.

"They wore dark grey all over, I think. Sort of like a uniform but with those hoodie things. I couldn't see their faces at all. The funny thing is that when they walked I thought of those American basketballers you see on TV sports news. Like a swagger" she said.

"Did they walk into the street or was there a car?" blurted Winston, breaking the routine, although she didn't seem to notice.

"I only saw them on foot, but I think there was a black or dark blue car what people call a AUV or SVV, whatever that means, further down the street that I didn't think I've seen before. Oh, something else I've just remembered. I think one of them must be left-handed because he looked down at his watch on his right wrist. I remember that!" Winston now stood up and took charge.

"You've been incredibly helpful Mrs Winter. Your observational skills are amazing. Miss Marple couldn't have done better herself. Would you be willing to repeat all of this to a police officer if required tomorrow? It could be very important."

"None of this Mrs Winter dear, I'm glad I could help; please call me Thelma and come for tea again. If the police are coming, does this mean I'll be part of a murder investigation?"

"I hope not," replied Winston with foreboding, "but I'm beginning to think we might be dealing with at least a kidnapping, although why anyone would kidnap my wife Laura I have no idea."

"You didn't say it was your wife at the start," she said remorsefully, "I would never have enthused about a murder investigation if I'd known."

"Our fault, not yours," said Winston graciously, "you have really been most helpful. Thank you so much and I will come to visit, hopefully to celebrate your detective work helping to find my wife."

They left and Winston walked Laura's two friends, home. He was touched by their solicitousness as they entreated him to let them know if there was anything at all they could do, even cook him meals, and to let them know if he had any news. Assuring them that he would, he then headed home himself.

He poured himself a stiff whiskey and made a sandwich. As he sat down to see the late news, his mobile chimed. It was one of the security team to tell him that Laura had left the library at about 5.25pm and had exited from the University grounds on the most direct path to their apartment. No-one followed the same path for at least 15 minutes after she left, he reported, plenty of time for her to reach home.

Winston was now extremely alarmed, but felt he had done everything humanly possible to discover what had happened and where she was. He decided to take a sleeping tablet as he was so wound up and distressed. There was nothing more he could do, so he would pursue it further the next day.

26

Winston awoke drowsily the next morning and checked again on the web that Laura had not accessed their bank accounts. As soon as he felt D.I. Rex would be on duty, he called him on his mobile to report his findings.

"Great work", Winston, he remarked, "You've saved us 12 to 18 hours with your prompt action. Phone Sarah Miles to update her at the 24 hour deadline and I'm sure she'll initiate an upgrade of the case. Meanwhile, I'll see if I can pull a few stings to get CCTV coverage of the main roads around the University, although identifying a dark coloured SUV with two passengers in the absence of a make, model and number plates will be like looking for a needle in a haystack,

I'm sorry to say. We don't even know they're involved in Laura's disappearance, where they came from, or where they're going."

Direct police action was activated that afternoon, with scanning of CCTV tapes, questioning of University staff and re-examination of neighbours and local residents. D.I. Rex had to admit to Winston that they were getting nowhere. Laura had disappeared apparently without trace. Winston was now obliged to inform Jeremy Wright who then called Winston for regular updates. All he could do was to tell Jeremy that the police were doing all they could and that, perhaps, in this case, no news was good news. Jeremy reported that Penny was under sedation at the insistence of their doctor who was concerned for her mental well-being. Winston felt hopeless and wracked with guilt that he had not called Laura and realised that something was wrong earlier. Wednesday night and Thursday passed fitfully as the investigation dragged on and D.I. Rex had nothing positive to report.

On Friday morning, Winston went to his office to do some research on the web to get his mind off Laura's disappearance. It was hopeless. He just sat there, staring at text and images but not being able to concentrate on their significance. He decided to check his mailbox again in case the last mail for the week had been delivered. There had been nothing at the apartment or work from Laura or about Laura so far. There were two pamphlets advertising conferences and a small square brown box used for posting DVDs. His name and address had been typed on to a label but there was no sender recorded in the space allotted. The postmark was smudged but looked like Heathrow. He ripped it open, found a DVD inside and tentatively and with growing trepidation, inserted it into his computer and checked the contents.

It was a video showing Laura standing next to a tall man whose body and head were completely covered. An image of Middle East terrorists shown on the TV News flashed through his brain. Laura was not gagged but looked totally disoriented with dim eyes.

A distorted voice – Winston immediately thought of digital voice modifiers – began to speak.

"Through your teachings Dr Frobisher, you have insulted Islam and the prophet Mohammed. Your people desecrated the Islamic Centre at Truro. We wanted you but we have your wife. Islam will be avenged." Through his utter disbelief that this was happening and that he could in any way have denigrated Islam, Winston saw Laura's lips move. He thought she mouthed, "Don't blame yourself, I love you," but wasn't sure.

The speech completed, the screen went blank with the sort of mild crackle Winston associated with lack of TV reception. Thank God she's alive, he thought. They don't want her, they want me. They'll probably resume the video with a request for my life against hers. He desperately grasped at the idea that he could save Laura. Suddenly, vision resumed with an image of Laura lying on what looked like a green tarpaulin with blood oozing from a deep wound in her neck. The distorted voice called "Allahu Akbar!" And then silence. My God, they've killed her; he gasped as he suddenly went cold and felt as if he were being dragged into a black void, knocking his head against the desk as he slumped forward.

A little later he woke groggily, as his mobile phone chimed in his top pocket. It was D.I. Rex with his twice-daily update.

"Come over immediately" croaked Winston, tears flooding down his face and his voice breaking. "I've received a video showing that Laura has been killed by Islamic extremists. How can that happen in Devon?"

"Stay where you are," growled D.I. Rex with urgency. "No mention of this to anyone, not even the parents. Turn off the computer. If this gets out we'll have a media scrum all over us, your life and her parents will be hell, and it will hinder what's now a murder investigation, if you're right." Winston, through a complex haze of shock, pain, guilt and despair realised that this was common sense, turned off his computer and waited. D.I. Rex arrived within about 30 minutes, viewed the video, ejected the DVD with a gloved hand, and put it together with the mailing box into a plastic bag.

"I'm terribly sorry that this has happened, Winston," he said, "such a senseless killing." He held Winston's shoulder in a gesture of sympathy. "Before we discuss what this could be about, I must stress that this is to be kept between you and me. No-one else can know about it. The main investigation will now be by Counter Terrorism Command or CTC, what you would call Special Branch of the Metropolitan Police in the good old days." He sighed, thinking of the increased paperwork, protocols and enquiries into police conduct that now paralysed the force. "This investigation and its wider context of identifying internal terrorists will be hampered if the press get a sniff of a Muslim connection, not to mention media scrums around your family and the University. If, and when Laura's body is found, we have to announce it's a murder not a slaying. Is that clear? We just have to hope there is no announcement of responsibility."

"I totally understand," replied Winston, "but what about Laura's parents. I feel so guilty about all this and she's their only child."

"From what you told me, the shock of this could seriously harm Laura's mother," he answered, "I think you have to live with your guilt. If I read her lips correctly, Laura absolved you of it anyway. Look at the bigger picture. The shock of murder by misadventure will be enough." D.I. Rex then questioned Winston about any Islamic connection, to which Winston replied that he was bewildered because there was no obvious connection. The only time he mentioned Islam and Islamic sects was in the context of his course on religion and conflict in which he mentioned all religions and the senselessness of sectarian violence when all beliefs had the same fundamental principles of peace, and goodwill and high moral standards.

"What about Muslim students in your classes? The Islamic Centre near Truro was specifically mentioned," asked D.I. Rex.

"I think there are very few Muslims in Devon or Cornwall, but, come to think of it, I did have two young men named Aazim and Najib in my class last year. They were short, probably of Middle Eastern descent, certainly not Negro nor as tall as the man in the video. Exeter is multinational and my class reflects it, but not to the extent of London or the northern cities, so I would have noticed."

"This is pretty tentative, but at least it gives us a starting point which we didn't have before. I'll check with CTC and then go down to Truro to talk to those students if the officers from Command agree." Winston left to mourn, plunged into deep guilty remorse, feeling terrible that he could not tell the Wrights the truth even after Laura's body was found, if it was found at all.

27

Winston spent a fitful night, finally resorting to sleeping pills again to bring him peace. In the mid-morning he called D.I. Rex, but there was still no discovery of a body and still no declaration of responsibility.

"I'm going to Truro today to interview those students and the leaders at the Centre, and I'll get back to you when I have something to report," he told Winston. "I suggest you go to work to get your mind off it. There's really nothing you can do at this stage."

Winston went to work and tried to concentrate. Maria was in and suggested a coffee. He agreed, but could not concentrate on her chatter about research papers and what she was doing. His mind went over the video. Was Laura really dead? Had the kidnapers doctored the images to make it look so? No, the more he thought back, the more sure he was that she had been killed.

"Are you OK?" asked Maria, "your mind seems to be somewhere else."

"Sorry," replied Winston, "I didn't sleep so well last night and I've got a bad headache. I didn't mean to be rude." The remainder of that Saturday was just a blur, much of it sitting and looking expectantly at his iPhone but there was no incoming call. He went home, made a snack, had an ultra-large whisky and a sleeping pill, after checking his apartment was secure at the insistence of D.I. Rex who was concerned about a direct attack on Winston.

He woke early the next morning and, restless, went for a walk in the dark streets but this simply reminded him of Laura's disappearance after dark. He bought a paper at the corner store which was just opening and went home for breakfast. For the first time for months, he read the paper from front to back, suddenly realising how violence, manslaughter and murder were becoming an every-day occurrence in the UK and globally: a further indication of decline, he thought.

At about 10am, his phone chimed. It was D.I. Rex, who reported in a subdued, solemn and respectful voice. "Laura was found earlier this morning by an elderly couple walking their dog. Her body was wrapped in a tarpaulin and covered with some small branches and leaves under bushes in grasslands near the Avon River close to Salisbury. They noticed there was a view of the Cathedral from the hiding place and that her body was turned towards it, perhaps suggesting religious significance."

"Was she assaulted or tortured before being killed?" asked Winston fearfully.

"We'll have to wait for a forensic examination to be sure, but the police on site don't think so. Her clothing was intact and there was no obvious bruising. The good news from our collective viewpoint is that the couple have no mobile phone, so no photos were taken that could be leaked to the press. As the location is also remote from houses and it's Sunday, the police were able to cordon off the area, take photos, and remove Laura's body to the mortuary at Salisbury District Hospital before any reporters could arrive. It's better than transporting Laura to a London morgue which could attract attention. The old couple have been told it's in the country's interest for them to be silent and they had no problem agreeing. We'll have to announce it as a murder, of course, because the area will have to be cordoned off as a crime scene to collect forensic evidence, which no doubt will attract attention."

"Will Laura's name be mentioned" said Winston, concerned about her parents, "and will her body be released?"

"No, not immediately, we'll inform the media that we are checking identity and will need a formal identification and to notify her family before releasing her name. If the perpetrators claim responsibility, CTC want you to deny having received any DVD. We can then try to let this cool down. At the moment, CTC feel that the purpose of this attack was a feeble excuse designed to test the nerve and skill of the perpetrators and to prepare them for a greater task of more importance to their movement. It seems that you and Laura were simply unlucky to be targeted."

"What do you mean?" asked Winston. "Why unlucky? Why was I targeted and why did Laura pay the price?"

"Sorry, I wanted to tell you about the discovery of Laura's body first, and got ahead of myself" said D.I. Rex softly. "When I went to Truro yesterday, the two young men you mentioned, Aazim and Najib, said that when they were in London for a student meeting recently, they discussed how great your courses were to other students and downloaded your digital notes that Najib had on a USB, on to other students' computers. There were four students who had access to the USB, two of them tall and of African descent. It seems that this is how the perpetrators read your notes, saw statements about Muslims and Crusades, shared it with others, and were presumably instructed to target you with this, and the past Truro incidents, as an excuse."

"So Laura's death instead of mine was totally pointless," cried out Winston, in incredible anguish.

"Yes, I'm afraid so," replied D.I. Rex. "The only positive is that you are really in no way to blame for Laura's death. It was a chain of circumstances that no-one could have predicted."

"If you've questioned the students and leaders at the Truro Centre, won't the Muslim Connection get out?" asked Winston angrily, thinking there was no positive in any of this.

"They have no desire for it to get to the media, particularly if their Centre is mentioned, as they would undoubtedly receive retribution as in 2008 when there was no obvious excuse for the desecrations. They are actually an extraordinarily pleasant, polite and co-operative group simply wanting to live peacefully, like the vast majority of the population. When things have settled down, they've invited you to join them for coffee and shared prayers for Laura as a sign of their deep regret that they played an unsuspecting role in this."

"Where to now?" asked Winston curtly, instantly regretting his discourtesy, as D.I. Rex had actually been most understanding.

"From what you tell me of Laura's mother, I think it would be best for her, and your peace of mind, if you go to Brighton as soon as possible and break the news of Laura's death personally. Just portray it as a random attack with no motive and indicate that she has not been violated in any way as far as the police can tell. Offer to visit Salisbury on your way back to Exeter to formerly identify Laura. The Hospital is south of the town and the Mortuary is Block 13."

"When will her body be released for burial? I'll have to discuss that with them," asked Winston, now in a gentler tone.

"Should be in less than a week, particularly if cause of death is clear and there are no other injuries" was the solemn reply. "I know it's of no comfort to you whatsoever, but CTC have had indications of planning for a major terrorist attack in one of our cities. For reasons they're not sharing, they think that this incident will help them identify members of the group involved and help them avert a disaster. This goes no further understand. I would be suspended if my superiors knew I 'd discussed this with you."

"I realise that you have tried to soften the blow for me," said Winston, "and I appreciate it. I'll take your advice and keep you informed of anything that happens. In turn, can you let me know informally of any developments? I want these men punished, but realise it would be better for Penelope Wright if there was no murder trial and the men were imprisoned instead, on terrorist or espionage charges."

"I fully understand Winston. Frank co-operation here will be the best result. There's a jealousy between us and CTC because we need to solve our quota of crime to survive, but in this instance we're working towards the common good. You can rely on me to do my best. Good luck with the family. I had to deliver bad news when on the beat in my youth, and it was a horrible experience, even when I had no connection to the victim."

28

Winston phoned the Wrights in Brighton to say he realised they were as anxious as him about Laura, and asked if he could come and stay with them for a few days. Jeremy was particularly pleased because he felt that Winston could keep Penny company while he attended to urgent mounting business issues.

"Life must go on" he said sadly, "however much we worry." Winston felt incredibly guilty that he could not inform them of the discovery of Laura's body, reassuring himself that he was doing was in the best interests of everyone. D.I. Rex had endorsed it and he could be dispassionate whereas Winston knew that emotion was his driving force at the moment.

As he had scheduled two classes and a tutorial early in the week, he called Maria to ask her to cover for him as she had done before while he attended conferences or hurriedly-called committee meetings.

"What's the problem Winston?" she asked consolingly, "this is very sudden."

"Family problems, I'm afraid. I'll explain when I return from Brighton," he said with as much calm as he could muster. As he considered he was too distracted to drive to Brighton, she insisted on taking him to the station and they had a coffee while he waited for the train after buying his ticket. As usual, they chatted about their research and papers in press and preparation. His train was called and he stood up, clasping her hand to thank her. She held it tight and reached up and kissed him on the cheek. Caught by surprise by the hot sensation he felt on his cheek, he pulled away, realising fully for the first time the depth of her burning brown eyes, her delicate cheek structure and her willowy body.

With a flustered, "Thanks so much for the lift Maria," he hurried to the train, feeling incredible guilt that he had felt admiration for Maria before Laura was even buried. He remembered that, in life, Maria was the only woman that Laura viewed as a potential rival. I must avoid any future social contact, he resolved. Nothing must erase my memory of my Laura. Nothing!

He arrived at Brighton station late in the evening and took a taxi to the Wrights. Throughout the journey, he had been rehearsing what to say. Having taken his overnight bag to the rooms he had shared with Laura, he suggested that they all sit down with a drink as he had news to share. As gently as he could, he explained the discovery of Laura's body in Salisbury. He said he wanted to tell them face to face and explained how he, in turn, had been told by DI Rex and how kind he had been. He stressed that it seemed to be a random attack, which was believable given the increasing number of such incidents in British cities, and that the police believed that Laura had died instantly and that there had been no other physical or sexual violence against her.

"Thank God for small mercies," murmured Penny, somewhat distractedly. "I knew she was dead. A mother always senses these things. I was just praying that she didn't suffer." She started to sob, Jeremy put his arm around her, and they both cried unashamedly. Winston, who had cried his tears beforehand, put his hands over his face to shield his lack of tears, but, surprisingly, where was no need as they suddenly poured down his cheeks. They sat there for what seemed like an eternity, each with their own thoughts and memories. Suddenly, Jeremy got up, refilled their glasses, and said in a choking voice, "Here's to Laura, the kindest, most diligent, polite and hopelessly romantic daughter that we could have ever asked for. May she rest in peace and reside in our memories forever."

"Yes" agreed Winston. "She was the most wonderful person I've ever met. There will never be anyone like her again. I can still feel her presence in this room through the people she loved and who loved her so much."

They drank a toast and Jeremy helped Penny to bed. The emotion, and her medication and the alcohol had been too much for her. When they were alone, Winston explained to Jeremy that Laura had to be identified following an autopsy in Salisbury and that he would do this unless Jeremy wished to or wished to accompany him.

It was agreed that, in the interests of Penny's health, Winston would go alone, although Jeremy would loan him his car so that he didn't have to do the train trip via London, but drive along the South Downs via Southampton. It would also enable Winston to return to Brighton so that the Wrights were not alone.

"There's one favour we must ask" said Jeremy, once the pragmatic decisions had been made, "we have a family burial plot in Brighton and Preston Cemetery, a tranquil spot on the Downs. We would like Laura to be buried there with us to be beside her in due time."

"Then, there's one favour I ask in return," replied Winston. "That you add a clause in your Will that I am to be buried there too, along with the ashes of my parents, provided I have not decided to scatter them at St Mary's or elsewhere."

"It's the least I can do. You're our only close family and close tie with Laura now," he replied sadly. "Of course I'll do that. It's an honour that you want to join our family in this way."

The remainder of the week passed in a frantic blur for Winston. He drove to the Mortuary in Salisbury and formally identified Laura. She looked so peaceful that he felt she had died suddenly without

warning or had prepared herself into a serene state. He was told that
he couldn't touch her but was allowed to kiss her now cold forehead,
as he had done so many times in life. He cried bitterly all the way
back to Brighton, having several coffee stops along the route, as he
mourned for Laura and their baby who the Coroner had reported
was a boy.

D.I. Rex phoned on Wednesday to say they had released Laura's
name as the victim and to expect some media attention. He suggested
they get a lawyer from Winston's father's law firm to represent them,
to avoid interviews and to stay inside together.

"It will blow over in a few days when the next tragedy occurs.
Such is the way of the press," he added from bitter experience. "You
just have to see it out." He also added that Laura's body would be
released on the Friday. Forensic tests had confirmed that she had not
been interfered with in any way prior to death. So far, they had no
DNA from the perpetrators.

"They must have covered their bodies completely and worn
rubber gloves when they abducted her," he said. "They have been
very professional. Looks like the CTC guys were on the ball and this
is a prelude to something on a larger scale in the future. There's still
no claim of responsibility, so at least the terrorist connection has
been submerged, at least for now. I'll keep you informed."

Winston rang Anita and Kate, Laura's friends who had been so
kind to him, as he knew they would be shocked at the news. He told
them the same as he had told Jeremy and Penny and asked them to
explain to her other friends. Promising to advise them of the funeral
date and time in Brighton once he knew details, he rang off.

When Jeremy arrived home, Winston gave him the news about
the release of Laura's body, and he managed to get a spot for a
service at St Peters on Tuesday morning, with a later burial at the
Cemetery, while Winston organised for Laura's body to be moved
to an undertaker in Brighton whom Jeremy knew. Everything was
now organised by phone as the media had started to camp outside.

Jeremy phoned the lawyer and asked him to come later to talk to the press, indicating that Penny was taking the news very badly and the family had no comment to make other than a written statement that he could read on their behalf. They would also provide a photograph of a smiling Laura to satisfy media demands, and, hopefully, help apprehend the murderer.

That evening Winston received a call from Maria to say that one of her friends had seen the story about Laura's murder on the TV news and phoned her to inform her.

"I'm very sorry for your loss Winston," she said using the phrase that had now become the norm when offering condolences, and hence sounded somewhat insincere. "What a terrible thing to happen and such a shock to us all. Is there anything I or the University Library staff can do? Where and when is the funeral? I and all her really close friends from the University would like to come and pay our respects if we can, based on my phone-around."

"The funeral's here in Brighton on Tuesday" answered Winston slowly, thinking of a suitable response. "You can really help me most by covering my backside until next Thursday. You know, giving my lecture course and tutorials, I'll be forever grateful. The funeral is likely to be a private affair as Laura has, I mean had, few relatives." At that point she heard his voice crack, and there was a pause before he continued. "So, there's really no point in anyone coming all the way to Brighton unless they really want to. If you could send wreaths from our staff and the Library, that would be great. Even better would be as many condolence cards as possible saying how much Laura was loved and respected. Her mother is taking this very badly and we're worried about a nervous breakdown. Lots of positive affirmation that she had a wonderful daughter might help. You could scan them as attachments to my email address or send them here." He gave the address.

"I'll do what you say" replied Maria softly, "don't worry about anything here in Exeter. Just concentrate on what you have to do

there. Love from all of us here. We'll be thinking of you on Tuesday.
I know the staff wish to close the Library for an hour on the day of
the funeral as a mark of their respect."

"Thanks, you've been absolutely wonderful over this. I won't forget
it." Winston said as he hung up. Maria almost purred at the other end
of the line. I will become indispensable in time, she thought.

29

The weekend came slowly, with the three of them in a sad house with
no gaiety or laughter, each of them immersed in their own thoughts
and grief. At least there has still been no mention of terrorism,
thought Winston guiltily. If that came out, I'd be in a very sticky
position with the Wrights. The media presence had diminished but
some reporters were still there hoping that the family would appear.

On Sunday morning, the media had gone. Winston scanned
the news bulletins on his computer to see if there was a reason for
this sudden departure. Apparently, two call girls had been savagely
murdered in Birmingham and bikie gangs and drug dealers were
rumoured to be involved. As D.I. Rex had predicted, if one was
patient, something else more newsworthy would appear and the
media would move on. All of them in the house were relieved. They
would go out for an airing, as Penny described it, have lunch and visit
the undertaker to see Laura and pay their respects.

Thank God she looks so peaceful, thought Winston. It will be a
help to Penny. Tuesday dawned a clear still day for the funeral. To
their complete surprise, St Peters was packed for the service. Jeremy
recognised that most of the staff and loyal customers from his
bookstores were there, as well as staff and customers from the local
library. Winston noted that many of his father's friends, his Nanny,
Maureen from Telscombe Cliffs and her family, and some of his

colleagues from southern England were there. They must have found out because of all the publicity, he thought, as he also noticed a group that he deemed to be reporters. Anita and Kate had got time off and came to represent Laura's library friends and colleagues. Whatever the reason, it was a wonderful tribute to Laura that so many had come. Winston quickly went across and whispered to Jeremy, who nodded and then went to speak to the clergyman.

All went according to plan. The service was held with some of Laura's favourite hymns and Winston presented the eulogy, covering all aspects of Laura's life and contributions to family, friends and community. Although an accomplished lecturer, he had to stop several times as a lump welled up in his throat and the tears filled his eyes. There was hardly a dry eye in the Church, with women openly grieving while several men shifted about on their seats and averted their eyes, subconsciously fearing an unmanly show of emotion. At the end of the Service, Jeremy stood up at a signal from the clergyman: "We are totally overwhelmed by your response to Laura's untimely death. We imagined a small gathering here today to pay their last respects. Penelope, Winston and I are so grateful for your loyalty and friendship to us and Laura. Normally, we would invite you back home to celebrate Laura's life, or have a wake as the Irish like to term it, but we have been effectively besieged in our home by media. If you wish to join us later this afternoon, there will an open slate at the Sutherland Arms, near Brighton College. Laura liked it there and they know the family well." Secretly he hoped that not too many would accept his offer as it was a small pub, but it was all he could think of at short notice.

The family moved to the Cemetery where Laura was to be laid to rest. They all knew she was gone, but the last moment when they dropped soil on her coffin was heart wrenching. It signalled a final farewell to someone they all loved, the Wright's only daughter and Winston's SHE or HER. He knew in his heart that no-one could ever replace what she meant to him. He felt bitter at the hand fate had played him with Laura's sudden death on a futile excuse by men he did not know, and whose cause was contrary to all religious beliefs whether they be Muslim, Christian, Jewish or other assorted religions. He also felt remorse that he, indirectly, had been the cause of her death and guilt that he could never reveal to those she loved.

"Oh Laura, I miss you so, my love," he murmured to himself. He vowed that he would return to spend time with her on his regular visits to Brighton to put flowers on her gravestone which, through agreement between he and the Wrights, would read Laura (Wright) Frobisher and JND in memory of the unborn Jeremy Neil Darcy who would still be remembered as part of Laura by them all.

30

In London, Adam Lampton was settling into his research position, impressing his supervisors and gaining their trust. He was a meticulous worker and actually enjoyed the job he did. Although he didn't seek out any close relationships with his colleagues, he did greet them and was happy to indulge in everyday chit chat when the occasion demanded. Over the months, he had assessed the security in the building which appeared formidable, as might be expected for immunology research. There was only one main entrance which had standard metal-detector arches and security personnel who checked every article coming into and leaving the building: briefcases, bags, lunch boxes etc. Employees had to hold security badges and then had to empty their pockets and were randomly selected for a body search. Access to any lab was initiated by punching a code, regularly changed, into a security panel. It would be very difficult to get past this system, considered Adam.

There was also CCTV throughout the building, both in the

corridors and in the laboratories. The only places with no CCTV were the cubicles in the toilets and the small sick bay, as CCTV was considered to infringe workers' rights when they were in a state of undress. Of course, there were smoke detectors there as well as elsewhere through the building. By accident, he discovered that the roof was also free of CCTV as there was a solid steel fence around it and a sheer drop of four storeys below that. One of his co-workers, when going up for a smoke, invited Adam to accompany him. Few employees smoked and Adam himself was a non-smoker but he recognised the roof as a potential space for future plans. What held his attention when he was first shown the roof was an old chimney, a relic from the original building, preserved to help disguise the true purpose of the research facility. He noticed that some of the bricks looked slightly loose with depressions and pits in the mortar.

So as not to attract suspicion, he gradually took up smoking using the roof once a week at the beginning and then gradually increasing its use to once a day. The mortar was loose and the chimney represented a potential repository if he could loosen the bricks. His research showed that geologists used small pen-shaped, hardened-steel scratching instruments to test the hardness of rocks and minerals. He bought one and inserted it into the shell of a large metal ball-point pen and smuggled it into the building as an innocent looking object. It would take several months, but initial indications were that he could loosen the mortar in the few minutes that he was smoking in isolation on the roof. It was the start of a plan that he was formulating in his mind, egged on by the his now more frequent visions.

One day, he feigned a migraine headache, and was admitted to the sick bay. It was small, with a single bed, first-aid equipment including a resuscitator, and a microwave oven used for heating food and drinks and small bags, that he knew were filled with wheat, to keep patients warm if they started to shiver. The facility employed a nurse in case of accidents and to apply first aid when needed. She doubled as a Laboratory Assistant when not required in the sick bay. Adam asked her to heat one of the bags for him, which she did. He noted that she set the micro-wave to two minutes, and the bag was warm, slightly damp, and had a faint burning smell when it was fully heated. He determined to buy one and experiment with varied heating times. When he said he was feeling better and would just sleep for an hour before resuming work, she left him alone, promising to return and check he was OK in half an hour or so.

The plan could now be extended. It was high risk, but he thought worthwhile. He had thought earlier that he would need someone in his inner group who was an expert in controlled explosives, but had put this on the backburner so far. Now he knew he would have to search for a person with this expertise. He needed someone living near London, who had experience as a quarryman, a miner, or a returned serviceman with experience of explosives in Iraq or Afghanistan. He would see if Helga could help locate such a man and engage him in conversation. No man in their right mind would ignore her, he thought, and no man had better take advantage of her. Adam understood that, in his own way, he loved her as well as admired her.

He would also need to recruit a fireman or someone familiar with the Fire Brigade who could access or steal a fireman's kit and backpack. He had learned, at his induction that the emergency procedure ensured that emergency services including the local fire brigade had sufficient knowledge of the building layout and the risks within the laboratories. He knew it would all take time as anyone he recruited would need to share his own philosophy and also become completely committed. He realised he could afford to be patient. He was enjoying life with Helga and the increasing power and control he was generating in *Vers Une Terra Verde*, particularly among his inner circle.

He had another important decision to make. He could not disclose his plan to the inner circle until the time it was to be activated, but he needed their total loyalty. Any leak would end in discovery and downfall, but how could he ensure that this would not happen. The answer came in the most unexpected manner. One night he was extremely restless, with flashes of bright lights flickering across his vision, so he got up to get a drink to settle himself down. As usual, he turned the TV on because he found it a total distraction from the thoughts rattling around in his brain. An old black-and-white movie was showing, the sort his father used to see when he went to the Saturday matinees for sixpence, as he told Adam countless number of times. The Indian chief was talking in a disguised American voice about 'Blood Brothers', to a cowboy. They cut themselves with the tip of a Bowie knife on the inside of their arms just above the wrist and then mingled their blood.

"We are now 'Blood Brothers' forever," said the Chief. Adam immediately saw the possibilities of his inner group becoming Blood Brothers. In these days of AIDs and other blood-transmitted diseases, where even sportsman were forced to leave the field with blood rules in team sports, this could be an ultimate test of total loyalty to each other and to him. He resolved to ask Helga when she woke up.

"It's a great idea," she said, "but I suggest a precaution that shows them you care for them individually as well. Why not announce your Blood Brother concept and ask for individual pledges to enact it. If they all agree, then announce that you'll organise blood tests to protect everyone in the unlikely event that someone has a disease that they're unaware of."

The idea appealed to the members of the inner circle as it had a Masonic secret-society ring to it. Within the month, it was done, with all showing trust and loyalty and only one needing stitches for an enthusiastically deep cut. Any new inductees would be subjected to the same test.

Luck was on Adam's side when another piece of the jigsaw of his plan fell into place. The viruses they were researching had to be stored below -20°C, commonly at -70°C, because they became non-viable within relatively short time periods, hours to days, at higher temperatures. The fear was that an evolved virus might develop, which was stable at room temperature, and hence was more deadly in a pandemic. Combined secret British, American and German research had successfully isolated such a virus, an adaptation of Swine Flu, and Adam had been chosen as part of the British team to research its properties and to attempt to develop a vaccine and/or an oral-inhalation drug like Rulenza to control its spread during an infection period in the future. The research was to be kept secret for fear that it could fall into the wrong hands. There had been evidence of chemical warfare in Iraq and Syria in recent times, and the western world feared that this might escalate into biological warfare in the future as unrest spread across the world, particularly in the Middle East and Africa, where Muslim extremist groups, including the feared ISIS, were starting to flex their muscles.

31

Following Laura's funeral, a disturbed and grieving Winston could not settle his mind. The first thing he noticed was how incredibly lonely it was without her. No companionship, no long conversations over meals or coffee breaks, no shared experiences or humour, and, most of all, no love. He missed the warmth of her body in his bed and the warmth of their meetings after they had been apart. He realised that he had taken their life together for granted, expecting it to go on for decades: they had lived their dreams together as time flew by. Now the hours dragged by interminably and it was as if a day in his new life was like a week in the old. He realised that he was starting to talk aloud to Laura whenever anything concerned him, and that others looked at him thinking he was talking to himself. He knew he had to avoid this at work or the students would think that, like many other academics, he was going senile, or crackers as Laura would have said, before his time.

He filled the days with teaching and research. He and Maria were incredibly productive, and papers were flowing into the press, but he avoided invitations to evening drinks or meals at local cafes, remembering that moment at the railway station which had been most disconcerting. She radiates sex appeal he thought to himself, but I must be loyal to Laura's memory, as she would have been to mine, or so he hoped.

His loneliness did have some positives in terms of his awakening perception of modern life and the rapidly increasing influence of films, TV and digital technology in a rapidly evolving modern world. He and Laura had rarely watched TV. They sometimes watched the News and liked archaeological programs or those concerning periods of history or historical characters which particularly interested Winston, or screen adaptations of Laura's favourite 19th Century novels. They shared these interests, although it was Laura who needed the tissues during dramatisations of *Pride and Prejudice*, *Sense and Sensibility* and the like, he remembered fondly. They only went to the cinema to see highly rated, Oscar-nominated American movies, British historical films, or foreign films recommended by the library group that Laura had joined. They simply had limited time so were very selective. Most of what was shown looked like crass, uncultured rubbish, Laura had said heatedly.

Now he sat in their apartment, trying to relax after long days teaching or thinking about research. He needed something to distract him, something mindless so he could relax his brain for the following day. A stiff drink and TV seemed the logical choice. As he scanned the numerous digital channels, he realised that most channels had excessive program breaks with tasteless adverts and that much of the content was 'reality TV', with almost total absence of reality in the sense he understood it. His active mind, however, always searching to understand history, suddenly realised that TV was a window into the minds of the population and could be a strong influence on behavioural patterns. Suddenly, he had a new mindless research topic. He decided early on that anyone watching the reality shows and believing in their reality must be naive. The excessive advertising of what was to happen next drove him to distraction, and the overacting of the judges on the talent shows he found obnoxious, but they were still very popular. These are interminable and inane, he thought, thinking of how Laura would have teased him for even watching these shows. So, he watched, or rather scanned, dramas, crime shows, so called 'soapies', and even cartoons. It took him a while to recognise, but he identified repetitive themes and found that after a while he could name the producers before the credits appeared. Some of them were incredibly prolific and he assumed that they were executive producers.

Something that had always intrigued him was the 'Americanisation' of world culture from his perspective in terms of dress, music, lack of discipline, distinctive attitudes, particularly towards increasing self-examination of motives and actions, and a desire to protect the environment when most of the population lived in large cities that had all but destroyed the local flora and fauna, polluted the soil, rivers and atmosphere, and consumed vast quantities of energy from fossil fuels.

Watching the TV programs gave him a new awareness of what he now understood was a cocoon that he and Laura had built around themselves, a sort of time warp of old-fashioned values, manners and behaviour towards others. He realised that whether it was news, crime or modern drama, it had to be seen as multicultural, something that had migrated to Europe as well. He was also aware that most of what Hollywood produced, represented a modern American outlook on life with the actors portraying American attitudes. The humour, which Winston considered often unsubtle and distasteful, was totally unlike British humour, with its self-deprecation and insight into real human behaviour. He found it difficult to recognise characters unless they wore distinctive clothes because most were glamorous or handsome with artificially whitened teeth. On his rare visits to North America, he had seldom seen anyone resembling these characters on the street. He could now appreciate the obsession with appearance that was making plastic surgeons, beauty consultants and hairdressers rich and famous, and causing those with non-perfect body shapes to emulate celebrities and to wear clothes that were often inappropriate and unflattering for them. Most of all, he noticed that even the cartoon characters, whether they be modern, or historical or stone-age people, dogs, cats, chickens, African animals, penguins, fish or sharks, most had American accents and portrayed American attitudes and values. I can see why 'high-fives' suddenly appeared around the world, he thought, along with everything else. He resolved to include these revelations into some new lectures on the role of entertainment in shaping cultural trends. No wonder the French try to keep their unique culture, he thought, whereas we Brits seem to be increasingly accepting the global norm.

He also became more aware of the increasing impact that modern digital communication devices were having on society. He had always viewed the internet as a priceless tool for his research as he could gain the information he required in seconds in most cases, using search engines like Google and Bing and databases such as Wikipedia. He and Laura had never seen the need to use any form of Facebook as they had real flesh-and-blood friends that they could meet and talk to. Similarly, they never used Twitter, but it was now a standard source of information and discussion for many organisations. He wondered how much productive time was spent on these digital outlets and how much was simply wasted time, cutting into productive work time or replacing physical activity with virtual reality. He guessed, from the rising level of obesity and related diseases such as diabetes, that it was the latter.

He now had more time to read the newspaper and, being obsessive, started collecting articles relating to problems linked to the internet. He was staggered by the volume of material he collected and the range of problems that were caused globally. Digital bullying on systems such as Facebook, and less-desirable competitor sites, it seemed was leading to increasing suicides among teenagers. Pupils were too tired to study at school because they were using laptops, notepads, I-Phones and the like until the early hours of the morning. Prosecutions for possessing and distributing vast amounts of both adult and child pornography on the web were escalating. Sportsman were inadvertently divulging confidential information from their clubs or posting messages on Facebook or tweeting them on the spur of the moment, leading to global condemnation and suspension. Celebrities were outdoing each other with more grotesque or sexy U-tube videos, and so the list went on. Young people even posted videos of themselves driving recklessly or committing crimes. There seemed to be an overwhelming desire to be recognised, to be an instant celebrity, whether it was for the right or wrong reasons.

Winston also noticed the major impact that modern mobile phones were having on social behaviour. When he travelled by bus or train, many of the younger passengers sat there with earphones on, listening to music from their I-Pods, while staring at their phones while messaging, playing digital games or waiting expectantly for a message. They had to be continually entertained, he thought. They are oblivious of the real world around them. His Australian colleagues told him it was even worse there, with teenagers texting while driving on probationary licences, killing themselves or their passengers, or crashing into houses or retaining walls while distracted. Even some train and aircraft mishaps or near misses had been attributed to these distractions. He wondered at the real economic cost through time lost at work on phones or the internet. Again, he resolved to include these observations in his lecture courses.

He called Jeremy Wright regularly to keep in touch, and, at his invitation, stayed over the weekend about once a month when the family always visited Laura's grave to place flowers and remember. Jeremy and Penelope liked to listen to Winston's observations as they had formed similar opinions on what they described as the advent of the 'new barbarians', a term that Winston thought appropriate from his historical viewpoint, as human history seemed to oscillate between periods of culture and growth led by visionaries followed by destruction and decline by barbarians.

They collectively decided that, despite all the advances, technology in general was not being used to develop a superior culture and social order, and that the western world was in the early to middle stages of decline.

"People are using technology to think for them," concluded Jeremy. "We're not far off what seemed an unbelievable, surreal scenario of a technological dictator building an army of robots under her command," he laughed out loud as he said *her*, "with the population unthinkingly obeying all commands that come from digital devices plugged in their ears." Winston wrote it down as a good punch line for his lecture course.

32

Winston's lonely existence was punctuated by fortnightly calls from D.I. Rex for them to meet somewhere private for coffee so that he could keep him informed of on-going investigations. He didn't want to discuss matters over the phone as it could be recorded. In the first few weeks, the reports were negative, with the D.I. trying to explain the reasons for lack of progress by CTC and his own detectives.

"With a population in the multi-millions today, the type of sleuthing and deduction portrayed by Sir Arthur Conan-Doyle in the *Sherlock Holmes* novels is virtually impossible. Criminals just melt into the crowd. We're so reliant on CCTV footage and DNA that, without either, the force struggles. What's shown on TV in shows like *Criminal Minds* and *CSI* is totally unrealistic, particularly in terms of the rapidity of analyses etc." He paused, waiting for Winston to intervene, but Winston fully understood. "If we had the vehicle make and registration, we could get somewhere," he went on, "but we have neither. In the old days, criminals used to burn vehicles involved in crimes, commonly leaving behind DNA or other evidence. Today, the clever ones check when people are absent, steal their vehicles, disconnect or digitally inhibit their speedometers, and add temporary number plates, carry out the crime, and return the vehicle as if it has been parked all the time the owner was absent. The vehicle then becomes untraceable. CTC think this is what's happened in your case."

About four months after Laura's death, D.I. Rex had more positive news. From the descriptions provided by Winston's Muslim students, CTC had identified two suspects, one a Nigerian and the other of Somalian descent. They had disappeared from London but were located in Manchester through their contact with a group that CTC had under surveillance, believing they were home-spun terrorists with links to Al-Qaeda or ISIS. Their association with this group had strengthened CTC's belief it represented a major national threat and it was now under close watch. Again, the D.I. stressed to Winston that this was totally confidential and that he would be suspended if their conversation got out. It was cold comfort to Winston that Laura's death may have been the catalyst in helping avert a national disaster.

Six weeks later, D.I. Rex called Winston and suggested they meet in a local park. Over the phone, he just said that he wanted to see how Winston was coping with life as a follow-up from their investigation. They met and moved to a park bench. The D.I. was clearly very excited and eager to share the news with Winston.

"You can read all the details in the newspapers in a couple of days time," he began, "once charges are laid. The group that Laura's executioners joined were planning to detonate a series of bombs at Old Trafford football stadium as the crown emerged to catch buses and trains after a local derby between Manchester United and City. They estimate that there could have been dozens to hundreds of deaths if this plan had been successful, so it has been a major triumph for CTC, with a bit of on flow to us locally," he added.

"Has there been any mention of Laura's death or the video," asked

Winston nervously, thinking that his lies, well-meaning as they might have been, may be discovered by Jeremy and Penelope and ruin their relationship.

"As far as I know, there hasn't" replied the D.I. "CTC's guess is that they won't reveal it now because it would be an admission of guilt of murder and would add to any sentence they might receive. Announcing it now would also lose impact after such a long time. But you can never predict what fanatical people will do."

"I guess CTC won't pursue it," said Winston hopefully.

"Unless there is an admission of guilt, all the evidence is circumstantial and a jury might give a not- guilty verdict without hard evidence," said the D.I. "The terrorist charges are solid and will definitely end in conviction so justice will be done, if only indirectly."

"I can't tell you how grateful I am to you for keeping me informed like this at potential personal cost," said Winston as they shook hands. As they started to turn away D.I. Rex turned back and, as an afterthought, asked: "Did you ever take up the invitation from the group at the Islamic Centre near Truro?"

"Oh yes, I did," Winston replied, "I should have mentioned it before. Friendly, hospitable and earnest people. As you suggested, I told them that no blame could be attached to the students. If nothing comes to light about Laura's death, it will be in the best interests of their Centre as well as Laura's family and me. As I try to emphasise in my lecture courses, the great majority of people in any religious group want to live in peace. It's only a tiny minority of extremists who ruin it for everyone and generate religious intolerance." He paused and went on, "sorry I'm pontificating again, an infectious disease amongst us academics." D.I. Rex smiled thinking how true this was.

"I hope this is the end of this matter for all involved" he said as he walked away. Thankfully for Winston, the lack of mention of Laura in the newspapers and TV news over the next few days suggested that it was, at least for now.

33

Winston spent the remainder of 2014 in what he considered to be a 'holding pattern'. He worked as hard as he could, concentrating on his historical research in order to push his guilty thoughts about Laura into the furthest possible recesses of his mind. It was the only way to remain sane. He had his monthly visits to Brighton, and sporadic visits to St Mary's, to check that all was well, although he missed Laura there more than anywhere else.

"It was our sanctuary: our special place," he said out loud as if Laura was there beside him.

He arranged to spend Christmas in Brighton, fully realising how it would contrast with the wonderful Christmas before when they had gone to Paris. Laura's last Christmas, he thought morosely. He scanned the web and booked as many events for the family as he could, to avoid sitting around, reminiscing and making everyone feel sad over the holiday break.

As always, the evenings and the periods when he woke up in a sweat from disturbing dreams were the worst times. He reflected that although Laura had found time for friends, his absorption with both Laura and his work had left little time nor inclination to seek the company of male friends with whom to share time at the pub, football or other social activities. He was incredibly lonely and didn't know how to overcome it. He felt that he was digging a deeper and deeper pit for himself and didn't know whether to climb out or wallow in despair. He genuinely didn't know the answer. Only time can heal, he thought, digging out an overused cliché.

His research association with Maria was flourishing, going from strength to strength, as she was now also getting invitations to present at conferences, join editorial boards and adorn committees. Despite her suggestions, Winston avoided mutual social events or attending the same conferences, inventing various excuses to avoid being thrown together outside the University environment.

As he became lonelier and the evenings seemed to drag on forever, she appeared increasingly attractive and alluring. He started to notice what she wore to work, her smiling eyes, her high cheek bones, her slender body, and her slim but muscular long legs. He fought the impulse to ask her out, despite repeated urgings from his students who all lusted after her themselves, always aware that he would be disloyal to Laura should he do so.

His Christmas at Brighton was pleasant if a little sombre. The Wrights clearly felt the contrast to the previous year, although they didn't want Winston to leave in the New Year and were effusive in their thanks for the theatre and other events he organised for the three of them. On the last chilly day, he suggested they walk to the Pier and have lunch there, to cheer themselves up. It seemed to work and the mood grew lighter as they shared amusing moments and remembered Laura's obsessively romantic nature and behaviour.

"She'll never be really dead while we continue to mention her name," said Winston at the end, remembering saying something similar about his parents on St Mary's. He closed his eyes and saw Laura, her skin glowing and her hair blown back in the breeze, emerge from the green-grey waves and crunch towards him across the pebble beach. He opened his eyes and she was gone, with only the ghost of a smile remaining.

A few weeks after returning to Exeter, Winston learned that his application for promotion to Reader, one rung down from full Professor, had been approved. It was announced by the Dean and soon he was being congratulated by the staff, some of whom were secretly jealous of his rapid promotion, and his students. A delegation of students came to his office and insisted that they have a proper celebration at The Fat Pig, a local pub, on Saturday night. Their leader, a somewhat pimply and bespectacled young man called Tim, explained with some fervour.

"We're not taking no for an answer this time. You're our most popular lecturer and we want to celebrate a rare good academic decision. You never join us for a beer, or darts, or to watch the Premier League games. You always make excuses, but no excuses this time," he paused, "Sir," he said as he remembered his manners. Winston was surprised as Tim was normally the quietest student in his classes.

"I can't say no to that," he said smiling. "Of course I'll come. What time?"

He arrived a little late, hesitating twice before going inside. The place was packed so that it was hard to move, but the students made way, patted him on the back, and bought him a pint of bitter, which they urged him to scull, laughing good naturedly at his failed attempt, with beer running down his chin. He looked around to see if Maria had come and saw her across the room surrounded, as usual, by admiring senior students trying to 'chat her up'. He noticed that she looked stunning in light clothes that emphasised her figure, legs and cleavage despite the cold weather outside. She saw him looking at her and waved airily without coming to join him. Somehow he felt deflated and relieved at the same time.

Against his better judgement, he was persuaded to trade vodka shots with his closest research students. They seemed to toss them down with no obvious effort, from long experience, whereas his throat experienced a burning sensation after each shot. He was certainly feeling a little drunk, a new experience for a man whose alcohol consumption was normally a glass or two of wine or two stiff whiskies a night. Suddenly, Maria appeared on his right, and the rowdy students insisted they share a shot, clapping as Winston and Maria clinked glasses and tossed the vodka back in unison. They insisted on a repeat performance while several took photos on their iPhones to mark the occasion. And bribe me later for higher marks thought Winston whimsically.

As he stood there, he started to feel dizzy, as if his surroundings were unreal. He tried to tell them he was a little drunk and should go home, but he couldn't hear his own words. My God, he thought in a daze, they've led me on and then given me some of that date-rape drug, Rohypnol or something like that, so that I can relax and enjoy myself with no inhibitions. It can't be just the drink. Surely, they didn't do it for me to make a fool of myself?

He felt as if he was going to sleep on his feet and would fall down unconscious. He felt Maria's arm go around his and the last thing he remembered was to hear her say, through a haze, "Don't worry, I'll take your drunk Reader home to make sure he's safe," to more clapping and some ironic cheers from the now excessively rowdy, intoxicated students intent on having a good time.

He stirred, half awake, lying on his back looking at an unfamiliar ceiling in the half light. He realised that he was naked in a strange bed with smooth silky sheets. He turned his head slightly, wincing at the ache in his neck, and saw a naked Maria looking at him with those deep brown eyes. Even half conscious, he could see that her upper body was as beautiful as he had imagined at unguarded moments at their meetings. Slowly, she moved towards him, alternately kissing him, licking and playfully biting him. Despite the feeling that his muscles were unnaturally relaxed, he was increasingly aroused and all his pent-up loneliness was released. She continued to play with him like cat and mouse, using all her experience from her sophomore days. Finally, when she felt he could bear the teasing no longer, she sat astride him with her pert breasts and small firm nipples inches from his face, and guided him inside her. Rocking rhythmically, she heard him sigh then moan as she increased the pace, until they were both satiated together, calling out each others' names as they climaxed.

Winston, already only half-awake, almost immediately slept. Maria, turned on her side, went to the bathroom, and came back to bed, pleased with herself. She had imagined this ever since Laura had died and she had seen his loneliness grow. Three hours later, when he stirred again, she put her fingers on his lips to silence any dissent and repeated the lovemaking again, this time with a more active role from Winston.

It was midday on Sunday when Winston finally woke feeling his normal self. He was now very self-conscious, somewhat embarrassed, and mortified at his betrayal of Laura. He wanted to ask Maria if she had engineered the events of last night but felt awkward to ask her. As if she read his mind, she offered.

"Before you ask, I think either you have alcohol intolerance or someone slipped something into your drink for fun. I promise you, it wasn't me. I'd never do that. But I did take advantage of it and I'm not ashamed of that. I've seen you looking at me and I've thought we'd be good together, and we were last night. It's the first time you've let go for months. All that emotion coiled up inside you like a snake is not good for you and certainly no good for those around you." He wondered if all Americans were as direct as she was. He would have found it difficult to have been as honest as she had been, fettered as he was by his natural reserve.

As he pondered, she said gently, reaching over to grasp his hand,

"Can we spend the rest of the day together, have lunch, talk about our relationship, and spend the evening together again?"

"I'm really sorry" blurted Winston," but I need some time alone to think this through. It's all so sudden and unexpected. You've removed my inhibitions and I have noticed you as a woman, actually for months now and you are as beautiful as I had imagined, but in my mind I feel terribly guilty. I really need to think this out. I don't want us to get hurt. I especially don't want to lose our research relationship. I'm just confused by all my conflicting emotions." He threw his hands in the air in a sign of uncertainty and despair, knowing he wanted her but fearing the consequences.

"OK," she said gently. "Go home and think about it. Take your time. I'll see you at work tomorrow as usual. Just promise me you'll have dinner with me next Friday and discuss it. No shots, no drugs, no sex unless by mutual agreement!" Her face lit up as she saw a grin on his still boyish face, followed by a rumbling laugh, and a nod that said OK.

Winston could not settle on Sunday afternoon or the following week. He was full of resolve to be true to his love for Laura until each time he met Maria at work, when he was totally seduced by her combined beauty and intellect. He tried to be calm in the day but imagined he was in bed with her at night and had disturbing lustful dreams about her. He realised that, at this moment, he was torn between his lingering love for Laura and his current longing for Maria. He decided to have dinner with Maria on Friday and explain his feelings honestly, in her American way, to her. He would tell her that he could not commit totally to her while Laura was still in his mind, however much it hurt. After checking that Italian food was to her liking, he made a reservation at Zizzi's.

Friday evening arrived and she drove him to the restaurant as he had walked to work as usual. They engaged in small talk over a pre-dinner cocktail, ordered pasta and chianti, and started to talk about themselves. Winston explained his feelings about her and Laura, stressing that he was incredibly attracted to her and had been thinking of her all week, but with guilty feelings. "I can't give you my complete love," he explained. "There is no certainty in the future of our relationship. I can't commit to you. I'm carrying so much baggage at the moment that it hurts."

"I'm a modern, realistic American woman," she said soothingly. "You can never replace the romantic love you enjoyed with Laura. Few couples ever experience that. I'm enough of a realist to know that half of all relationships fail at some time. Love is a form of madness that can fade as fast as it can bloom. I'm happy with a relationship based on mutual attraction. Why don't we just enjoy what we can bring to each other and see how it goes?"

Winston couldn't disagree with such logic, and his desire for her was growing each minute they were together at their intimate table. So she took him home to her apartment where they languorously undressed each other and made love, Winston marvelling at her suppleness and ability to arouse all his senses. His anxieties fell away, swept aside by his passion. He thought he had to give it a chance and reasoned that it was a good compromise. He knew there were many guys out there who would kill to have a relationship with Maria. He had seen it in their body language and in their eyes when they looked at her. Importantly for Maria, he didn't run away in the morning, but initiated the lovemaking himself, bringing her bagels and coffee in bed, after a quick check of her small kitchen.

Later that morning, they drove to Exmouth for lunch. Maria was happy. She had broken down his resistance, strengthened their bonds, and found a handsome man intelligent enough to be worthy of the love and sex she had to share. Tomorrow was another day.

34

For the next few months, Winston and Maria carried out their mixed work-related and social relationship. By mutual agreement, they attempted to be discrete so that their affair would not become common knowledge in the Department. They were totally professional, as before, in their joint research programs at work, went to any University social events independently, only teaming up after the events, and avoided public displays of emotion in cafes and restaurants in town. Of course, this subterfuge was useless as all the students fully understood that they were an item since the party when Maria had taken Winston home. They all noticed the softer relationship between them and that Winston, as well as Maria, now regularly went to social events related to the University, but pointedly ignored each other.

To keep their propriety, they each lived in their own apartments, meeting for dinner and passionate lovemaking once in the week and at least once on the weekends, sometimes at a hotel elsewhere in Devon or Cornwall. When in Exeter, they always slept together in Maria's apartment. She had wanted to sleep with him in his apartment but strongly sensed, quite correctly, that Winston felt that the ultimate betrayal of Laura was for her to sleep in the bed that they had shared together. She decided to be patient, fearing that pushing Winston would terminate the relationship which she enjoyed so much. She also understood his need to visit the Wrights and Laura's grave in Brighton once a month or so, and for his desire to keep their relationship from them. Their professional relationship blossomed with joint international papers relating to social changes that developed due to conflicts and advances in technology throughout history, flowing from their co-operative research efforts.

From Winston's perspective, he really liked Maria and admired her for her active mind and, at the same time, lusted after her. When they were in bed together he forgot everything else, soaking up the exhilaration and pleasure of the physical moment of lovemaking with such a gorgeous woman. However, he could not recapture the spiritual love he had felt—still felt—for Laura, and, afterwards he inevitably felt guilt at betraying her memory. He had read about the sex addiction of numerous celebrities, the most notable being Tiger Woods, and wondered if that was his affliction. He sensed that Maria loved him, although she had never declared it verbally, and wanted to love her in return, but something was holding him back. He often wondered whether it was just Laura or was there something else missing from their affair.

As their relationship settled into a routine, another steady period of life as Winston considered it dispassionately with his academic mind, he continually pondered this question of what was missing. Gradually, he realised that it was the nature of their relationship outside work and outside bed. He and Laura had accepted the digital revolution and used it to their advantage in their work, including joining LinkedIn and Students Circle Network, but had never become involved in social media such as Facebook, Myspace and Twitter, and never sent nor received blogs or tweets, using only email for correspondence. They had often laughed together at problems caused to politicians or sports personalities from inappropriate tweets sent off on the spur of the moment. On the other hand, the younger Maria seemed to be increasingly obsessed with her iPhone and tablet, contacting her many Facebook friends, tweeting and blogging as well as emailing, or listening to music through headphones on her iPod. Her social life was therefore one largely of virtual reality, thus isolating her from Winston when they were relaxing together. Winston had noticed earlier how teens and younger adults often sat together in virtual silence, messaging or playing games on iPhones, or isolated behind their headphones. The art of conversation and discussion was dying, he thought, and this is the fundamental difference between shared times with Laura and Maria. Instead of togetherness, there was largely isolation, with each partner living in their own virtual world. This was most annoying, he realised, when Maria sat up in bed, utilizing her tablet after they had made passionate love, when he would have liked to have talked to her and savoured the subsequent languid moments.

He wondered whether he was alone with these thoughts as a conservative academic, so started reading articles that he would otherwise ignore. He was particularly taken with the comments of Clifford Nass who worried that technology would rob people of the ability to concentrate, analyse information or even feel empathy for others. He was particularly attracted to the term 'Emotion Atrophe' describing short attention span and the increasing habit of dealing with emotional issues through social media instead of face-to-face.

Always questing for answers, he wondered if the massive modern-day increase in divorces and relationship break-ups relative to his parents' time was at least in part due to the somewhat unsatisfactory relationship—incomplete relationships he thought—that he was experiencing, combined with more satisfying, more remote relationships with seemingly perfect partners that could be developed through social media. Of course, the growing emphasis of physical appearance and attraction and sex over love and companionship was another, somewhat related factor, at least in his opinion coupled, of course, with the growing financial independence of women.

On his part, he did not want to return to the utter loneliness, almost despair, that he had experienced before Maria came into his intimate life and so was reluctant to discuss his concerns with her. I'm guilty of the modern malaise myself, he thought wryly, putting sex before companionship in the short term. Perhaps Maria will change, he thought. After all, we are writing papers together on social change brought about by advances in technology, and her own experience in the New York power outage has led her into her current research because of the realisation of excessive dependence on technology. He reflected on this for a while, concluding that many academics think about problems in an abstract way, seldom connecting their deductions and conclusions to their own lives, fully realising that he was also guilty of this himself.

I'll give Maria time, he thought, and try as subtly as I can to influence her to reduce her reliance on social media, although in his heart he knew it was almost certainly a lost cause. It was one of the growing addictions, together with drink and drugs, of the new generation of affluent western teenagers and young adults, with numerous business organisations predicting the emergence of an underclass poorly equipped for the workforce and society, together with professionals who would be too distracted to carry out complex tasks. In his ponderings, he wondered where the addiction to iPhones and related devices would end. He remembered Jeremy's comments about some evil IT mastermind inventing a group of super-intelligent robots sending messages to the world population on their iPhones to do their bidding, because as Clifford Nass had discovered, people are most flattered by praise from computerised voices. The ultimate reversal, he thought, with robots controlling humans rather than the other way around. Perhaps this was the glimmer of an idea for a new paper with Maria. He chuckled to himself as he thought that she could provide the technical input, at the same time chastising himself for disloyalty to someone who had rescued him from the brink of despair with her love and support for him. I'm an emotional head case, he thought, why can't I just accept things as they are, like everyone else does?

35

Over the next few months, Adam had cemented his relationship with Helga, both declaring their love for each other and their commitment to fulfil Adam's grand plan. Their Green society flourished, with increasing numbers attending meetings as climate change remained high on the agenda of most western governments, although warnings of worldwide global warming were gradually being replaced by those predicting increases in extreme weather. This advantaged Green movements worldwide, as the 24 hour news channels seized on any extreme weather, whether it be record snow levels or record high temperatures, major cyclones or hurricanes, or record melting of the Arctic ice sheets, and brought on their experts to discuss it. Interestingly, the growth of the Antarctic ice sheets and recent sporadic growth of Arctic ice was never mentioned. It simply wasn't newsworthy.

Adam had assembled his group of 15 Blood Brothers with the important inclusion of Dermott O'Leary, a somewhat mad Irishman with extensive experience with explosives, including an apprenticeship with the IRA in a former life, and Matt Bryant, a fireman who had taken up the profession to lead an exciting life, but was now bored and disillusioned as his time was often taken up with fairly simple rescue operations, while serious fires were infrequent. He had even confessed to Adam that he had once contemplated starting a fire in his fire district to get his adrenalin pumping and get into action.

Adam's grand plan, which had taken shape over time and come to completion after he had watched how passengers travelling between countries in West Africa had played an important part in the spread of the Ebola virus in 2014, and vigilance at airports had prevented the development of a pandemic, had not yet been revealed to the Brothers. He ensured, however that their discussions continually came back to the concept that the ultimate reason for all the world's environmental issues was over-population of the Earth. It was emphasised continually that this was causing land and soil degradation, pollution of rivers, oceans and underground water reservoirs, pollution of the atmosphere, not only with CO_2 but other more noxious gases, and accelerating near-extinction of some fauna and flora. Only the insects seemed to be thriving in new environmental niches was the conclusion of several of his group, particularly those who enjoyed camping. Both Adam and Helga were satisfied that, when the time came, the group would act as a team to carry out their daring, and somewhat dangerous, plan.

At work, Adam had used his 'geological scratcher' as he liked to call his hardness-testing pen-like device, to loosen the mortar around the bricks on the chimney during smoking breaks on the roof. It was painstaking work and he often despaired that it would all be in vain as he loosened a few millimetres a time. Only the persistent hallucinations that told him that he had been chosen to save the Earth drove him on with increasing determination. He also enjoyed the excitement generated by avoidance of discovery by other smokers who could venture on to the roof at any time, despite resenting any intrusion that might restrict his mini-excavations. He could now imagine how tense it would have been for prisoners of war trying to escape their prison camps, like the Stalags he had seen in old war films, via tunnels, or prisoners trying to escape from stone castles in past centuries by prising loose stones in the walls or iron grids serving as light and air sources to their cells.

After several months of effort, by late 2015, Adam had loosened sufficient mortar to make a cavity inside the chimney, on the opposite side to the access door to the roof, by removing two inner bricks from the thick walls. He could re-align the outer bricks and cement them close together using mortar-impregnated chewing gum that he had chewed after smoking on the roof. He considered it would escape casual inspection and could see no reason why there should be closer inspection as the chimney was dirty and already crumbling due to disuse and inattention. The two loose bricks were a problem, but he decided to cover them with dust from the roof and place them against the wall perpendicular to the one enclosing the door, hoping that no-one would notice, particularly as it was getting cold and fewer staff members were visiting the roof.

He left any further action until he was certain that no-one had detected his handiwork. As he had expected, the security-cleared cleaners simply removed the cigarette butts from the sand-filled tray opposite the entrance once or twice a week while the rain effectively removed any dust from the roof area itself. Meanwhile, he continued to eat lunch at a nearby café most days but brought in his lunch once or twice a week in two polystyrene cooler boxes, the larger for his sandwiches and the smaller with a plastic container inside, to hold mixed berries and yoghurt. The security guards joked about this at first, but it soon became routine, as did Adam's habit of placing the smaller box with its plastic container inside the larger box when he went home. On these days, he ate lunch on the roof, making sure he smoked after lunch and left his butt in the tray as normal.

When he was sure no-one had detected the cavity in the chimney, he left the smaller polystyrene box on the roof, out of casual sight, and exited the building that evening with only the plastic container in the larger box. If the security questioned him, he would say he must have forgotten it while having lunch and then retrieve it and show them before exiting. He need not have worried. The guard on duty was tired at the end of a long shift and took only a cursory glance at Adam's lunch box after a close examination of his briefcase. There was nothing inside the lunch box, so there had been no security breach. Adam breathed a sigh of relief and went home to tell Helga of his success, with champagne and some tumultuous lovemaking to celebrate. He woke at 3.00am with a vision of Charles Darwin congratulating him for his persistence, and urging him to complete his mission. Next morning, he went for a smoke early to avoid contact with others, retrieved the polystyrene box and hid it in the chimney space. A month later, he successfully repeated the procedure.

He now had a storage space for the virus, and was ready to take the next step in his master plan.

36

Winston and Maria continued their relationship, with Winston unable to directly broach the subject of excessive digital disengagement on Maria's part, at least as he perceived it. She, for her part, was somewhat aware of his disapproval but could not cut herself off from the many Facebook friends she had collected over the years. She felt that they were an integral part of her social life. She did not even consider that she was shutting him out by listening to music on her iPod. It was simply a way of life for people of her generation to entertain themselves through their headphones. She never thought to suggest that they play a DVD and enjoy the music together.

Her concern was always his inability to put Laura out of his thoughts, except in their most intimate moments together. Several times she had tentatively suggested staying the night at his apartment and he had always found an excuse. Finally, she realised that she would have to push him into making a commitment to her or break up the relationship if he could not. She sensed that he was wrestling with the same issue, but somehow neither of them seemed to be able to raise it directly.

"The weather is improving, and it will be summer soon," she said when they were alone in her apartment. "You'll have to go to St Mary's to check on your cottage. Why not take me with you? I've never been to the Scilly Isles, the history sounds interesting, and I'll have you all to myself for a long weekend." Winston started to find excuses, but then realised that this was the ultimate test of their relationship. Hollingbury Cottage had been at the heart of his relationship with Laura and he intended to keep it for the future. He wondered if Maria would see it in the same positive light as Laura and could he overcome his feelings of disloyalty and spend time with Maria there?

"OK," he said after a pause, "let's do it when we have no Monday morning commitments. We can go over on the ferry on Saturday, spend Sunday on the island, and fly home on Monday morning. That should give you a sense of St Mary's and give us some quality time together."

"That's great," she replied, flying into his arms, as she had expected more resistance. "Let's go to bed and celebrate," she stopped short at saying "a defining moment in our lives," fearing it would generate second thoughts on his part.

She was happy when he gave himself up to her completely. She sensed this was a turning point in their relationship and hoped that it was in a positive direction. At least she had a fall-back plan if it was negative. She just needed to make sure that they visited St Mary's within the next month to keep open her options. She now realised that she truly loved Winston, despite his conservatism, or perhaps because of it: she wasn't quite sure. She also knew that she had her own life to lead and that pursuing a relationship that could never be completely fulfilled would lead to recrimination and bitterness as it progressed. She had experienced this second-hand through several of her Facebook friends, whose confidence had been shattered and lives devastated through their love of uncommitted or unattainable men.

37

The Saturday morning of their trip to St Mary's dawned fine with Winston and Maria already on their way by car to Penzance. Their voyage to St Mary's was relatively calm, although Maria felt a little seasick on her first ferry crossing, particularly after having a snack and coffee as a late brunch. Like Winston, on his first visit to the Scilly Isles, she was captivated by the view as the islands came into view on the horizon and historic sites loomed larger as they approached St Mary's.

After disembarking, Winston took her to Hollingbury Cottage to drop their bags. Although looking rather neglected, Maria was captivated by the rustic charm of the cottage, and entranced by the village and its associated spring blooms. Her only obvious irritation was the intermittent iPhone access and the slow internet as she checked her social media sites prior to and after arrival. After settling in, Winston made coffee and they ate pastries they had brought at the local store. He showed her round the garden before taking her on a short tour of the key historical sites of the settlement, giving her a potted history of the island. She was highly animated at each site, but still pre-occupied by her iPhone as they walked along, muttering to herself about sub-standard access, although Winston had found it adequate for his purposes.

He took her for an *al fresco* dinner at one of the local restaurants, ordering seafood with French white wine. They chattered about their research and papers in review and in progress and deliberately left her iPhone alone, realising it was important to give Winston all her attention if she was ever to get him to commit to her. While drinking coffee, she remarked:

"Isn't it rather isolated and lonely here, with limited entertainment relative to even Exeter, let alone London; what do you do here?"

"Laura and I were happy just relaxing from our work, a spiritual vacation if you like. We'd read, talk, watch DVDs, listen to music, and take long walks along the coast or inland. We often ate out and of course we did quite a bit of gardening. Sometimes we'd take a boat to visit the famous Abbey Gardens on Tresco. Laura loved it and the other islands too. You see we planned for the future here: this was where we wanted to retire to." Winston could see from her expression that this was not her cup of tea, although she smiled at his reminiscing and chattered on, changing the subject.

They walked back to the cottage, chattering about the joint work they shared ahead in the next few weeks. As they undressed to go to bed, Winston had a panic attack, realising that making love to Maria here in this bed was the ultimate betrayal of his love for Laura. He tried to calm his emotions and to look away from her now naked voluptuous body as she moved suggestively close to him.

"I'm very tired from the driving and the very long day," he said jerkily. "I think we should just sleep tonight. Tomorrow is another day."

"OK," she replied slowly, "if that's what you want Winston," as she reached for her flimsy nightdress and pants. It's bloody Laura again, she thought to herself. I'm never going to come out of her shadow!

Both spent the night fitfully, facing away from each other, Winston for fear he might rescind his decision and weaken his resolve, and Maria in pique and frustration. They awoke very late, and said good morning to each other rather stiffly. Winston dressed hurriedly and went to make coffee and breakfast from the meagre provisions he had bought on arrival. By the time he had made breakfast, Maria had bathed and dressed and sat down at the table with him. She was angry with Winston and frustrated that their relationship could not take the final steps, but, deep down, understood his agonising issues. She sensed that he wanted to break their relationship but was too sensitive a man to do so. His British reserve, politeness and introverted character stood in the way. She decided that it must be up to her to make the break, however much it broke her heart to do so. She must also do it gently as she didn't want to lose him as a research colleague.

"Look Winston," she said gently, looking into his rather soulful and confused eyes, "I've fallen in love with you over the past months, but you can't give me the full love I want in return. Laura's always there in the back of your mind, and, although you're strongly attracted to me, you cannot commit to me while you remember her like that." He made a move to reply, but she waved him away.

"Just let me finish what I have to say," she went on, "I've realised this was the situation for some time: frustrating for me and an internal torment for you. So, as my current post-doc with you is coming to an end, I've applied for another post-doc in New York without telling you. I knew you would find me an extension to my current position if I wanted it, and I would have taken it gladly if our love had been fulfilled. However, I've been offered the position in New York and last night decided to accept it. I think it's best for both of us." Winston again tried to break in, but she silenced him.

"Look," she said, "I know it would have been better for me to wait longer before consummating my desire for you but the opportunity came up at that party and I seized it. You are not over Laura, and if I stay, we'll have recriminations. If I leave now, we can still be friends and colleagues in our research, and we can leave our love connection as an option for the future. It's best for both of us."

"I hate to admit it," said Winston slowly, "but I think, as usual, you're right. I am confused in my mind. You're an intelligent gorgeous woman that any man in his right mind would desire. You've brought me out of my pit of despair. I do want you and love you, but my memory of Laura haunts me and inhibits my commitment. I'm a stupid sentimental fool and I'm really sorry if I've hurt you." Tears welled up in his eyes as he thought of the loneliness that would reappear when she was gone.

They spent some time reflecting on their own thoughts, until Maria got up and said firmly, "We're wasting a beautiful sunny day, in all likelihood my last on the Scilly Isles. Let's walk and see all the sights and any historical sites you didn't show me yesterday." This broke the gloomy spell and conversation again became animated as they discussed common interests in the history of the British Isles. Walking towards home, Winston asked, "Shall we try a different restaurant for dinner tonight?" Maria thought for a moment, wondering if she dare make a provocative suggestion to avoid another embarrassing moment when they returned to the cottage after dinner.

"Why don't we just take a picnic dinner, some champagne, and a couple of blankets and have our meal along the shoreline. If we can find a private spot, we could make love for a final time. It would be a bit of excitement before we leave and a reward for our abstinence last night." She giggled girlishly as she made the suggestion.

"How could I decline such an invitation," replied Winston, frantically trying to think where they could avoid the attention of someone from the village. He could imagine that they would never let him forget it if they came upon him with Maria making love out on the grass, and he had a sudden flashback to the time he and his father came across a couple copulating in the grass while on their ramblings near Hollingbury Camp, when he was little. It all seemed so long ago.

Later that night, they found their secluded spot, ate their food, drank their champagne, toasted their future joint research and publications, undressed each other slowly while kissing passionately, and finally making love on the now wrinkled blanket. The possibility of discovery made it all the more exciting, as Maria had predicted, such that they were lost in their desire for each other, living for the moment with no recriminations. Winston had never been so satiated in his life and, for a few moments, was tempted to plead with her to stay. However, reason returned as he remembered the problems that would reappear to restrict them from fully consummating their love. After a while, they dressed and walked, arm in arm, laughing at what they had just done all the way home. This time, they slept side by side companionably. Equilibrium had been re-established.

38

Three weeks later, after a lengthy discussion in which Maria insisted that it was not necessary, Winston drove her to Heathrow to take her flight to New York. They were both rather subdued, realising that an important period in both their lives was coming to an end. They renewed their strong commitment to continue their research relationship as Maria's post-doc position was designed to allow her to build on her growing reputation with a view to taking up a professorship at some level in due course. They agreed to have regular Skype conversations to maintain their work relationship as long as feasible given the physical separation. They chattered desultorily as they travelled, Winston glancing across from time to time to soak up her image, and Maria sneaking glances at Winston and wondering if she could ever find anyone to replace him in her affections. She realised that she was attractive to men, but knew it was difficult in the modern world to find someone intelligent, kind and trustworthy, as well as physically attractive, such as Winston.

Finally, they arrived at her check-in counter and she prepared to go through security before heading for the Departure Gate. Winston made the first move, embracing her with a hug that almost took her breath away. She hugged him back, and they stood like that for a few minutes, neither wanting the moment to end. With both trying to hold back the tears, they kissed for the final time. Winston looked at her beautiful sad face and soulful brown eyes, and wondered yet again why he was letting her go. I'm a bloody stupid fool, he thought to himself. Maria, as usual, broke the silence.

"If you're in the States for a conference, please stop over in New York and see me. I've not given up hope that we'll get together again when you release those pesky varmints from your mind. But don't leave it too long," she said with emphasis.

"You'll be swamped by admirers," he replied realistically. "I know I have to release those demons in my head very soon, or I'll just be a pleasant British memory as you move on" he continued wistfully, "I'll see you on Skype next week to see how you've settled into your new position." They hugged again, kissed briefly, moved apart and walked away. As she went into security, she waved and he waved back. She walked through without a backward glance, tears streaming down her cheeks. You're a damn fool, Winston, she thought, we could have conquered anything together. He didn't look back either. It was not considered manly for an Englishman to cry, but he couldn't help himself.

As he was close to Brighton, he drove down to sit at Laura's grave and talk out loud to her as he often did. He felt emotions of guilt and betrayal mixed with sadness for the departure of Maria and wonder that love for someone who was now gone could live on through their memory and persistent spirit.

39

For Winston, the next weeks stretching to months, were lonely. He became introverted in Maria's absence, politely refusing invitations to social events unless he was required to attend as a University professor. Consequently, he made no new contacts. He looked forward to his monthly visits to Brighton, which broke the monotony of life. He found himself waiting impatiently for his regular Skype discussion with Maria. Each time they connected, his heart leapt involuntarily as he soaked in her beauty and enjoyed her insightful comments on their joint studies. Gradually, he forgot his misgivings about living with someone, even as attractive as Maria, who was so involved with social media. If you can't beat them, join them, he thought, as he experimented half-heartedly with Facebook as a starter. He was also starting to think that Laura would want him to get on with his life, particularly since both Jeremy and Penelope Wright told him so repeatedly. To their knowledge, of course, he had had no romantic relationships since Laura's death and they were concerned about him, believing, quite correctly, that he blamed himself for her death.

Hence, when an invitation came at short notice for him to attend a conference in Boston in late 2015 to replace a keynote speaker who had become seriously ill, he emailed Maria to arrange a Skype connection. She came on screen looking particularly radiant, something he had noticed over the past month or so. Winston was extremely nervous as he spoke to her, hoping that her reaction would be positive.

"At very short notice, I've been invited as keynote speaker at a conference in Boston," he commenced. "I've accepted and plan to fly to the US in ten days time. Could I accept the offer you made at Heathrow and come via New York and stay with you, or even meet with you, for a few days on my way to Boston or on the way back?" He imagined that she was taken aback by this, and her eyes became rather misty as she thought how to reply.

"Of course I'd love to catch up with you in person again, Winston," she said softly. "However, I can't ask you to stay. I missed you so much in the first few weeks that I just moped around hoping you would call and say you'd got your act together and wanted me. Finally, I gave myself a kick in the 'ass' and got on with my life. Now I've met a great guy, a young professor in IT, who, like me, is fascinated by social media and is introducing me to sites I didn't even know existed. We've become an item and he's already jealous of you. I've told him nothing of our relationship, but he said he's sick of hearing your name and I probably do go on about our research together. So, I think, it's impossible for you to stay with me, and we should just meet privately if you come to New York." Winston felt and looked crestfallen.

"So, I've missed my chance," he said finally. "It sounds like you've got a good thing going there."

"I really loved you Winston," she said softly, "but, on reflection, I don't think it was just Laura getting in the way. The few years difference between us, and your special relationship with Laura, meant that you didn't need social-media friends, whereas I just naturally accepted the new technology as part of my life. Jake is more on the same wavelength as me and I think I can be happy with him outside my professional life. That is if he doesn't kill any of those 'pieces of work' that pay much too much attention to me."

"OK," said Winston after a short pause, "I hope it works out well for you. I'll fly directly to Boston and Skype you from there. Better that I don't come to New York. Thanks for all the wonderful memories. At least we're an item, as you put it, with our names nestled together on our seminal papers," he continued light-heartedly. "See you soon on Skype."

"Take care, Winston. We'll probably meet at conferences or even ceremonies to collect our future joint research medals sometime soon," she replied in similar vein. The images faded and Winston put his head in his hands. Another window of opportunity had closed through his own stupidity. You can't move slowly in a fast-moving world, he thought philosophically, as he contemplated the lonely flight and impersonal hotel room in Boston and compared it to his imagined love-filled stay in New York with Maria.

40

At the same time that Winston's and Maria's frustrating love affair was over, Adam Lampton completed the next stage of his master plan to save the Earth as he viewed it, from its swarming, self-destructive population. Over the past year, he had secreted eleven small vials of the new high-stability flu virus into one of the lined polystyrene lunch boxes in the chimney on the roof. He had managed this by taking two vials each time for his repeat experiments but using only one and falsely recording the second result within error of the first. He did this over irregular intervals to avoid any fellow researcher or Director noticing a repetitive pattern as there were anomalies between repeat experiments in about ten percent of cases. These had to be followed up to determine the cause. In the other box, he had managed to secrete a lesser amount of the new vaccine, together with the new neuraminidase inhibitor designed for inhalation to replace Rulenza. He was assisted by the protective clothing he was required to wear while in the lab. He had found a way to push the vial up the sleeve and into a pocket which he had stitched into the inner sleeve of the jumper he wore when intending to steal a vial. Each batch of virus was labelled with a series of digits from 1 to 10 to record their relative time of storage in the chimney. He needed to prioritize them in case some of the early vials of virus became unstable over time.

Several times during the past few months he had narrowly avoided detection by smokers coming unexpectedly onto the roof. Instead of dampening his enthusiasm, it actually heightened the excitement of his 'Crusade' as his visions increased, encouraging his actions with thunderous acclamation.

He now needed to have a meeting with Matt Bryant, the fireman in his inner group, to arrange the next stage of the scheme to retrieve the polystyrene boxes from the roof. Finally his plan was coming to fruition. It had been several years since its inception so that now, to be almost at the point of execution was exhilarating. Although the inner circle would not be told of the ultimate plan until everything was in place, Adam decided to discuss the minutiae with Helga. He needed her trust and access to her superior analytical mind, in addition to her plain common sense. The two of them went over the details several times, modifying some of Adam's original ideas, to perfect a relatively risk-free plan, such that there was a high certainty of success. In particular, they considered the 2014 Ebola outbreak in West Africa, how it had spread, how it had been contained, and which factors would have resulted in a pandemic if isolation and treatment centres had failed to effectively restrict the number of virus-affected people arriving in North America, Europe and Asia.

Helga was secretly relieved that Adam had trusted her with the final details of his plan. She sometimes worried that he was too intense, and appeared to internalise his thoughts over activities related to *Vers Une Terra Verde*. She was particularly concerned that, at odd times, he seemed to lose his sense of place for a few seconds at a time, and didn't answer if she asked him if he was alright. As he rapidly returned to normal each time without seeming to notice it had happened, she was fearful to raise it with him in case it increased any anxiety he was feeling.

41

Winston returned from his trip to Boston in a despondent mood. His keynote lecture had been very well received, but his proximity to Maria without being able to meet her had proved frustrating. This had been enhanced by seeing her radiant face and highly animated conversation on their Skype call. She was obviously happy, whereas he was full of remorse for his ongoing procrastination.

His mood improved dramatically when he read an analysis of climate change by one of his students, Caitlin Prescott, who was taking his course and chosen the subject for her main assignment. She had carefully analysed the reports of the Intergovernmental Panel on Climate Change (IPCC), endorsed by the United Nations General Assembly, in the light of the book *Heaven and Earth* by Ian Plimer, an Australian professor of geology, and a 2013 article on *www.climatedepot. com* that presented a variety of evidence for a potentially cooling, not warming Earth in the longer term. Winston had read *Heaven and Earth* earlier, and had found it highly interesting and provocative, but had been distracted by other issues and had not fully absorbed the consequences of the conclusions. Caitlin had obviously enjoyed the challenge to the current conventional view and had done a wonderful patient job of synthesising all the critical evidence and producing an elegant précis. In her summary, she proclaimed that a variety of evidence, particularly geological evidence for global-scale ice ages when atmospheric CO_2 levels were much higher than present, argued against CO_2 in the atmosphere as a major driver of climate. Instead, there were strong correlations between solar activity and relatively warm and cool periods in historical times.

Winston's interest, as a social historian, was particularly aroused when she presented evidence, derived from *Heaven and Earth*, that periods of social and cultural decline, and the advent of major military campaigns that resulted in new empires, were strongly related to past climate change.

He was highly amused by her succinct summary of what she termed 'yo-yo predictions' which alternated between global catastrophe resulting from a cooling Earth and that caused by a warming Earth, with none of the computer-based models able to predict future change. From her synopsis, it seemed that the bulk of the evidence favoured a warming Earth from the mid-1970s to about 2000, followed by a slowing warming rate or even cooling of the Earth together with all the other planets since then, although news bulletins suggested the opposite. It was difficult to know what to believe because of the development of urban heat islands caused by the ever-expanding concrete and paving jungles that represent power-hungry modern cities.

Caitlin had assembled a variety of interesting facts that he was unaware of. It seemed that the lowest temperature ever recorded on Earth, -94.7°C, was measured in Antarctica in August 2010 and that Cairo had its first snowstorm in 112 years in December 2013. The photos of a snow-covered Sphinx were very impressive. This was followed in January 2014 and again in 2015, by the giant freezes that affected most states in the USA, closing airports across the country as the similar extreme winters had done across Europe in 2011 and

2012. In 2014, Californians were also blaming three years of drought on global warming, but analysis of growth rings of sequoia trees showed that similar conditions existed in 1580 when Sir Francis Drake first arrived in California. Winston thought that Caitlin showed wisdom beyond her years when he read one of her conclusions that it was arrogant for Man to think He influenced or controlled Nature when it was clearly the other way around. Many ancient civilisations had revered or worshipped the Sun, a pulsating star formed from recycled stardust, as the giver of warmth, light and life itself. It was only modern Man who was in a state of denial, she wrote astutely. The sun produces more energy in one hour than all humans produce in one year.

In conclusion, she had agreed with Ian Plimer and several of the scientists who had reviewed the IPCC reports, that these reports did not follow scientific principles but delivered dogmatic political propaganda. Human-induced climate change provided a much-needed fear factor for Green movements to maintain their global influence, and for governments for whom it provided an additional tax in their capitalist system. Climate change had been a feature of Earth long before humans evolved, and humans now played a miniscule role in its direction, she concluded.

Winston made a note in his diary to have a coffee with Caitlin and try to persuade her that she should join his postgraduate group on obtaining her degree. He would flatter her truthfully by telling her she had the ability to become a successful academic in the future, and would also seek permission to post her assignment on his lecture notes on the web for other students to read and set as their standard. Whether her conclusions were totally correct did not matter to Winston. It was her ability to analyse both sides of an argument and come to an independent conclusion that impressed him.

Researching the relationship between solar activity and climate that her assignment had stimulated was also a much needed distraction for Winston. He yearned for some social interaction to replace his shared times with Laura and Maria, but his male colleagues were all married and tied up with their families and all the single women he met seemed to carry impenetrable emotional baggage. His closer postgraduate students had goaded him into trying cyber dating sites, but two women he met had only a remote similarity to their much exaggerated and digitally-enhanced images on their web profiles, so he stopped looking.

As he reread *Heaven and Earth* and researched climate change, he became convinced that the Earth's weather patterns were cyclic on a variety of historical time scales of 11, 22, 87, 210 and 1500 years, coinciding with cyclic solar driving plus cosmic-ray forcing of climate. He was particularly impressed by the broad relationship between sunspot activity and climate, with higher sunspot activity relating to higher global temperatures. He was also concerned at the potential catastrophic effects of solar flares and geomagnetic storms, similar in scale to the much-publicised supervolcano eruptions such as Yellowstone and Toba, or asteroid impacts, such as that postulated to have caused the extinction of dinosaurs. According to his understanding of what he read, the largest solar storm, recorded in 1859 as the Carrington Event, would have had a disastrous effect on 21st Century power grids and communication systems if they had been in operation at the time of the storm. This prompted him to regularly visit websites that monitored solar activity from space, using satellites such as that of the Solar and Heliospheric Observatory (SOHO) a joint NASA and ESA project. He found that the US Space Weather Prediction Center was a particularly valuable source of information and resolved to adapt his lecture notes with all these new insights.

42

It was a cold wintery morning when Adam met with Matt Bryant and David Bryce, two of his inner circle. Adam checked when Matt would be off duty in the coming weeks and made sure that he and David were available on that day. He asked David to hire a small van with no windows in the rear doors. He was to hire it for three days, from the day before the vials were to be removed from the research facility, until the following day. David was also instructed to replace the van's number plates with a set provided by Adam, previously taken from a wrecked car, and to use the fake driver's licence Adam had organised from a contact in Soho, when hiring the van.

On the appointed day, early in the morning, David drove the van and parked it in a commercial loading bay about 20 metres down from Adam's workplace on the opposite side of the road. He pulled his cap down over his forehead and read the paper as if as waiting for someone to arrive or an office to open. Matt sat quietly in his fireman's uniform in the back of the van. Adam had learned, at his induction, that emergency procedure ensured that emergency services, including the local fire brigade, had sufficient knowledge of the building layout and the risks within the laboratories should there be a fire and he was satisfied that this would not impede his plan.

When he arrived at work a little later he was complaining of a splitting headache. Soon after, he staggered a little and asked to go to the sick bay. The part-time nurse, Jenny McDermott, was summoned, took Adam's temperature and felt his pulse. Satisfied that it was nothing more than a headache or fatigue from the party he described from the night before, she gave him a codeine tablet and suggested he lie down for an hour or so when she would come back and check on him.

As soon as the coast was clear, Adam got up and took two more codeine tablets so that he would appear drowsy and sedated later in the morning. He picked up the small wheat-filled warming bag, wetted it, and placed it in the microwave. He set the timer for 10 minutes, considering that anyone who would somehow check this might think he had meant 1.0 minute and set 10 minutes by accident, and pushed the start button. After four minutes, there was a strong smell of burning wet wheat and after seven minutes it began to smoulder. He stopped the microwave by opening the door, releasing intense and noxious smoke into the room. Fire alarms sounded throughout the building, and a recorded deep voice boomed instructions to assemble in the emergency staging area. Adam staggered into the corridor as Jenny McDermot, the nurse, came rushing to make sure he was out. Then coughing and with a blanket drooped around his shoulders, he was escorted by Jenny to join the other employees who were moving to their meeting place in a walled courtyard with a guarded exit behind the building.

Two fire brigade engines from the nearby fire station with sirens blaring pulled up outside within minutes of the alarm. Fire fighters in full uniform jumped from the vehicles and moved into the building. Matt Bryant, in his uniform, leapt from the back of the parked van and joined them unnoticed. Making his way, he hurriedly climbed the stairs two at a time directly to the roof using the memorised instructions Adam had given him. He retrieved the polystyrene boxes, put them in his pack, put back the bricks, and made his way back to the front entrance of the building. The whole manoeuvre had taken less than three minutes, and a crowd had not yet gathered to witness the drama. Coughing violently so that he could avert his head, and provide an excuse for an early exit before security could stop him, he went behind one of the fire engines and David drove up, using it as cover while Matt jumped aboard, shut the back door, and they drove off. Both experienced an adrenalin rush like nothing they had experienced before, not even Matt when he had experienced danger while attending serious fires in the past. They couldn't wait to meet up with Adam and Helga that evening to celebrate their successful operation.

Meanwhile, Adam waited nervously in the emergency staging area for the investigation he was sure would ensue. The smoke inhalation, codeine tablets and nervousness made him shiver genuinely under his blanket, such that Jenny had to sit him down and ask if anyone had any water to give him. Within 15 minutes, the fire alarms had been turned off and the fire engines were prepared to leave. The firemen were given a cursory check by security before leaving. The Director of the research group, Cameron McKenzie, who had talked to the chief fire officer before he left, walked purposefully into the courtyard.

"You can all relax now," he said with authority. "It seems it was a false alarm caused by a hot sack overheating and smouldering in the sick bay microwave. Luckily the microwave door was opened before it could ignite. Will the person responsible please step forward." A now severely shivering Adam stepped forward, the nurse holding his arm.

"Right!" he paused looking at Adam, and pursed his lips. "There will now be a thorough security check which will apply to all staff. After that, please remain in the courtyard while security make a detailed search of the building to ensure that there has been no tampering with equipment or products during this distraction. "You" he pointed at Adam, "come to my office as soon as you've been checked. And you too Nurse McDermott."

After security searches had revealed nothing untoward, Adam and the nurse made their way to the Director's office accompanied by one of the security guards. Once there, the nurse described what had happened up until the point she left Adam in the sick bay. He then explained that he had started shivering, noticed the hot bag sitting on the sink, and put it into the microwave to heat for one minute.

"Then I felt nauseous," he went on, "and lay down on the bed. I must have fainted or dozed off because I woke to a burning smell and smoke coming from the microwave so I opened the door to check and was overcome with smoke. I heard the alarms and the directive to assemble in the staging area and then Jenny appeared and got me out. I'm really sorry if I've caused a problem." The Director stared at Adam as if he could see right through him. He noticed that Adam was sweating and that his head was shaking slightly. He asked Jenny to check his pulse which she reported feeble and unsteady.

"OK for now," said the Director slowly. "Jenny, take him back to sick bay and stay with him. I'll let you know when the all clear is given. You can then escort him through security for an exit check and put him in a taxi to take him home." The fire chief had indicated that it would be reported as a false alarm, so Adam realised there need be no more action unless security discovered anything untoward. He breathed an inner sigh of relief, feeling wobbly at the knees from the stress and effects of the codeine. Inwardly he was delighted to have got away with it and planned to have another day off before returning to make sure the chimney bricks were cemented back firmly, on his first smoke break.

Later that evening, Adam exchanged 'high fives' with Helga, Matt and David as they celebrated with takeaway pizzas and beer. In the early hours of the morning, Adam's sleep was interrupted by visions of Darwin praising his actions, extolling his cunning and courage, and exhorting him to take the final stage of his plan to save the Earth before Doomsday arrived.

43

The next day while at home, Adam checked the availability of the inner circle of Blood Brothers and set a meeting for an evening the following week. Once they all arrived and settled down, he stood up and asked for attention. He had previously outlined his overall plan to reduce world population in general terms, but now provided more specific details on how this was to be achieved. He explained to them how he had secreted vials of a new resistant strain of the flu virus and extracted them under cover of a fire alarm with the help of Matt and David. He then went on to outline their critical role in releasing the virus at selected international airports around the globe. He and Helga watched for any sign of dissent that could jeopardise the mission, but sensed accord among the group. They had chosen well in terms of each individual's predisposition to cleanse the Earth at whatever cost, and their subtle indoctrination over the months and years had cemented their resolve.

"Monday 17 July will be D-day," said Adam. "The weekend is usually less busy with fewer business travellers and security may be lower due to staff rostering. We need space to make things ready and then we can plant the vials on the Sunday. Then Monday will be ideal for the action to begin, as there should be numerous international business people travelling all over the world at the start of the business week."

"What's the plan and what will we be required to do?" asked Matt Bryant, anticipating that everyone in the room wanted to ask the same question.

"You already played a critical role when you got the vials out of the research building Matt, replied Adam, "but you're welcome to join the others in the next task if you wish." He paused and stuck a poster of a world map to a book shelf. "I want each of you to prepare yourselves to take leave from at least 13 July to as long as possible afterwards. I'll allocate you an international destination and you must book to be there before Friday 14 July and to depart on Sunday 16 July. I'll provide funds for the tickets, but you must all ensure that your passports and travel documents are in order and that you have any required visas for the travel. You also need to have thought of a valid reason for travelling to your allocated destination."

"We'd better each use separate travel agents to avoid any connections being made?" interrupted David.

"Exactly," replied Adam, who had been about to suggest it. "Use your local travel agents, particularly if you've booked through them before, or transfer the funds to a credit card and book on the web."

"What are the destinations?" David interrupted again glad he was the one asking the questions.

"I've chosen hubs for international travel where security is less intensive than in the USA and the UK." He pointed to each place which had been highlighted on the map to emphasise his point. "We'll target Johannesburg and Nairobi in Africa, Hong Kong, Singapore, Bangkok and Mumbai in Asia and the subcontinent, Dubai and Cairo in the Middle East, Sao Paulo and Mexico City in South and Central America, and St Petersburg for eastern and northern Europe. These all service densely populated countries as well as North America and Europe," Adam concluded. Greg, another of the Brothers queried how they would be allocated.

"Talk to me at the end of the meeting and we'll allocate by mutual agreement," replied Adam. "If any of you have been to any of those destinations, it would be an advantage for you to return as you have prior experience." He added as an afterthought, "Let me know if you have any special people to protect and we can discuss strategies," knowing few, if any, would accept. He explained how they would all be vaccinated and inhalers would be kept for emergencies. He had already bought tickets for a cruise of Australia and New Zealand for his parents, knowing his father would be on leave at that time and he hoped they would accept his gift, and that this would keep them safe. There was muted discussion between the members and someone asked, "What do we do when we return?"

"It would be wise for us all to find a remote location for a few weeks, just to be on the safe side. I'm thinking myself, of a hiking trip in the Outer Hebrides or Orkney Islands," he said to muffled laughter. After further talk, Adam produced a spread sheet and asked the members to consider their preferred destinations. They were then allocated the airport where they would hide their vial of flu virus.

Adam concluded the meeting by going over all the main points of the exercise and making sure that everyone was absolutely clear about the actions required of them prior, during and after their mission.

44

In the Spring and Summer Terms of 2017, Winston had tried to keep busy at work to alleviate the loneliness he increasingly felt in his apartment during the evenings. His interaction with the Wrights had become less frequent, mainly via phone or Skype, partly because Penelope had become less mobile and excursions were more difficult. His research co-operation with Maria still continued, but the frequency and duration of Skype discussions decreased as common social interests declined and Winston watched her beautiful animated face with regret. He was mentoring Caitlin as much as he felt appropriate in an academic environment where there were always jealousies and potential gender issues. However, he looked forward to supervising her research once she graduated. Promising intelligent and hard-working students were becoming more difficult to find in the modern world, where instant digital entertainment was ever-present, and web-based friends were in constant communication, he reflected and grinned to himself thinking, I'm just getting old and out of touch.

He watched the development on the climate debate with interest. The rhetoric had continued to change from global warming to climate change involving more extreme weather, whether it be extreme heat, extreme cold, or extreme storms. No-one in the media seemed to emphasise the greater problems with a cooling, rather than warming, Earth. Most people believed the polar ice caps were still melting whereas both the Antarctic and some parts of the Arctic appeared to have had increasing ice areas in recent years. Over Christmas 2013, icebreakers had been unable to rescue tourists from a Russian research vessel because the Antarctic ice was unusually thick. He became increasingly cynical about news broadcasts on the weather, many of which were self-contradictory with the newsreader seemly oblivious to it. It also constantly annoyed him when almost all newsreaders talked about hot or cold temperatures, knowing that any thinking person would realise that temperature is a measurement and can only be high or low. Why hasn't it been picked up he thought?

He had continued to follow sunspot activity and variations in the Earth's geomagnetic field through websites. In the early part of the year, sunspot activity had been low, as widely predicted, in concert with cooling of the Earth and other planets. Some experts had suggested that the lull in solar activity was similar to that known as the 'Maunder Minimum' which had coincided with a 'little ice age' in the 17th Century. However, in early June, to his surprise he started to notice reports of increasing solar activity. Logic told him that this was simply a minor anomaly, but his intuition suggested otherwise. He remembered that he and Laura had bought Hollingbury Cottage in part as a refuge in the event of a world crisis and had adapted it and stocked and restocked it for the future. He hadn't bothered since Laura had died but now he felt it was time. In a week or so, the summer break would start and his teaching commitments would end. He would go to his neglected cottage for a few weeks, clean it up, tidy the garden and check the stock. He would use the rest of his time to complete two papers he was writing and put together a proposal for the textbook he had been asked to write by a publisher for the past two years. He was not to know that his premonition about danger from a solar source and his decision to spend his summer break at the cottage would fortuitously protect him from another looming threat.

He suddenly remembered the Wrights, so he Skyped them to tell them of his decision. He wondered whether he should tell them of his concerns about imminent climate issues because it sounded fanciful for an educated man. In the end, he explained that he had decided to spend his break on St Mary's partly due to needing a change and partly to an impulse based on inner concerns that something threatening was about to happen. Urging them to stock up with food and fuel just as a precaution, on the vague possibility that he was correct, he promised to visit on his way back to Exeter. He wasn't normally a person who had premonitions although he did have a sixth sense about some things. Laura was the one whose intuition was often correct. Thinking about Laura made him sad, and he thought that maybe loneliness was making him more reclusive, entertaining bizarre thoughts. Still he had told the Wrights that there was nothing to be lost by being prepared and he thought it was about time he checked and updated his own stock at the cottage. After all, any preserved food, bottled drink and fuel would not go to waste.

In early July, he was firmly ensconced in his cottage, spending the mornings on long walks, gardening or making minor repairs to the cottage. The afternoons and evenings were spent on his work, with irregular trips to the village for some social interaction and an evening meal. He was beginning to feel much better and more normal now that he was filling his time with physical work and he enjoyed the company of the people who frequented the pub in the evenings.

45

The week of 9 to 16 July arrived and all the chosen members of Adam's brotherhood who had been prepared and vaccinated had arrived safely at their delegated destinations all over the world. They had each been given a small box marked bath oil in which there was a vial, packed in cottonwool, and a small plastic-coated detonator and timing device produced by Dermott O'Leary, guaranteed not to be picked up by security X-ray. As he put it, the device only needed to shatter the vial, so a noise like a fart would be produced and hence go unnoticed. As instructed, the boxes had been placed in their toiletry bags and carried in their check-in baggage to reduce the possibility of detection. All agents had been given disposable cell phones for convenience, and instructed to enter only contact numbers for their hotel, taxis, restaurants and the like: on no account were any *Vers Une Terra Verde* or brotherhood members' names or family and friends to be included and they were not permitted to take their own iPhones. They had also been ordered to remain anonymous and under no circumstance to contact any of those people. They were on their own. On arrival at the chosen airport destinations, each member passed nervously through immigration, picked up their bags, checked into hotels and operated as typical tourists, seeking out the main attractions, and eating out in local cafes, as they had been briefed.

On the Saturday, each visited the airport as instructed, on the pre-agreed pretext of checking their tickets in the unlikely event anyone asked. It was highly improbable that any of them would be noticed as crowds of people passed in a continuous stream in and out of the entrance areas of major airports, checking in and farewelling or meeting friends and family. They reconnoitred the departure terminals for secure places to secrete the small boxes where they would not be found by cleaning staff and disturbed, even on a Sunday night when the airports were relatively quiet. Modern airports were large open spaces with few secure hiding places which were periodically unattended. Most shops, restaurants and bars were clearly out, with rare exceptions.

It was a challenge to find safe, protected places. However, before Sunday dawned all Adam's agents had found a suitable hiding place for the vials to be detonated on the Monday. It had been difficult for some to find a place where the infection could be spread to the most advantage and where they would not be found before the virus was discharged. A couple did find suitable places in shops but others were more innovative in their choice of spaces. Some chose toilets where the area was restricted, realising that often passengers made

last-minute trips to the toilet before passing through security where
there could be long waits. In Bangkok, one agent was propositioned
by a passenger who considered he was loitering in the toilet to be
picked up for sex, but otherwise the operations were uneventful.

On the Sunday, they arrived at their allocated airports, several
hours before their own flight home and loitered close to their selected
hiding place, as if waiting for a flight call. For some it was agonising
as they waited for the areas to be free of passengers, particularly
the toilets as people were constantly emptying their bladders before
passing through security. Once the areas cleared long enough to
deposit the boxes, which were set to detonate at 7.30am local time
on Monday, the agents did so. It only took a few seconds and then
they were able to proceed through security to their boarding gates.
They each experienced profound relief after the stress caused by fear
of discovery, and a few suffered pangs of guilt from their actions.
As normal, there were some delayed flights which caused further
concern, but all were on their way home to London by late Sunday
evening, to continue on to the destination of their choosing where
they felt they would be protected. On arrival at these safe places, they
messaged Adam on their disposable phones to say they were OK,
and then immediately destroyed and disposed of them.

Once all were safely in the UK, Adam and Helga set off to Wick
in northern Scotland as they planned to stay in the Harbour Guest
House B&B, where they could get high-speed internet and follow
world events from a remote location. There was also easy access to
the Orkney Islands if required. Adam's parents, who had somewhat
reluctantly accepted his gift of a cruise, as they had had renovation
plans for Andre's leave, were now sailing around northern Australia
which was always warm regardless of the time of year.

46

In Scotland, Adam and Helga scanned search engines for web-based news outlets to find any indication that their operation had been successful. Although research on the virus was incomplete, Adam estimated that the first victims should start showing symptoms within two to three days and that they would be infectious for up to seven days after that. He expected early deaths to result because the strain was potentially more deadly than that of the Spanish flu in the 1918 pandemic. However, he realised it might take several days before the media realised that an outbreak had occurred, with such a high daily death rate simply the result of the huge global population.

Wednesday and Thursday went by and Adam stated to imagine that the virus had become unstable as it had been subjected to variable temperatures and long storage times, or that the devices had not detonated to release the virus. On Thursday night, the visions assured him that he would be seen by history as the saviour of the Earth. On Friday, the first news of a potential flu epidemic broke. People presenting with symptoms, such as sore throats and severe coughs, alternating fevers and chills, body aches, fatigue and vomiting, were appearing at multiple locations around the world, predominantly in Asia, Africa, South America and the Middle East. These were the regions served by the airports prioritised by Adam and Helga to receive the most recently acquired and hence potentially most stable vials of virus. The global media reported that isolated cases had presented on Wednesday, with more on Thursday, reaching potentially epidemic proportions on Friday.

By Saturday, it was clear that, as in the 1918 pandemic, some infected people were dying within 24 hours of having symptoms and the mortality rate was becoming high. The heterogeneous geographic spread was now pronounced, with only isolated cases reported from North America, Europe and Australia. By Sunday, media coverage worldwide abounded with conspiracy theories that the west had used biological warfare against the developing world. In response, the US President, British Prime Minister, Canadian and Australian Prime Ministers, and the German Chancellor, on behalf of the European Union, in turn emphatically denied such involvement in formal TV news bulletins and in written statements. They emphasised that severe cases were now emerging in their regions. This somewhat calmed the sabre rattling, from countries like North Korea, Iran and Pakistan where anti-American sentiments, in particular, were escalating. No-one seemed to be able to pinpoint the source of the virus. It had appeared almost simultaneously around the globe, and was spreading rapidly as world travel was continuing unabated. Only the Hong Kong and Singapore airports were automatically monitoring passengers for flu-like symptoms and isolating those who had a fever. However, health authorities realised they had a serious flu epidemic on their hands and warnings were being given on all news bulletins for people to cease travelling, unless absolutely necessary, to wear medical masks when in crowds, to get medical help if showing any symptoms, and so on.

As it was early days, no-one had yet reported isolating the virus, but Cameron McKenzie, the Director of the research unit at which Adam worked, suspected it was the virus that they'd been researching or something very similar. He hastily organised a telephone conference on secure lines with his counterparts at sister research units in Chicago and Berlin. They decided that they should urgently inform their respective governments, despite the fact that each believed their security was impenetrable and could not see how the virus could have been dispersed from their laboratories. They feared their jobs were on the line, but suspected they might survive via governmental cover-up, as each of their heads of governments had formally denied any connection to the virus in interviews with the media which had gone global. They need not have worried.

Within hours, orders from each of the governments were essentially identical: keep the matter under wraps and provide enough vaccine for the cabinet members and senior military and police staff to ensure continuity of leadership during any crisis, including a pandemic, if it eventuated. The laboratories were to suspend research but produce as much vaccine and other preventative medication as possible to ensure that those who worked in emergency services and those who maintained essential facilities in their communities could be protected if an epidemic ensued. They were also to investigate the effectiveness of Rulenza, for which there were already supplies from previous crises, in this outbreak. Other labs throughout the world, who were researching strains of influenza, were similarly instructed by their governments to work on vaccines and preventative medicines. Self-preservation had inevitably become the dominant driver during emergencies throughout history.

47

In St Mary's, Winston had a continued sense of foreboding that something was about to happen. He couldn't explain it, and was annoyed because it was illogical, but the premonition was always there. He wished that he had experienced the same uneasiness before Laura went missing, because he might not have left her and, if so, she could be alive today. He pushed the thought that he might be dead instead to the back of his mind.

Due to this fixation, he regularly watched the global news bulletins on TV and checked media reports on the web. On Friday morning, 21 July, he saw the first reports of the flu epidemic on TV and by early Saturday cases were being reported around the world with some people dying within 24 hours of contracting the virus. Good God, he thought, is this what my intuition has been all about? He had gone to St Mary's thinking that some natural phenomenon was imminent but he had never considered a disease epidemic. He called the Wrights to check on how they were. They said they had been watching the news of the spreading epidemic and, as there were now almost 100 cases in the UK, Jeremy had decided to close his business for the time being to see what would eventuate. Luckily they had stocked up with staple provisions as Winston had suggested, although with misgivings.

"We're OK," Jeremy reported. "We'll just stay put and sit it out. I'm sure the authorities will find a way of preventing the spread of this flu fairly quickly, but we'll bunker down in the meantime. What about you? I think you ought to stay on St Mary's. They should be able to isolate the population before any outbreak occurs there."

"I hope so," replied Winston. "Actually you've just given me an idea. I might go to the Council Office and see what they intend to do. I haven't heard anything locally, only what's on the news." He told them he'd keep in touch and to take care before finishing the conversation.

Winston watched the midday news and was dismayed to find that the virus was spreading, and that twelve people in London and five in Glasgow had died, with many more being infected. With some misgiving, he went to the Council offices at the Town Hall to see if he could find the Council Chief Executive whom he had met several times and who knew most people on the islands. The CEO knew Winston to be a world-acclaimed historian and was happy to meet him when contacted, and listen to his reasons for spending his long University break in St Mary's, only showing surprise when Winston directed his attention to recent flu outbreaks.

"This is as safe a place as it probably gets anywhere in the world," stated Winston, "as long as St Mary's avoids contact with the outside world before the epidemic spreads. Does the Council have a plan for such an eventuality?"

"As a matter of a fact I did have a meeting with our three GPs last night. One of them is the Chairman of the Health Committee who's been in contact with the NHS to see if we are able to get any vaccine from the mainland. Our pharmacy does have a small stock of flu vaccine but it's doubtful that it will prevent any new virus. I'm meeting with him this afternoon to assess the situation and to see what he has been told by Community Health in Cornwall. Would you like to accompany me?"

"I would, thank you very much." Winston nodded "I've been thinking that possibly you ought to isolate the islands for the duration of the epidemic." The CEO thought for a while, sensibly deciding that he had everything to gain from listening to Winston's opinion if it provided a potentially good outcome.

"We've discussed emergency situations as a full Council," he replied, "but mostly about preparing for extreme events of Nature, dealing with marine disasters or preventing acts of vandalism. What's your opinion of the current situation?"

"Well, it looks pretty dangerous as it isn't confined to Britain and people are beginning to die. Personally I'd be inclined to call the Council together with your Health people and suggest a plan of action that will benefit all those on the islands and keep the local residents happy. As Britain is beginning to really feel the effects of this epidemic, locals will want to come home and probably tourists will want to return to the mainland to be with families as well."

"So, you're suggesting evacuations from St Mary's for the tourists and an immediate return of our residents from the mainland, consistent with policy," interrupted the CEO, eager to share credit for the idea.

"Exactly," said Winston. "There's only one ferry and one air service to the island. I'm sure with your influence, you could arrange a one-off exchange of existing tourists with returning residents, within a short timeframe and then persuade both the ferry and the Skybus to cancel services for a period while you assess when it is safe to resume. You could offer some compensation if required. That way you can isolate the island from any epidemic."

"You may be right," agreed the CEO. "We have contingency plans drawn up for various emergencies such that they can be adapted for most situations. I'll get a list of absent residents and of course school students and their contact numbers within the next 12 hours, and I'll ring both Scillonian and Skybus operators at the Isles of Scilly Travel Centre in Penance. If they're coming over in an emergency dash, I'll also get the stores to order in at least triple their normal supplies to make sure we can survive an extended period without starving. I'll call the Council members right away to arrange an emergency meeting for this afternoon in the Old Wesleyan Chapel. The Chairman of the Health Committee is on the Council too, so we can hear what he's got to report at the same time. Most councillors live in St Mary's anyway and we can phone any on the other islands who are unable to attend." Winston could see that he was now fired up with the opportunity to demonstrate leadership in a potential crisis, and asked: "When do you think special ferry and Skybus services will be in place?"

"I'll phone them straight away and see what I can do. Then I'll call the Council together and see if we can gauge whether your fears of a serious epidemic are founded, and then act accordingly. The school holidays with an increase in tourists will start later next week, so swift action would be an advantage. We can get Radio Scilly on board to instruct people once we've decided. I'll call you after the meeting and let you know what's happening. Would you be willing to assist in any way, if it appears necessary?" asked the CEO.

"Sure, I'd be pleased to help," replied Winston with enthusiasm. "We need to keep a close watch on developments of the outbreak so as not to be caught unawares."

When he got home he decided to Skype Maria to see how she was faring and to warn her to be careful. She told him the situation in the United States was similar to that of the UK and that people with the virus were beginning to die. She laughed nervously and told him not to worry that she'd be OK and would take extra care to avoid infection.

By Saturday evening, the global media were recording thousands of cases of infection, which was now rampant in overcrowded cities, particularly those with poor hygiene. By Sunday, media estimates were that tens of thousands of people were displaying symptoms from those well-populated regions where communication was possible. Over half of those infected were dying. Some countries were controlling media reports to stop mass hysteria, so the total number was probably higher. At this rate, it will be hundreds of thousands by Monday or Tuesday, estimated Winston, remembering that approximately 30 percent of the world population was affected by the 1918 pandemic, with an estimated 50 million dead, over 650,000 in the US alone, when the world population was much lower.

That evening the Council CEO phoned Winston to tell him that his medical people had been informed that there was no spare flu vaccine and that they needed to make sure the elderly and very young had been inoculated before the commencement of winter, and to use what they had sparingly for anyone who might be at serious risk. There was no guarantee that it would work considering the virility of the new virus. Also Council had tentatively approved the planned 'evacuation', for Tuesday, if the epidemic continued to spread. Winston hoped that this was early enough, as more cases were being reported throughout Britain, although mostly around London and Manchester, and Glasgow in Scotland with their international airports and large populations.

The Council had also agreed that anyone arriving by private boat or yacht was to be quarantined there for a week before coming ashore, and that vehicles would be parked across the airport runways on Tuesday evening to avoid any arrivals from the air. St Mary's would adopt a siege mentality as the Council fully realised that if the virus arrived in the small community it would decimate it. Isolation was the key to survival in such circumstances. Living in a crowded, totally serviced environment could be a death warrant. As Winston had predicted so long ago, St Mary's would be a safe haven if all precautions to isolate it were taken.

48

By Monday, the world media had stopped interviewing the relatives of victims of the flu virus as they would in normal circumstances, instead speculating on how the virus had appeared almost simultaneously in many countries and commenting on the probable death toll. Terrorism was the word now being whispered by the media but, being a global epidemic with no-one group boasting responsibility or blaming another, coupled with lack of motive, there could only be speculation. They could not make a realistic prediction of the number of victims, but it was estimated to be already in the hundreds of thousands.

Irrespective, it was enough for the St Mary's Council to confirm their 'evacuation' plan. Council workers visited all tourist accommodation sites to inform visitors of an emergency meeting that evening at 5pm. The Council Chief Executive had ascertained that only a handful of island residents were on the mainland as the main tourist season, the village's lifeblood, was about to commence. They had all confirmed that they wished to return and would do so on Tuesday by plane or ferry, together with the Year 12 and 13 students who were at school on the mainland. The Isles of Scilly Travel Centre had agreed to cancel all subsequent travel to the island for a week, on a watching brief, with only partial compensation for cancelled tickets as they would incur no ferry or plane operational costs. Residents were told to keep tuned to Radio Scilly for updated information and any instructions deemed necessary.

Tuesday dawned sunny and relatively calm on St Mary's. The CEO couldn't contain his apprehension as he remembered his father, who had been a Fire Warden in London during the blitz, recalling how people had pulled together in those dark days to save Britain. Two visits by Skybus had cleared all the tourists with plane tickets, and Scillonian II arrived with massive food and fuel supplies which took over two hours to unload. Finally, all but two of the tourists who had return ferry tickets boarded the ferry, those departing electing to stand by their close families on the mainland rather than remain in the safety of St Mary's. Winston considered them brave and perhaps a little foolhardy until he considered how he would feel if Laura and his parents were alive. He would go to them without hesitation, he thought, as he justified himself that he had done all he could from afar for the Wrights in Brighton and for Maria in America.

The two women who had elected to stay behind were Fiona McDougall, a widowed doctor with snow-white hair in her early seventies, who was suffering withdrawal symptoms after retirement from her practice and felt she might be useful at the hospital in any medical emergency. Her daughter had migrated to New Zealand many years ago and she had no close relatives in mainland Britain. The other was a smart, rather attractive, willowy brunette, as Winston viewed her, in her late thirties, or so he estimated. Kathryn Fletcher had a rather sad, haunted look, enhanced by the lack of make-up, and explained to Winston when they got talking after the Monday meeting that she was an orphan, raised by an elderly aunt and uncle, who had died when she was 19. She had become an English teacher, and five years ago met and married her future husband, Mark Fletcher, an army major. He had been killed by a roadside bomb in 2014 on his first mission to Afghanistan and one of the last involving the British military. She was understandably bitter about this, and had been depressed and unable to cope with the world at large ever since.

"How come you're on St Mary's before the school holidays start," Winston asked inquisitively.

"Oh, my courses and exams were over," she explained quietly, "and I thought I'd beat the summer rush and get here early to enjoy the peace and quiet. My Head was happy to grant me some leave I'd accrued and I decided not to go back to the mainland when the Council gave us the option to return home, as I have no family and I feel safer here. The lack of other tourists will be a big bonus," she added with a smile which turned into a laugh as Winston chuckled at the comment.

"That's why I'm staying too," he said, "I can get on with writing my textbook without interruption." She knew he was a university professor as the CEO had introduced him, together with councillors, medical staff and others who would be contacts during the imposed quarantine of the islands, and thought that it would be good to have an academic with whom to discuss current affairs and literature over the coming days. Interestingly, he was thinking the same thing. The next few weeks may be safe but would become boring without good company.

As night fell, the island stores were still open as residents queued to buy their ration of supplies as defined by the Council. Winston was glad that he had thought ahead and stocked up on Monday to supplement the emergency supplies in his cellar. He felt satisfied that the Council had done the right thing by the residents and was pleased that he had played a role in it, making him feel part of the St Mary's community, not just a visitor as before.

49

On Thursday afternoon, the CEO personally visited Winston at the cottage to thank him for stimulating the rapid response to a potential crisis that was predicted, but not yet reality, just a few days before. The media reports were now extremely alarming, with infection spreading like wildfire in countries with inferior hygiene and overcrowding, particularly major overpopulated cities. Traditional funeral pyres were burning 24 hours a day in some countries, while cremations were overstretched in others. 'Experts' trotted out on TV stations such as CNN and BBC World were now predicting the probability of millions of deaths worldwide unless there was some global agreement on how to halt the advance of the epidemic, which had clearly reached pandemic proportions. Populations worldwide were panicked.

Infected citizens were now appearing in increasing numbers in North America and Europe. In Britain, the flu outbreaks were mainly in and around the large cities in the southeast, Midlands and north, but local outbreaks were appearing in Scotland, Wales, Ireland and southwest England. The CEO reported to Winston that staff working for the Scilly Steamship Company that ran the ferry had asked to seek asylum at St Mary's ahead of the epidemic which they had feared was coming. They, and some staff from the Travel Centre and Skybus Ltd who had been stood down at least for the next week, had agreed to live on the ferry for the incubation period, estimated to be up to four days, to ensure that no-one who was infected arrived on the island. They were on their way the next morning with additional food and fuel supplies. There was now plenty of accommodation for them on the island, and the ferry provided a link to the mainland in an emergency. It was a win-win situation.

As epidemics worldwide seemed inevitable, western governments took stock of how well they were placed to meet the problem in their countries. All were faced with the same basic problems related to ageing population, inadequate funding for hospitals, limited isolation wards, shortages of skilled nurses, and shortages of doctors. Medical practitioners who were not involved in essential medicine, such as cosmetic surgeons involved in the beauty industry, or those involved in clinical trials for research, were now ordered into theatres to assist with minor operations or into wards and Outpatient Departments, to help hospitals cope. Overcrowded emergency centres, clogged with self-harmed drink and drug- induced patients, did not help. The inevitable results were long waiting periods for surgery and overcrowding in most public hospitals and full beds in private ones. In a serious epidemic as this one threatened to be, the authorities would need space to isolate infectious patients, so using school buildings seemed the most suitable choice to many governments, particularly in the northern hemisphere, since the school holidays had now started or were about to commence. They would also need to inoculate all medical staff with whatever was most appropriate and provide protective clothing, particularly for the facial area, to avoid the risk of infection causing even further problems.

Several governments realised that even these measures would not be adequate if the worst was to happen, and hundreds of thousands to millions of people were infected, as some government advisors were predicting in agreement with the media 'experts'. Self-regulation would be required, however harsh it might be for the individuals concerned. The governments knew the main behaviour drivers were greed, self-interest and fear. After all, they routinely used these drivers in campaigns to be elected to power. In this case, fear was the logical driver to induce populations to co-operate in halting the pandemic or at least bringing it quickly under control.

The problem was how to get rapid decisive action in a modern democracy. Over the past 50 years, democracies based on the Westminster System had progressively failed to deliver real progress, partly because the Upper House stymied the bills introduced by the elected government. The same applied to the USA, where Democrats and Republicans waged open war to score political points such that the President's reforms were pushed aside and financial crises such as the 'Debt-ceiling' episode of 2013 ensued, threatening world financial stability. In some countries, like Australia, the problems were further enhanced by the appearance of non-majority governments, where minority groups, who had received 10-20 percent of the vote, effectively defined government policies. The end result was inevitably indecision, public dissatisfaction and policies that harmed the economy. Benevolent dictatorships would be able to handle crises much better despite their obvious downsides.

After frantic phone conferences, the heads of government of some of the most powerful countries approached the World Health Organisation (WHO) of the United Nations to make a strong statement on a global strategy to limit the pandemic. The individual government authorities could then adopt this strategy in a state of emergency worldwide.

The WHO treated this request with caution. The United Nations, in general, were widely perceived as an ineffectual, even inept, group who had made serious blunders, at least in the public perception, in their engagement in conflicts in Iraq and Afghanistan, and to a lesser extent, Libya, and most recently in dealing with ISIS in Syria and Iraq. Their Committee on Climate Change was coming under increasing criticism for failed predictions. The WHO, themselves, had been criticised for spreading fear and confusion in the 2009 swine flu pandemic, which killed more than 18,000 people, although they had justified this by pointing out that many new vaccines had been developed quickly due to their intervention.

In the end, they looked at lessons learned from the 14th Century 'Black Death' plague, even though this was caused by bacterial not viral infection. Community-imposed and self-imposed isolation of infectious people had helped keep the death toll from rising above 75 to 200 million in a global population of only about half a billion people. It was impossible to contemplate a similar proportional death toll in a population of about 7.5 billion in 2017 with a yearly growth rate of 80 million. The responsibility to halt the pandemic was mind blowing.

A formal, politically-correct statement in legalistic jargon was released that confirmed the pandemic and essentially pointed out that hospitals and government quarantine areas were already saturated or would be very shortly. People displaying symptoms should essentially quarantine themselves within their own houses, isolating themselves from their families as far as possible, and call the relevant authorities to seek medical assistance. Travelling themselves to medical centres would cause chaos around these facilities, increasing the chances of serious infection for those doing so. Everyone was strongly advised not to travel by plane or ship, and to avoid public transport if possible.

By arrangement with major governments, the WHO announced that governments would arrange delivery of face masks to every household while stocks lasted, to avoid mass purchases from limited suppliers that could accentuate local epidemics. These governments were also manufacturing vaccines as fast as possible, and these would be distributed by random ballot based on the first letter of surnames, as had been done in some countries for armed services conscriptions. Governments would also advise employers to allow non-essential workers to take leave for the duration of the epidemic. The WHO also advised that cremations should be carried out in preference to burials to further reduce the advance of viral infections.

Overall, world governments were pleased with this sensible, measured advice from WHO. Importantly, it placed responsibility on individuals and local communities to take self-regulatory actions because no government could cope with a pandemic of these proportions. They hoped that the population would be sensible and responsible, while fully realising that there had been a growing tendency for irresponsible behaviour and risk-taking in the increasingly undisciplined younger generations, particularly in affluent western societies.

50

In Scotland, Adam and Helga spent their time on short hikes when the weather allowed. Otherwise they watched the news channels to keep up with reports on the 'Global Flu' pandemic. TV reports from all over the world had similar vision. Overworked doctors were shown treating distressed patients. In more sophisticated medical centres and isolation wards prepared for the 2014 Ebola crisis, the doctors looked like spacemen in their full protective suits or had Perspex head shields, whereas elsewhere they were protected only by simple face masks akin to those used during surgery. The cameras inevitably panned to lines of bodies, similar to those after natural disasters, awaiting burial in mass graves, or cremation and then on to cremation towers belching smoke. As usual, there was little sensitivity in the media coverage: sensationalism was the name of the game. Studio coverage involved endless interviews with experts on viruses, epidemics, the plague, and anything else that was topical. Experts predicted at least millions of casualties and, by making comparisons with the 'Black Death' and the 'Spanish Flu' pandemics, estimating up to 2 billion deaths.

Adam had the same mixed feelings he had with his father in the African refugee camps. When he viewed the news dispassionately and simply listened to predictions of casualties of faceless people, he was pleased with his operation. With knock-on effects that no-one was yet factoring in, the world's population would be significantly reduced and, hopefully, birth-rates decline as the population took time to recover from the crisis. However, when he saw the personal tragedies he had caused, he felt remorse for his actions which were causing suffering and extreme grief to families. After a while, he let Helga watch the TV news, while he simply kept up with developments via the web. His visions seemed to have deserted him, but the disturbing images of bright lights flashing before his eyes remained.

His intrusive feelings of sympathy for others led him to worry about his parents. He was having trouble calling them, perhaps because they had turned off their international roaming on their iPhones. His email enquiry, however, was answered swiftly. It appeared that, despite sporadic outbreaks, Australia and New Zealand, with their relatively small populations and forward planning, were well equipped to deal with epidemics. The cruise company however, had decided to keep their passengers at sea and were servicing the ship wherever possible at anchor away from the docks. Andre Lampton had volunteered his services should any emergency develop on the cruise, which had become rather monotonous, but otherwise everything was fine. He told Adam how puzzled he was that influenza outbreaks had occurred all over the world at the same time, but said nothing more about the epidemic, to Adam's relief.

As agreed, there had been no contact between the Brothers for fear that it might incriminate them at a later time. The world was too busy now trying to halt the advance of the epidemic and concern about its source was not the top priority. Only the media repeatedly asked the question, but global populations were only interested in what level of danger it posed in their particular communities.

51

Winston watched developments on TV and websites from the safety of St Mary's, checking every second day that the Wrights were still safe in Brighton. Most of the available news inevitably came from the western world. Governments had been quick to implement the WHO recommendations, providing both national and local authorities with advice on controlling the spread of the influenza virus. Despite this, the epidemic was spreading more widely every day, particularly among the younger generation who viewed wearing masks as 'uncool', and still tended to congregate in overcrowded pubs, hotels and nightclubs with a self-admitted feeling of invincibility.

By early August, the epidemic was global, spreading rapidly through North America and Europe despite the delayed onset relative to Asia, Africa and South America of infected people displaying increasing symptoms of fevers, coughs, rapid breathing, severe vomiting, grey skin colour followed, in a high percentage of cases, by respiratory failure and death. In many cities, essential services were starting to collapse as key workers were infected or simply stayed away from work, fear triumphing over concerns for their future employment. Looting and attacks on pharmaceutical companies and chemist shops were being reported. Authorities simply did not have the ability to deliver the limited supply of vaccine available to the population rapidly enough, and the dilemma of who should be a priority to receive any vaccine was causing unrest. It seemed that only isolated rural communities or religious sects who clung to conventions of previous centuries had so far escaped the onset and advance of the epidemic.

By the first week in August, Winston noticed that most reports were now coming from TV studios, not from reporters in the field who had been reporting the crisis. It was reported by rival channels that some infectious reporters among the media packs had themselves caused infections that had effectively wiped out the population of large refugee camps in Kenya and Turkey and had been warned off by international aid groups. The mortality rate in individual countries it seemed, would depend on socio-economic factors, underlying medical conditions, nutrition and access to fresh water. Experts were now confidently predicting that the pandemic would kill over 1 billion people worldwide.

On an impulse, Winston Skyped Maria in New York. She said she was still well and had heeded his warning, stocking her apartment at first appearance of the virus before panic buying set in. She reported that many Americans were also taking leave at short notice with disruptions to services, that roads were clogged with commuters who were reluctant to take their normal trains or buses to work, and that looting had broken out in some cities where food supplies were declining. A state of emergency had been declared in many towns, as well as night curfews, with the army, reservists and National Guard intervening in extreme cases.

"I'm really fearful of that will happen here in the States if the pandemic continues to accelerate," she said to Winston, who noticed worry furrows on her forehead for the first time. "The irony is that the capitalist system just charges on throughout the crisis. The New York Stock Exchange has recorded record trading with retail businesses and import firms plunging while pharmaceutical stocks have soared along with precious metal prices. As usual, the rich will benefit from the crisis while the poor suffer. As you often said, Winston, democracy is an ideological concept not a pragmatic reality."

Winston wanted to ask her how her romance with Jake was progressing, but decided he didn't really want to know. She would have told him if there had been a change in relationship. He simply said: "Goodbye Maria, keep in touch," as she faded from view. He hoped not for the last time.

As an afterthought, he called Kathryn to see if she would like to share a simple meal with him: he was rationing his food in case the pandemic was prolonged. Although he noticed that she was rather guarded, they talked animatedly over a precious bottle of wine, hardly noticing how late it had become. The conversation inevitably came around to the global pandemic.

"What do you think is the source of this world-wide virus?" Kathryn asked.

"Well, the apparent simultaneous world-wide onset of the infection strongly suggests a human hand," Winston paused. "However, it's unlikely to be a terrorist act because no-one has claimed responsibility and it has affected all nations and all religious groups more-or-less equally, if we can believe the news channels."

"Well, in your opinion, what else could it be?"

"My guess is that it's a group who see reduction of the global population as the only way to save the Earth from escalating disasters that will culminate in the extinction of humans themselves. They might also see it as a wake-up call to global politicians to admit that efforts to reduce world population is the number one priority for our survival. You see many countries wipe out part of their population through war, and Mother Nature plays her part with natural disasters. Then there's disease and outbreaks such as AIDS, flu epidemics and the recent Ebola virus, but in some countries the population is multiplying so fast, much of it from immigration that even these disasters cannot stop it escalating further." He looked at Kathryn and smiled. She frowned and asked, "So, you believe reduction in population is essential." Winston could see her concern and he thought very carefully about his reply, not wishing to place himself in a poor light and appear insensitive.

"Yes, our population is rushing headlong out of equilibrium with our planet. We're rapidly depleting resources such as clean air and water and fertile soils that are critical for our future survival. We're inhabiting niches of cleared land that are prone to earthquakes, flooding or drought, and we're depleting our natural food supplies and natural resources. Yes, we are facing a crisis." He paused and thought for a moment, "The Chinese have already realised it but Africa, for example, has a birth rate of 5 children born to each woman in her child bearing years. Even here in Great Britain the population has risen more than 400,000 in one year and more than one third of that is down to immigration. The rest of the world is in a similar situation."

"Well" said Kathryn somewhat taken aback by his answer. "Do you condone what has been done if your idea that the epidemic was deliberate is correct?"

"No," said Winston emphatically, sensing her dismay. "I'm an academic, who believes in discussion and management, not direct action such as this. Like you, in my heart I'm shocked at the suffering this is causing and I'm relieved that we've escaped it, at least so far. Having said that, I think that the world community will come to see this as a pivotal moment, which will give world leaders a 20 to 50 year breathing space to take a more moderate measure to curb population growth. It'll take a superhuman effort with all the ethnic and religious obstacles in the way." Kathryn nodded and muttered that Fiona had said something along the same lines, although Winston could see that she was still a bit shocked at the honesty of his answer. So he quickly said "Let's talk about more pleasant matters, because all this is simply speculation about events which we can't influence."

Winston walked her home to make sure she was safe. He would be very glad of her company if the current crisis was prolonged, he thought, although she's clearly carrying some emotional baggage. It takes one to know one, he laughed to himself.

He suddenly realised that he had been so preoccupied that he hadn't checked his Space Weather and other websites for several days. To his surprise, he noted that there had been anomalous solar flare activity over the last two days and some minor, but significant falls in the Earth's magnetic field over the past month or so. Tired, he vowed to investigate this more fully the following day, Saturday 5 August. His intuition was again kicking in. The world certainly doesn't need any natural disasters at the moment, he thought before going to bed.

52

The next morning dawned bright with a sunny day forecast in southern England. After breakfast Winston scrolled through the news items on the web. Undeniably, over 90 percent of the news related to the flu pandemic, with estimates of tens of millions deaths worldwide and tens of millions more already infected. Fear gripped the world with communities now trying to enforce quarantine where self-isolation was ignored. Shades of the 'Black Death' thought Winston where houses of the infected were marked to identify them.

After a while, he found two obscure reports confirming what he had expected. Apparently, the Kitt Peak Solar Observatory near Tucson, Arizona had recorded a medium-sized solar storm two days before and this broadly coincided with reports in the USA of unusual phenomena such as involuntary rise and fall of automated garage doors, intermittent internet access, flickering TVs, erratic GPS location data, and minor problems with aircraft navigation systems due to secondary radiation. Having recently read articles on overdue magnetic reversals which could be catastrophic for life on Earth, Winston prayed that these were simply isolated events and not the precursor to something more serious. The media reports reminded him of phenomena that Maria had described from a major power outage in Canada when she was talking about her experiences in New York in 2003.

Winston discovered from a small item in a news bulletin later that evening that the Kitt Peak National Solar Observatory had now recorded a gigantic solar flare or 'canyon of fire', in NASA terminology, that had erupted close to the centre of the Sun. The item was sandwiched between lengthy bulletins on the pandemic.

What wasn't picked up by the media was that records showed this eruption was at least ten times more energetic than that of March 10 1989, which had sent an enormous gas and plasma cloud hurtling towards Earth causing the Quebec power outage three days later. As required when set up by the National Science Foundation, on-duty Observatory staff reported the solar flare as a matter of urgency to the White House and to the Federal Emergency Management Agency of Homeland Security. The President's office immediately asked for an estimate of risk, but was told that it was unclear. The Earth's outer atmosphere would be impacted by ultraviolet and X-ray radiation within a short period, probably minutes, but the main threat would come from geomagnetic storms at the earliest 24 hours from now, they were told. These were likely to be severe, potentially affecting satellite systems, aircraft and shipping navigational systems, and power generators, they were informed after posing the relevant questions.

The President was informed of the potential crisis immediately. He was already overtired and under pressure as fear and panic raged through the USA due to the flu pandemic. There was no point raising further alarm bells without good reason. He called several of his closest scientific advisors who were given access to the Kitt Peak Observatory data. They unanimously agreed with the conclusions from the Observatory itself, and pointed out that it was a global problem and needed a global response to protect satellite communications and ensure passenger safety during the danger period. There seemed little else that could be done except attempt to limit electricity usage during the critical days of potential danger to global power. No one could categorically define the danger period, with estimates of two to seven days.

The President called the heads of government of his closest allies to discuss further action, who then made the decision that the President should immediately call a press conference to announce the impending threat. Each contacted their own air traffic control agencies, such as Civil Aviation Control in the UK and Eurocontrol, and their maritime equivalents. The hope was that if they agreed to land existing flights, terminate new flights and close airports within the next 24 hours, agencies in most other countries would follow suit. The companies who controlled the hundreds of satellites orbiting the Earth would also be contacted and put on alert. They all agreed that there was no need to further alarm the public given the global chaos caused by the flu pandemic. After all, there may be no serious global effect from the solar storm.

Winston checked the news and web for further publically available information but could find nothing, and didn't pursue it. He went to bed at 10pm, only to be awakened by the peal of his iPhone just after midnight.

"Hello," he said sleepily, "I hope this is important; it's just past midnight," he mumbled as he fumbled for his watch.

"Sorry Winston," he heard in a voice he immediately recognised as Maria's, "I just forgot the time difference in my excitement. You know how you're always going on about climate change and the sun, well the President is just about to give a press conference about a large solar flare earlier today. I thought you might like to watch on TV. I'm sure CNN will pick it up."

"Thanks Maria, you're forgiven for calling so late. I saw a small news item earlier but couldn't find any follow up. Must be important for the President to speak. Are you psychic because it was the last thing I was thinking about before I went to sleep?"

"OK Winston. Glad to hear you're OK and still enquiring after the truth," she laughed. "Watch now and we can talk tomorrow." Winston turned on the TV and watched the President's press conference. He noted the references to potential threats to navigation systems and thought to himself that the solar flare must be very large to attract such warnings. He checked the Observatory website again. He didn't understand the scientific jargon, but his opinion was confirmed.

Early on Monday morning, he noted that most airports and ports had closed globally, despite a massive media campaign pointing out that the relevant authorities' actions during recent volcanic eruptions with ash clouds had been over-the-top. He called the office of the CEO to seek an urgent meeting. On arrival, he explained his fears that the solar flare could potentially cause communication problems and probably localised power failures and asked if he thought it worthwhile to send the ferry back to Penzance to pick up additional supplies for an extended emergency.

"Although he was unaware of this threat, the ferry captain suggested doing just that a couple of days ago," said the Chairman. "I think he and the crew have grown restless with the inactivity. Anyway I phoned around to see if supplies might be available. The answer was uniformly no. Apparently, the epidemic is raging in London and to the north, though there are fewer outbreaks in the southwest. Unfortunately, however, food and other supplies have almost come to a standstill due to heavy casualties among truck drivers and absenteeism of unaffected drivers reluctant to risk infection. The transport system is apparently a shambles and many stores are closed."

"Looks like we'll just have to make do with what we've got then," said Winston, "and play the situation by ear." The CEO nodded agreement: there was nothing else they could do apart from warn the residents of potential problems.

53

Winston went home to briefly Skype Maria as promised and to re-educate himself about the effects of solar flares. On the webpage (www.solaraction.ord/SWchapter1.html), he found a wonderful piece of prose that described the physics of a solar storm in layman's terms. The paragraph explained:

> *Silently, the storm had impacted the magnetic field of the Earth and caused a powerful jet stream of current to flow 1000 miles above the ground. Like a drunken serpent, its coils gyrated and swooped downwards in latitude, deep into North America. As midnight came and went, invisible electromagnetic forces were staging their own pitched battle in a vast arena bounded by the sky above and the rocky subterranean reaches of the Earth. A river of charged particles and electrons in the ionosphere flowed from west to east, inducing powerful electrical currents in the ground that surged into many natural nooks and crannies. There, beneath the surface, natural rock resistance murdered them quietly in the night. The currents eventually found harbor in the electrical systems of Great Britain, the United States and Canada.*

Although the literature on solar storms was full of controversy, it seemed to Winston that the severity of effects on Earth depended on how massive the solar storm was and by how much geomagnetic field strength was lowered. He gathered that human life would only be at serious risk if a magnetic reversal occurred involving a dramatic decrease in Earth's magnetic field. Such events were measured by 'magnetic stripes' on the world's ocean floors where the volcanic lavas containing magnetic minerals were alternately positively or negatively magnetised, representing periods when the magnetic North and South Poles switched over.

He noted that this happened on average every 450,000 years although the length of time between magnetic pole reversals was highly variable. The last one had occurred 780,000 years ago, so Earth was overdue but only in a statistical sense because of the variable periodicity of the events. Some authors suggested human life would be extinguished during a reversal, but Hominins, the ancestors of Hominids and Modern Man, had been around about 5.8 million years ago, the period of several magnetic polar events, indicating that survival was possible. Despite this, he hoped sincerely that the coming solar storm would be relatively uneventful. The flu pandemic was more than enough for the world to cope with just now.

He was just about to cook his rationed evening meal when his iPhone pealed and he answered the call.

"Sorry to disturb you Winston," he heard from a voice he recognised immediately with some surprise, as Kathryn. "Fiona, you know the retired doctor who opted to stay here, well she and I wondered if you'd like to have dinner with us at the guest house this evening. The proprietor says it's OK as long as you bring some alcohol in exchange for the food. He's originally a Scot," she explained and chuckled as he reacted predictably. So Winston took a bottle of French wine to dinner with the two women and a small flask of Scotch whiskey from his precious supplies for the Scot. Before they sat down to eat, he asked them how they were coping with life in isolated St Mary's. Kathryn was wearing makeup that enhanced her rather haunting beauty and Winston was glad he'd exchanged jeans for trousers before going out.

"We love the place," Fiona answered his query, "it reminds me of my early life in Scotland. But, with no medical emergencies so far, no tourists, and school holidays with children at home, it's all a bit quiet. Otherwise, we wouldn't be dressing up and seeking your company, young man," she said cheekily, reminding him of someone with such wry Scottish humour from his past. His mind raced to define a face and name.

"Yes, we've read all the books we've brought with us and even resorted to downloading books on our tablets when we can get the web connections," smiled Kathryn, "although we both like the feel of a paperback. Habit I guess. I wish the Five Island School was open. They go up to Year 11, so I could have volunteered to help the teachers in some way with the children of the age I'm used to teaching in my secondary school."

"I can solve the book problem, as least for a while. I've got a library built up over a number of years. Come over and pick up what you like," offered Winston.

"I saw it when I came over the other evening," said Kathryn shyly.

"Why else do you think we invited you over to dinner Winston?" added Fiona with a knowing smile, glancing over at Kathryn for an expected blush which was not forthcoming. "Come on you young devil, we can chat over dinner, if you can call what my countryman in the kitchen has cooked 'dinner'." Winston now remembered the name of the distant relative of his mother's whom he had met as a child. It was Nan Campbell MacDonald. He'd subconsciously stored it in his memory because he knew as a historian that the Campbell and McDonald clans had been bitter enemies for centuries and wondered whether Nan's droll sense of humour was a product of a difficult childhood at school, like his own, which could be blamed at least in part on his name.

Winston did most of the chattering over dinner, something that amused him as he thought that two women together normally took up 90 percent of the conversation. Both Fiona and Kathryn were, at the same time interested in, and fearful of, the impending solar storm. Both had been interested in climate change but followed the rhetoric about dangers of CO_2 in the atmosphere and had not followed counter arguments about the dominant role of the sun, and wanted a summary from Winston: a 'self-proclaimed expert' as Kathryn called him.

He did his best to explain it in simple terms, realising that neither he nor they understood the physics. He outlined the evidence that climate change had been directly related to solar activity long before any supposed intervention from humans, and tried to explain about solar storms. However, it was difficult to do so because of controversies about causes and effects and the time scale of those effects.

"So we're due for uncertain calamities at uncertain times in uncertain places," summarised Fiona succinctly with the wry smile that Winston had now come to expect.

"Yes, you're technically correct," replied Winston after a pause. "However, my observations on sun spots and premonition of a crisis led me in part to return to the isolation of St Mary's. I know that there has been the flu pandemic, but my intuition was suggesting problems related to the Sun. I know it's illogical but the strong feeling is still there."

He paused expecting a sarcastic or ironic comment from Fiona, but none came, so he went on. "Also your speech and wry jokes reminded me of a distant Scottish relative, Nan MacDonald. My mother told me she was a bit fey and always disliked the month of August. Her father had died that month and other unhappy events of note had occurred in August throughout her life. I remember that my mother told me that Nan herself died in August. You can never underestimate the mystical powers of the Scots."

"*Touché*," replied Fiona. "You've convinced me there's cause for concern. Can we walk you home, pick up some books, and lie low inside for the next few days?" After they'd chosen their books, Winston offered to see them home, but Fiona insisted it wasn't necessary. Kathryn lingered for a moment, then moved towards Winston, leaned over and kissed him on the cheek.

"It's a comfort to have you around, and call me Kate please," she said quietly, moving away before he had a chance to respond to the kiss or comment.

54

Subsequent reconstruction of events showed that it was around lunchtime in Britain, near sunrise in the western USA, sunset in India, and night in China and Australia on Tuesday 8 August when the first signs of the solar storm appeared. In space, communication satellites that sensed the Earth's magnetic field in order to point themselves, flipped upside down as the local magnetic field polarity reversed with all attempts for them to be repointed manually from Earth failing. Most satellites in orbit tumbled out of control and could not be recovered. Weather satellite communications were also lost indefinitely. The governments of the USA, UK, China and Europe scrambled to gain access to the handful of satellites still operational which were controlled by companies under their jurisdiction. These would be made unavailable to the global population, and instead be used for military and anti-terrorism purposes in a time of crisis.

The first to detect the impact were pilots in commercial airlines from aviation companies in 'rogue' countries who had defied the proposed global shutdown of airports. Their navigational systems signalled what appeared to be haphazard flight paths as their Global Positioning Systems collapsed. Attempts to use backup conventional compasses failed as the Earth's magnetic field was strongly affected. Within minutes, all external communication had failed.

When these aircraft attempted to land, the pilots found that their navigational radar was also offline. They were effectively on their own to use emergency old-fashioned navigational and landing techniques. Luckily, airspace was not crowded and airports were virtually deserted, so there were few major incidents, and only limited loss of life. Without flight bans, there would have been chaos and multiple crashes in the overcrowded skies, as approximately 1000,000 flights took off daily, with frightening density over North America, Europe and eastern Asia.

The global air traffic control agencies had made the right decision despite media criticism and pressure. Even if the planes were grounded indefinitely, they had been preserved for the future. Shipping was less affected, but all ships returned to port as soon as possible, most anchoring offshore due to the pandemic on land.

55

In New York, unaware of the dramas unfolding in the skies above, Maria was making herself a light late breakfast before commencing work which she had decided to do from the apartment she and Jake shared, to avoid infection from the flu epidemic in the city. Jake had decided to go early to the College where he worked to make sure his students were catered for, at least on the web, while the pandemic lasted. Maria had not been happy as she was afraid he was risking becoming infected. She had made sure that he wore his mask and took a spare along with a small box of disposable gloves, with instructions to text or ring her when he arrived and when he was returning to the apartment. She had BBC World on for background information, having come to prefer this to CNN since her stay in the UK. Although the constant self-advertising of future programs on the BBC annoyed her, the obsessive reporting of world politics from an American perspective on CNN irritated her more.

Suddenly vision on the screen started to break up, and then was gone. She tried other channels, and came to the realisation that all satellite-based channels were unavailable. As she was flicking through the channels her computer started to blink on and off, emitting a shrill beep as it did so. She grabbed her iPhone and found that there was no response whatever button she pressed. At the same time she was startled by a series of muffled explosions as the toaster popped and the electric kettle stopped humming. She checked her other appliances and tried the light switches. There was no power whatsoever. She shivered as she relived the anxiety she'd felt in the power outage that seemed to have happened many years before, although something was different this time. Trying to think what to do, she realised that her computer and iPhone should still be operating on batteries even if there was a power outage. She still had a landline that she had been meaning to cancel, but hadn't got round to it so she tried to phone Jake and found that it too was dead. Swearing out loud, it dawned on Maria that all power and communication systems had failed at the same time. On impulse, she turned on the tap, luckily having the foresight to put a jug under it. There was an initial flow of water, then a dribble, then nothing.

She walked to her balcony and looked out. There appeared to be spot fires all over the city, at least one near a power substation near their apartment, and another more intense one near where she had seen workmen digging around a gas main a month or so ago. As usual Winston was correct, she muttered to herself. He was always ranting on about the escalating level of human over-reliance on sophisticated technology that had infiltrated into every single niche of modern society, and how social media was running that society. She fully realised with a sudden shudder, that without power, computers, mobile communication devices, wireless and the internet, cities like New York would be doomed. All facets of life in the city would be affected: heating and cooling, transport, communication, access to food, medical help and money, everything. This would compound the problems caused by the flu pandemic which had already stretched scarce resources to the limit.

Her train of thought was interrupted by a frantic knocking on the door. Looking through the peep-hole she saw it was Susie, a near-neighbour whom she barely knew.

"Thank God you're in," Susie exclaimed, "everyone one else seems to be out. Has your power and cell phone gone down?" Maria said that it had and invited Susie in. They sat and wondered what they ought to do, coming to the conclusion that it was safer to stay put for the time being. Susie assured Maria that she had food, bottled water and coke to drink and went back to her apartment after both had promised to let each other know if one of them decided to leave for any reason, should the blackout go on indefinitely.

We're stuffed, Maria reflected later as she anxiously tried to think of some way that she could link up with Jake. Her thoughts turned to Winston and how reluctant she had been to stock up on his advice. She'd laughed at herself for doing so, but now muttered that she would never doubt his intuition if she ever heard from him again. She considered this was a big if. She realised that she was already thinking of the withdrawal symptoms that she would feel from lack of her social media sites and zero contact with her numerous Facebook friends, as Winston would have predicted had he been there. She felt like an addicted smoker who 'would give anything for a fag.' Instead, she would give anything for a call, text or tweet.

She would have to think logically about this, as Winston would do in his obsessive, focussed way, and imagine potential scenarios in order to deal with them and survive another crisis by taking advantage of logical reasoning.

Involuntarily, she went to make a coffee, her usual practice when she had a problem to resolve only realising as she turned on the tap that there was no water and no power. She imagined that everyone in her neighbourhood had the same dilemma, and shuddered at the thought of thousands of workers who must be trapped in elevators on this working day if the outage was right across New York and how it would impact on the flu epidemic. Of course, she had no way of knowing that it was global and that such problems would be compounded in ultra-modern cities like Dubai with its complex escalators and sky lobby system in the Burj Khalifa at the cutting edge of technology in the tallest building in the world.

Sitting down without her coffee, Maria took a pen and notebook, and tried to prioritise a survival strategy should this crisis last several days, as did millions of city dwellers throughout the world, albeit with varying degrees of intuitive thinking. Thanks to Winston's weird premonition, she had stocked up with food and drink essentials. She couldn't cook her perishable food which would soon be inedible as the temperature in her fridge/freezer rose. Then suddenly she remembered an old fondue set that she had picked up at a flea market and had a couple of fondue parties ages ago, for fun. The little ceramic pot worked over a wick lit with methylated spirits. Elated she searched out the pot and burner and found that she still had more than two thirds of a bottle of meths.

She knew she needed to be disciplined about rationing herself just in case, but decided to boil enough of her bottled water for a cup of desperately desired coffee. Drinking the heavenly brew, Maria sat back down to the task of considering a survival strategy if needed. She decided to cook what she feasibly could, from her fridge, and eat that first. She jotted down 'rainwater', thinking that she could catch rainwater from the spout at the far end of her balcony when inevitably rain came. After all, it was New York.

Feeling an urge to go to the toilet, she realised that she couldn't flush nor wash her hands. Luckily she did have a stack of sanitised hand wipes, as she always carried a packet in her bag. Flushing the toilet was more of a challenge. She would have to try and collect as much water as she could from the spout when it rained, and hoped she could catch enough to flush out once a day at least. She wondered at the same time whether it would flush away if there was no power at the sewage station. The realities of a totally serviced system where one took everything, however small it seemed, for granted, were starting to really sink in.

Trying to imagine what the US Government would do if the emergency in New York had extended further into the States, Maria pondered that crises bring out both the best and worst in people. Being a historian, she remembered what had happened in the aftermath of Hurricane Katrina in New Orleans in 2005, the major earthquake in Haiti in 2010, and Super-typhoon Haiyan in the Philippines in 2013.

There had been riots and widespread looting, not only by the usual criminal element but also by people desperate to get food and water from stores and relief agencies. She imagined, quite correctly, even if the whole country was affected, that the US Government would have a back-up system to mobilise the National Guard and other agencies to protect food outlets from looters and, if the crisis was prolonged, to distribute essential rations to the population while they lasted.

The immediate worry was, not knowing what was going on, what had caused the outage, and who was affected. Maria could see nothing untoward from her balcony. Some of the fires still burned across the city and there was sporadic yelling but otherwise everything seemed eerily quiet. She decided that if nothing had changed by the morning and Jake had not returned, she would pick up Susie and venture down the six flights of stairs, go to the local stores and see what the food situation was and find out if anyone knew what was happening. If there is no power, petrol supplies are likely to be limited unless gas stations have emergency power generators, and there may be long delays in replenishing food outlets, she thought.

She laughed at herself, thinking how much Winston's pedantic attitudes and his compulsion to think way ahead of problems that might arise in the future, 'to be prepared for the worst', had rubbed off on her. She wouldn't have been amused if she had known the global extent of the problem she was experiencing and contemplating in a country that was relatively well organised to deal with national disasters. She could not even envisage the chaos that would erupt in less-disciplined societies with poor disaster planning, and in countries where rainfall was low, where most water supplies depended on complex pumping systems, or from desalination plants, or where sanitation was poor. However, she was reminded of her father's words about the modern world with inter-dependent technologies teetering on the edge of a cliff waiting for the first domino to fall.

56

As Maria sat on her balcony that evening with Susie, after they had
shared some of their perishable food to make a scanty meal, she
wondered what Jake was doing and if he'd try to get back to their
apartment. She knew that it was over ten miles to his College and
that he usually took the tube, and she thought that he might just stay
put too, until this was over. She and Susie made up their minds to
go down to investigate what was happening and visit the stores in
the morning. They had both agreed that it was safer to stay put for
the time being and when they ventured out they would go together.
They tried not to worry as they marvelled at the spectacular 'Great
Aurora' which painted the sky in pulsating intense colours normally
seen in much higher latitudes. The red colouration looks like blood
in the sky, Maria thought and wondered what primitive man, or even
remaining remote tribesman would think of it. A foreboding celestial
sign from Hell itself!

In the morning she and Susie, both wearing jackets and boots over
their jeans, masks covering their mouths and beanies on their heads,
tackled the stairs down to the street. Maria had decided that it would
be prudent to each carry something they could use as a weapon if
need be. She took a heavy torch but Susie had a tiny Derringer that
her father had given her when she came to New York: just to be on
the safe side, he'd said. Now as they climbed apprehensively down
they noticed that no-one else appeared from the other apartments,
but as they reached the bottom the Super put his head out his door
and greeted them.

"Mind if I ask where you're going?"

"As there's no power yet and we haven't heard anything, we thought
we'd come down to check out what's going on outside, and go to the
store to see what we can get," they both spoke over each other.

"Well you need to be careful; it's not too safe out there. Most
everything's come to a standstill except those intent on making

mischief. Give us a hoy when you get back so's I know you're OK."
They nodded their agreement and tentatively opened the outer door.
At first they couldn't see anything untoward but as they dared to go
further towards the shops they saw that windows had been smashed
and some shop fronts had been jemmied open. A number of furtive
looking youths were dotted around on both sides of the street and
when Maria and Susie arrived at the Supermarket they were shocked
to see that it had been emptied, probably from some panic buying,
but also from looting as shelves and windows were smashed and
graffitied, and the few packeted goods still there had been emptied
over the floor. It was surreal; neither of them could believe that this
had happened in what they had always thought of as a good and safe
neighbourhood, and in one night. Realising they wouldn't be stocking
up from any of these shops they made their way back to the comparative
safety of their apartment building, avoiding the eyes of the youths who
watched them. They stopped to talk to the Super who told them that
he had heard from some of the residents, who had come back to their
apartments during the night, that it was a pretty bad scene all over,
especially nearer to the centre of New York.

Meanwhile Jake was witness to the same looting and even bashings
near the College where he worked. He had holed up with some of his
colleagues in their faculty building and they'd raided the Canteen for
any food to keep them going. However, after three nights of sheer
frustration, he and two others who lived in close proximity to each
other decided to make the ten mile dash to home. They had watched
carefully to try to pin point the safest time to go, and had decided that
between four and six in the morning everything became quieter. They
took bottled water with them and jogged till they became tired, but
still kept a good walking pace until they were in familiar surroundings.
Once or twice they ducked into streets off the main route when they
encountered gangs of youths loitering with seeming menace. Jake
was the last of the three to reach home and it was with great relief
that he let himself in through the main door to the apartments. He

spoke briefly to the Super before wearily climbing the six flights of stairs to Maria, who greeted him with tears and a strangling hug.

The sanctity of their apartment saved them from witnessing the riots, shootings and lootings that took place in New York over the coming days as authorities inevitably lost control. Primeval self-preservational instincts were aroused in a frustrated population as food and water supplies dwindled in the panic, transport evaporated, buildings were airless, and uncollected filth began to line the streets. Hell was the correct term to describe the situation that unfolded, and the overall lack of fuel and transport meant there was no escape from the stricken cities.

57

In Scotland, Adam and Helga had been hiking since morning, only returning to Wick in the afternoon. Preoccupied with the progress of the flu pandemic, and being in a remote corner of the UK, they had not picked up on the airport closures and impending solar storm. When they arrived back, they found many of the locals in the street having animated discussions. They were told that, apparently 'out of the blue', all power had gone off and that computers, mobile phones and even landlines were currently out. Some residents had earlier seen some TV news about airport closures but ignored it as it didn't concern them. Others had heard solar flares mentioned. Adam went to buy some newspapers and had to pay cash because the EFTPOS machine was not working.

He and Helga went to their room and scanned the papers, which, as expected, were almost entirely about the flu pandemic which had resulted in the closure of cinemas, theatres and major sports grounds around the country, so other normal news was not forthcoming. They found the relevant article concerning media criticism of what was deemed the unnecessary closure of airports on the possibility that a solar storm might upset aircraft navigation.

"The solar storm must have hit at least the north of the UK," reasoned Adam. "Nothing else could knock out all communication systems as well as power; I wonder how widespread it is?"

"Without any way of getting information, I guess we'll just have to wait and see. How would a widespread event like a solar storm affect the pandemic?" queried Helga.

"I guess there would be negatives and positives," he replied. "Without thousands of flights a day, the spread of infection would slow, particularly if other transport was also affected. We don't know how widespread the effects of the storm have been but any communities, say for example in refugee camps or in drought-stricken countries, which are totally reliant on outside supplies, wouldn't get any foreign aid. If not already infected, they'll soon perish without support. If power outage is global and lasts for a significant period, hospitals will struggle to operate, and populations in cities at high latitudes or altitudes or currently in winter in the southern hemisphere will suffer most."

"So, it would be the ultimate test of the principle of survival of the fittest?" suggested Helga.

"Yes, the fittest, the best prepared, and the most resourceful," said Adam.

"The cities would become unbearable without services such as electricity and gas to heat and light them and the CBDs would become canyons of despair," he said theatrically, feeling a little faint, from the excitement of images conjured up in his semi-neurotic imagination. As events would unfold over the next few days and weeks, most of his logical predictions would come true.

The little café near the B & B where Helga and Adam were lodging managed to provide a basic meal by candlelight, which they felt was quite romantic with only the soft noises of insects to serenade them. Walking hand in hand back to the B & B, Adam asked Helga whether she might consider marrying him when they finally went back to London. He said that he would like her to be with him to face what he termed as the brave new world, echoing the sentiments of George Orwell in 1949. He said that after what they'd shared he needed her to share the rest of his life with him. Helga was stunned. Although she loved Adam and knew that he loved her in his way, she never dreamt that he would want to marry her and live a comparatively normal life. She was overwhelmed and kissing him passionately and near to tears, she told him she would always be with him.

When they sat down later on the oak bench outside their door, as dusk materialised, the night was lit up with bands of bright lights, dominantly of white, red and green, that danced like dervishes across the night sky. Adam sat bolt upright, recognising the flashing lights he had experienced for many years. Had they been a warning to him about his fate or were they a celestial sign that life on Earth was ending. A cacophony of sound arose in his head, followed by a cadenza that sounded like cannon fire. The coloured hues of the aurora danced before his eyes, with a sudden dazzling explosion of light. He fell over backwards to the ground and did not move. Helga quickly put him into the recovery position and felt his pulse, first in his wrist and then in the neck. There was no pulse. Frantically, she tried to resuscitate him using CPR and blowing air into his mouth but Adam was dead. Helga sat on the ground cradling his head and moaning softly as the tears ran down her face. She was devastated. The future she had planned with Adam in that brave new world was dashed in an instant. She would have to reconnect with the Brothers alone, and complete the mission that Adam had initiated.

She discovered later that Adam had had an anomalous form of cerebral aneurism. The local pathologist asked her if Adam had been hallucinating, and though she answered that she had noticed times when he seemed distracted, she realised that this among other signs of odd behaviour must have been a symptom of the aneurism, which caused his death by rupturing. This is no way diminished her belief that Adam had been guided by a greater power to save the Earth from annihilation from a growing voracious human population that were relentlessly destroying fauna and flora, and using resources, including water, in a non-sustainable way. Others could see her as fanatical, but she would always see herself as a courageous realist and a Green warrior who had lost her spiritual leader, but would fight on in his memory.

58

In St Mary's, Winston spent the Tuesday morning alternately pacing around and checking network news sites for information about the impending solar storm. His cellar was prepared so that he could shelter there when the storm arrived. He was unsure whether it would be safer there or not, but he and Laura had decided that as they had built the cellar for storage and emergencies, he would honour their agreement to shelter there in times of crisis should they arise. He had been too distracted to shave and to changes his clothes from the previous day.

As with Maria, the first sign of trouble was the flashing on his computer, followed by a blank screen. Checking his iPhone he found it non-operational, at least in terms of phone and email connections. He turned on the light switch. The lights came on for a few seconds and then went out. He checked his appliances. The power was definitely out. He immediately came to the conclusion that the solar storm had been severe, causing disruption of the Earth's geomagnetic field. He hesitated for a few moments and then descended into the cellar to light the Tilley lamp and wait it out for a few hours.

He had regrets that he had not invited Fiona and Kate to share his cottage and its safe haven, the cellar. However, he hardly knew them and though, besides the main bedroom there was a spare room with two beds, it might have seemed inappropriate if he'd asked them to stay the night. He debated what to do in the evening if everything appeared clear but decided it was probably safer for them to remain where they were. He didn't know what the after effects of a severe solar storm might be. He was only familiar with earthquakes where aftershocks were common immediately after a major quake. He knew from his reading that significant weakening of the geomagnetic field could deplete the ozone layer, causing rising temperatures and threats to human life. His thermometer indicated normal temperatures, but he was uncertain of the time scale of magnitude of change he should be detecting and decided to play it safe.

So it was late afternoon when he emerged, unshaven and dishevelled, from his cellar with his clothes rumpled from lying on a camp stretcher. He talked out loud to Laura, about perfect storms, premonitions and safe havens, wishing she was there to share his predicament. There was still no power, nor web or mobile phone access, and no-one stirring outside on land, sea or air as far as he could tell. Only the shrill cries of the ubiquitous seagulls pierced the quiet of the deserted shoreline. So, despite the fact that the temperature was still in the normal range, he made the decision to return to the cellar, make a snack sandwich and brew some coffee on the old primus stove before going to bed. He had no way of knowing how severe or widespread the effects of the solar storm really were and decided to assess the situation again in the morning. He turned off the Tilley lamp and lay down, using his reading torch to try and read. It wasn't long before his book fell from his fingers and he fell asleep. In doing so, he missed the spectacular aurora, even more vivid and widespread than that of 1859, and which others were viewing all over the world that night from the Arctic Circle to within 1000 km of the Equator.

Instead, he spent a fitful night disturbed by his thoughts as he subconsciously relived the events that had brought him to this time and place, with vague shadows of an unknown future should he survive.

59

Winston awoke with a start the next morning. He realised that he had slept for over 12 hours, an anomaly he put down to the high stress levels of the previous days. He looked out the window, noticing again how little activity there was outside, except for the seagulls standing expectantly along the beachfront or swooping with their distinctive shrill cries. The skies were still free of the sign of passing aircraft, the power was still off and the internet and phone service still down. There was absolutely no way to connect to the rest of the world to learn of the current situation with the pandemic or how widespread the effects of the solar storm were. St Mary's was now essentially an isolated, unserviced community that would need to pull together with a strategic plan to survive, even thrive, for an indefinite period until power and communications were restored and the flu pandemic had run its course.

Winston pondered that this was essentially a return to the days before the industrial revolution had led to the present version of civilisation in which technology pervaded every niche of modern society to the extent that survival skills had rapidly disappeared. Luckily there were some advantages to being at St Mary's as the islands had stocked up on non-perishable food due to the flu pandemic. However, with his historian's view of societal change through time, he felt that he might have a leadership role to play in what happened on the island over the next few days to weeks or months, whenever the current crisis was resolved. He decided to check on Fiona and Kate before going to the Town Hall to see what action would be taken initially if the situation continued. First he ate a breakfast of cereal and some of his normal milk. It would be long-life or powdered milk soon he thought unless there are dairy cows on the island.

Winston was ushered into the office of the CEO who looked frazzled to say the least. The Chairman of Council and the Chairman of Health were already seated and after beckoning Winston to take the

remaining seat, he told him that they were about to set up an Action
Committee. Based on the earlier experience, he considered Winston
an asset to the community and welcomed any suggestions. They all
agreed that they needed to plan for the long term as no-one had any
idea how long they would remain isolated. Knowing from experience
that five or six people were ideal to get things done with minimum of
debate and bickering, the CEO suggested that they have a Committee
of six, with himself as Chairman, Winston to represent the non-
residents, the medical officer, as a councillor, to act for the health
workers, the ferry Captain to represent the crew and company, the
Chairman of Council and a Police representative. To avoid discussion,
the full Council, at least the 13 of 21 Councillors in St Mary's would
meet to ratify, or otherwise, any actions suggested by the Action
Committee: essentially, similar to the parliamentary system of cabinet
and backbenchers. The CEO would get his son to ride his bike to the
relevant houses and the ferry, now alongside the dock, and inform
them of the agreed plan and ask the chosen Committee to meet that
afternoon. They would then formulate a proposal to put to the full
St Mary's Council who would be summoned to a meeting in the Old
Wesleyan Chapel the next day. Once immediate action was underway,
a boat would be sent to the other islands to inform Councillors there,
but fuel was deemed too precious for full meetings.

After lengthy discussion by the Committee, several priorities were
defined. First, everyone agreed that people needed to be active and feel
worthwhile. With normal Council activities limited by lack of power
and limited fuel, it was planned to have each group of Council workers,
who themselves made up nearly 10 percent of the inhabitants, oversee
essential tasks and activities such as rubbish collection and assistance
to the elderly. With the same principle applied, it was decided that
the Five Island School should be re-opened and any local teachers
asked to act in a supervisory capacity. Lunches would be provided to
all children to ensure they were nourished during the crisis. Winston
remembered his father telling him of such a scheme after World War

II. The island bus service would be used for transport while fuel stocks lasted. All perishable items such as meat were to be cooked and consumed as soon as possible. Residents would be asked to pool wood and charcoal supplies and Council workers would provide communal barbeques in the late afternoon for those unable to cook at home. The St Mary's Boatmen's Association would be asked to set up fishing crews for their charter boats, the Kingfisher and Sapphire, to provide fresh fish when the meat supply was exhausted. Using these boats or the two lifeboats at the lifeboat station, a stocktake of cattle, together with horses and ponies in case of extended crisis, would be made on all islands. The same would apply to fruit grown in gardens or orchards. Owners would be compensated by the Council once banking was restored. For the moment, sharing or bartering were the only options.

Once ratified by the Council with varying degrees of discussion and self-interest, the Committee sent out messengers on bikes to all households to invite them to a series of meetings in the Apollo Theatre which could squeeze in about a quarter of the adult population at a time. Updates of news and information would be posted at various points throughout St Mary's each morning and those with rowing boats would be enlisted to exchange information between the islands.

It was Fiona and Kate who pointed out to Winston that there was no entertainment now that TV and radio stations were off air, social media sites were closed down, and there was no power for DVD players or computers. They suggested that concerts could be arranged at the school or Apollo Theatre using anyone who played a non-electronic instrument, particularly if there were organised groups or even amateur bands. They could also have dramatic readings of popular books, and even charades for the children. Winston relayed this to the Committee who embraced the idea and asked the teachers, aides and volunteers to get on board. As the days went by, these became so popular that repeat sessions had to be organised in mid-afternoon and late-afternoon before it got dark, with only torches and candles to light the night. Fiona was a particular hit as she read her books with her melodious Scottish accent, making up different voices for the key characters. She and Kate also helped out the teachers with organisation of a drama group. The entertainment was often more amusing than professional, but no-one seemed to care.

At the end of the first ten days of isolation, the residents were rapidly becoming a community in the old-fashioned sense. It hadn't always been a united community, but the events of recent times had pulled them together out of necessity. Several of the older residents remarked that the uplifting spirit was like that at the end of World War II when Britons came together to rebuild their country so wounded from German bombing and rocket raids. Everyone was keen to join in communal activities and volunteer to help wherever required.

As a historian, Winston was incredibly interested in these social developments. The past was repeating itself he concluded. Triumph of the spirit and a strong sense of belonging often comes out of adversity.

"The modern generation in the western world have been protected from wars and real crises in general, which has led to attitudes of self-interest and lack of social responsibility" he said to the CEO at one of their meetings. "Perhaps the western world needed a catastrophe to change social values and community responsibility." The CEO nodded in agreement.

Winston was thrown closer to Fiona and Kate as the days rolled on, even getting involved in presenting potted histories of Devon, Cornwall and the Scilly Isles to children at the school who, surprisingly, knew little of the history of that part of Britain. He could see that Fiona was in her element, with parents seeking her advice and several children treating her like a second, rather amusing grandmother. Winston suspected that she had found her retirement niche to end her loneliness and be needed again. He strongly suspected that she would settle on the island after the crisis provided she could find permanent accommodation. Kate, on the other hand, was harder to read. She was far more radiant and animated than when he had first met her, and much less conservative in her limited traveller's wardrobe. Winston imagined that her eyes sparkled more brightly when she was with him, but she would change the subject if the conversation turned to more personal matters. She always gave him a hug and kissed his cheek when they parted, but so did Fiona, so there was nothing to read there. He wondered why he was looking for signs of affection at all. After all, they had just been thrown together by chance in an emergency situation. He tried to convince himself that he didn't find her attractive, but when he described her to himself he always used descriptors such as understated beauty, gorgeous bone structure, intelligent, companionable and sensitive, and all this with a great figure and curvaceous legs. I'm becoming hooked again he thought, but what are her inner feelings, if any, about me.

60

Over the next few days, radio hams on the island reported hearing snatches of conversations that suggested the pandemic was coming under control, at least in western countries. One of them was shocked to hear the phrase 'over two billion dead and still rising from a combination of the pandemic and chaos during the solar storm' in one of the intercepted messages. The death toll and the disposal of so many bodies was unthinkable.

Almost a month to the day that the solar storm had hit, the power came back on, but it was only for a short time. After a few hours offline, it resumed for a short period. The Committee decided that there must be rationing of available power in southwest England, suggesting that life was returning to some semblance of normality on the mainland. It was agreed that it was time to send the ferry back to Penzance to determine the situation and bring back supplies if possible. The ferry captain, restless from the extended stay on the island, was happy to sail at first light in the morning and, hopefully, return before nightfall as the GPS was non-functional and navigational aids potentially not reliable. However, he knew the waters well and assured the Committee that he would have no problems.

The next evening, he returned as promised with limited additional food, drink and fuel supplies. The Committee met him at the dock to discuss the situation. He reported that the pandemic had been brought under control in Western Europe, including the UK, but the situation was still unclear elsewhere in the world, although limited reports from North America and Australia were positive. There had been massive disruption to power supplies with many power generation plants suffering damage beyond repair, with limited back-up generators and limited power to produce more. It would be months to years before the situation was back to normal. The power failure had also closed petrol and diesel outlets that were unable to pump fuel except from emergency generators in some garages. Transport had been curtailed with massive food shortages, particularly in the larger cities.

"Devon and Cornwall, with their low population, numerous farms and fishing ports, got off very lightly," he reported, "that's why I managed to scrounge some supplies for St Mary's." He went on to explain that the company in Penzance had requested a resumption of ferry services to St Mary's now that the peak of the crisis had passed and there was still some Indian summer weather ahead to try to recoup some losses. The Committee had no hesitation but to agree as tourism was the main industry for the island, and all tourist services had lost money with no trade during the past weeks.

Winston, Fiona and Kate had a candle-light dinner that evening with a welcome bottle of French wine brought back by the ferry Captain.

"What will you do now, Fiona?" asked Winston.

"As if you haven't worked it out, young man," she replied with a smile. "I'm going to stay on and look for an apartment or cottage. I feel at home here. I know things will revert now the crisis is over but I still think I've got something to offer."

"And you, Kate?" Winston queried, as Fiona winked at him secretly. He somehow felt that this was one of those 'step in the long spiral staircase moments', a decision that could change the direction of life, and was surprised at the thought. After a pause, she answered:

"I've decided to stay on for a few extra days before going home to teach next Monday. I need to see what's been happening at school and what the Head needs us to do." She smiled, "these weeks have made me realise that there can be purpose in my life. I'd been wallowing in self-pity, but what's happened has put all that in perspective. I'm ready to resume my life and would like a few days to sort it out." Out of Kate's view, Fiona gave Winston a thumbs-up sign. You're a perceptive old bird, he thought as he replied to Kate, "That's great. I'm so pleased for you. Can I have the pleasure of some of your company and show you the historical delights of the islands before you go." She beamed at him and nodded. He thought he saw her eyes brighten with the hint of tears and a slight blush tinged her cheeks.

Like a flash in his mind, a vision of his future emerged from the turmoil of the immediate past and the chance encounter with Kate. It was his personal epiphany. I've also got to move on, he thought. This experience has shown me I've got leadership qualities and I want to make a difference in the new world that emerges from these catastrophes. I want to have my own children who can share my life and follow on afterwards. I can never replace the ultra-romantic love with Laura nor the intense sexual desire with Maria, but I've met a marvellous attractive woman who could be a wonderful companion and lover. I don't want to lose her now. He had a sense that the spirit of Laura was releasing him.

He decided not to rush headlong into anything. Kate might still feel the same way about Mark as he had felt about Laura during his failed relationship with Maria. He didn't want to experience the personal rejection that Maria must have felt, so he had to be sure that she was ready for a relationship and that it was a partnership with him. He was almost certain that this was a mutual attraction, guarded on both sides by emotional baggage. He decided to test the waters in the next few days, before she went back to the mainland, and find a suitable time to tell her how he felt about her – that he was falling in love with her – in a suitably romantic setting on the island. Then he would have to return to Exeter to check the situation at the University and also travel to Brighton to visit Laura's grave and check on the Wrights and see how they had fared during the 'Digital Apocalypse' as the media would dramatically term it, in the printed press, on screens when Television finally returned, and lastly on line, to describe the repercussions of the two concurrent crises.

Later, he, along with the rest of the world, would discover that large cities had been left with no power, no transport, no fuel and no communication as in the aftermath of a nuclear explosion. One journalist coined the same phrase as Adam, 'Canyons of Despair' to describe the long city streets in the shadow of skyscrapers and other tall buildings. The phrase echoed around the world. The solar storm arriving on the back of the flu pandemic had caused massive deprivation and loss of life particularly in modern cities, while smaller, more isolated communities coped better, with fewer deaths from the flu virus and a greater ability to deal with the lack of modern technology, electricity and communication, as in St Mary's.

Countries like New Zealand, which were isolated, with a relatively small population, abundant farm animals, orchards and vegetable crops, combined with massive resources of water in lakes and rainfall, long fish-abundant coastlines and natural thermal energy, survived the best. In contrast, cities like Dubai, with its large population in modern, high-rise serviced buildings with most of its food imported and 99 percent of water provided by desalination plants, suffered the most. Like their ancestors, their most precious resource was water, but essential supplies were now non-existent. Throughout most of the Middle East, only the abundance of hydrocarbon resources, for power generation to keep desalination plants operational, or dammed rivers, like the Nile, saved those living in an overpopulated desert from total disaster.

Winston would later think about this in historical terms, in that the ancient world understood the importance of sustainable natural water and food supplies. These, in fact, restricted the population of each of the Earth's habitable niches to sustainable levels before the onset of the technological age. The world population was then in equilibrium with the Earth, due to attrition of the weakest, and Nature was understood and given the respect it deserved. He reflected on how our ancestors thought in terms of seasons and solstices, not minutes to microseconds, and knew better than to build on fertile flood plains or storm-and tsunami-ravaged coastlines. Most modern crises, apart from the current extra-terrestrial one, arose from a combination of an unsustainably large population with a lack of understanding of Nature and past history, he would argue to himself, and it would reinforce his decision to try to make a difference in the world, not just teach historical social perspective to a handful of students. After all, the perceptive historian Winston Churchill had shown he was a man for crisis and the western world had long rued their decision to ignore his warnings about Stalin at the end of World War II when most others relaxed in the euphoria of victory.

However, for the moment, his priority was to find a non-confronting way to express his feelings to Kate without driving her away. The emotional rollercoaster of nervousness and expectation that he had felt when he first courted Laura had returned with a vengeance.

61

Four months after the virus epidemic had been contained in Britain, and the country was returning to some semblance of normality, Helga organised a meeting of *Vers Une Terra Verde*. She had asked a prominent Green to address the society on the implications of the recent virus epidemic and the effects of the solar storm for a Green Earth. This was originally just a front to get together with the Brothers without making their meeting too obvious, but the attendance was larger than ever before, with not enough seats to go around. The Green movement was obviously going to benefit from the crises, perhaps to her benefit. When the other attendees had left after drinks and nibbles and Helga had warmly thanked the guest speaker, she privately welcomed the Brothers, who had all survived the epidemic, and started by saying:

"As you all know, Adam died suddenly on the night of the aurora. It was probably an inherited genetic problem with an aneurism," she told them. "He would have been extremely proud of your dedication to the Brothers and the success of your collective missions. There's been a significant decrease in world population and, more importantly, as you heard from our speaker tonight, realisation of the extreme dangers of overpopulation, particularly in large cities where failure of services during emergencies such as we've just experienced, results in absolute chaos. Although there has been much written and discussed about the possibility of a new world pandemic, of possible major earthquakes and tsunamis along the tectonic plate faults, and even about solar activity and how it could affect the Earth, the world has been shamefully complacent."

Some of the group were not really proud of causing so many deaths and were relieved that news channels were mostly off air during the worst of the crisis. Talking about casualties was one thing, but seeing graphic images of suffering on TV was another. Some were consoled by the fact that a significant proportion of the deaths were attributed to lack of proper medical facilities in the west and no airborne relief supplies in drought or war-stricken parts of the developing world. However, others later suffered trauma similar to the stress disorders experienced by servicemen returning from active duty abroad.

Dermott O'Leary, being a garrulous Irishman, acted as a spokesman for the group when he asked Helga: "Some of us are extremely anxious that Adam's plot will be discovered by the authorities and we'll be apprehended in due course. I think we're all fearful that any knock on our doors could be the police or Special Branch to take us in pending an investigation. I've been through this before in Ireland, and not only is it stressful but there's always the danger of a careless word." Helga thought for a moment and then, speaking as persuasively as she could, she explained to the group that Adam, as the intelligent man he was, had always considered that the British, American and German consortium that ran the secret research facilities, and the governments that supported them, would have too much to lose to admit that a virus which had caused a global pandemic could have originated from their unmarked laboratories close to urban populations. He had always envisaged a cover-up and, although he might be implicated, he believed he would not face public prosecution with the inevitable media frenzy over the secret research.

"The fact that they've never admitted it's their virus shows he was right," she explained. "He was worried that you might be implicated if the authorities checked travel to airports where the virus could have originated, although he anticipated that travellers carrying the virus would disperse and it would be difficult to accurately define the source or sources."

"I presume the solar storm will help us there," Dermott interrupted. "With all computers going down, they'll have to rely on a paper trail to discover passenger movements and recover Customs records on the critical days. I suggest we all destroy any paper E-tickets or travel itineraries we have and, if there is any hint that we're being investigated, then we should burn our passports. We have been lucky that the storm has caused so much chaos as it will be difficult for authorities to find evidence at this stage."

"That's right," agreed Helga. "Even with the data, it would only be circumstantial evidence that could tie us to the virus, and Adam, the direct link, is now dead. I think you'll find that the whole affair will be hushed up to avoid media attention. We'll just have to keep going as we have been in the society in the past, and support the Green proposals I anticipate will now be put forward to legislate for regulations to keep the population and associated pollution to sensible and sustainable levels in the future. We've scored a big victory for future generations." My ancestors in Germany would be proud of me, she thought as she concluded, "A stronger and purer world."

The Brothers toasted Adam as a final respect, gave each other brotherly hugs, kissed Helga, and disbanded for the last time. As Helga had predicted, an investigation never came, but she had the feeling at times that they were under surveillance, and hence restricted the temptation to apply for a political position where she could better influence future global policy. She was convinced that, with her looks, she could snare a high Green official and become his partner if he was attractive to her and the situation arose at an appropriate time. She could influence events from her bed, she thought, and chuckled at the thought. Adam's legacy could live on through her.

62

It was now 2021, four years after the viral flu epidemic and solar storm crises. Britain as an island with a temperate climate, had been moderately affected compared to some other parts of the globe, and was now returning to its pre-crisis state, although damage to the power grid had been so extensive that some more remote regions still had power rationing. Although communication satellites orbiting the Earth were still fewer in number, fast communication, GPS navigation, and coverage of world events and global sports was being provided. The internet, while slow, was available, although people were more wary of only using digital storage for personnel files and the like. During the recovery phase, the communities had been too busy reconstructing the country and rebuilding their lives to concern themselves with trivial matters such as the anti-social behaviour or pregnancies of celebrities, although celebrity and sport magazines and social media sites were starting to proliferate again as life returned to the normality of the second decade of the 21st century, albeit with a twenty percent reduction in population.

A similar situation existed in North America. In New York, Maria had moved on from Jake. Once the internet went down, she found they had little in common, often sitting in silence with nothing to say to each other. Choosing a partner was far more than sexual attraction she learned from the experience. She had since taken up with a progressive Democrat Senator who had come to one of her lectures, was attracted to her as an animated intelligent and beautiful woman, and saw potential for her in his political world. She was now a member of the Phoenix Committee, named after the mythical bird associated with the Sun who obtained new life by rising from the ashes of its predecessor. The aptly named group represented a Senate Committee for Economic and Social Reform and Reconstruction following Disasters or SCESRRD, as it was named in Washington DC, a city that loved acronyms.

She had called Winston to re-establish contact, asking him if they could continue to collaborate professionally as she missed his intuitive and incisive input into her research. He had agreed, after discussions with Kate who threatened him not to take his relationship with Maria any further than joint publications. After all, she told him, half-jokingly, it's 'No Sex You're British' that rules as far as she's concerned."

In the Houses of Chambers of the Parliament in Westminster, newly-elected MP Winston Frobisher was about to stand up to give his maiden speech. At their new home, close to the University and the school where she had found a part-time position, Kate Frobisher sat on the sofa with three year old Laura and one year old Mark to proudly watch the event through the parliamentary broadcast on TV. She recalled that evening in St Mary's, at a picnic near the Giants Castle, when he had nervously revealed his feeling of love for her and how she'd sprung into his arms, crying and whispering, "Why did it take so long, Winston? I was so scared I would leave here and lose you forever." He hadn't answered because he knew in his heart that she understood the reason. After all, why hadn't she told him of her feelings, as he commented later. She laughed at the recollection and relived their small private wedding at St Mary's, followed by a communal party with their new-found friends afterwards. She remembered their joint agreement on naming of any children they had.

"The energy of the past flowing into the future," Winston had said at the time.

In Brighton, Jeremy and Penelope Wright also sat and watched the TV. Winston had insisted that they be 'adopted grandparents' of Laura and Mark as the children had none of their own. They welcomed Kate as a daughter and, as he had hoped, they still felt Laura lived on through the connection.

For his part, Winston had been rehearsing and re-rehearsing his speech nervously since arriving in the Chamber, mainly because it was crowded with other Members who wanted to hear from the man who had won his seat with a record majority. While he realised pragmatically that it might be a pipedream, his obsessive side understood that one needed a well-focussed vision to succeed against the odds. After all, did Winston Churchill have a real chance of halting Hitler at the English Channel? Did John Kennedy just dream of Americans on the moon and spaceships visiting Mars? Did Hilary and Tenzing stay in Base Camp looking up at the peaks of Everest?

To quell his nerves, Winston resorted to his usual method of retreat: recollection of the past.

63

After his momentous decision to stand for election and convince the relative Conservative authorities that he was a worthy candidate, Winston had used his knowledge of historical cycles, his recent experiences in St Mary's, and Kate's tempering wisdom to set out a draft platform for election that he thought would strike a chord with a population totally disillusioned with government and politicians generally. When he wrote it, he realised he was promoting democracy with a dash of benevolent dictatorship, but it had worked in Britain and elsewhere before, and China's rise to power was a result of the fusion of Beijing and Hong Kong ideologies, or so he thought. Someone had to fight the political correctness that stifled honest debate and allowed uninformed, but passionate, minority groups to bully weak governments who were too influenced by what was reported in the media. Australia between 2007 and 2016 was a classic example in his opinion, where the Greens, Independents, and minority parties had set the agenda and stifled economic progress.

He knew it was difficult, if not impossible, to achieve reform in a democratic society, although, against all odds, William Wilberforce had helped abolish slavery, and Emmeline Pankhurst had helped secure women's' rights, among many others who had been successful. The important thing, he felt was to have a clear vision of ultimate success and to be content if that vision was even partly realised.

When he was ready, he had shown his draft to Kate and sought her opinion. After clarification of some points, she'd said, "Winston, my love, this is all good, sensible stuff but it's too stiff and starchy.

You've written in a mixture of 'academic and lawyer speak'. I'm not sure that your potential constituents will warm to this. You have to have something that appeals to the human soul, not just their logical minds. Subjects like dealing with population growth are taboo and political suicide at this stage. You can only raise them once you have the power to influence them. We need some other opinions thrown into the mix." Winston was silent for a moment, as he had expected her to praise him and stroke his male ego with her enthusiasm. He resisted the temptation to defend himself, reluctantly agreeing with her point of view.

After some heated discussion, Kate got her way and they invited Fiona, as she had come over from St Mary's to do some shopping and was staying with them anyway, and also Caitlin Prescott, now a postgraduate student in her final year with Winston, for a discussion over dinner.

"It'll be great," Kate assured him. "Both Fiona and Caitlin are straight talkers and will provide you with clear perspectives from different generations of the voting public. You have to remember that once you make public your proposals, there will always be people who disagree with you and it's good for you to be prepared."

Of course with three women at the table, an impatient Winston had to wait until the social chatter had waned before he could raise his draft platform for discussion. Caitlin had first explained to Fiona that, unlike most British students who moved on from the university where they had completed their undergraduate degree to study elsewhere, she had stayed at Exeter both for family support and because of Winston's inspiration. Fiona in turn, brought them up to date with her fulfilling life on St Mary's, interrupting her narrative with anecdotes about Winston and Kate and how they weathered the solar storm and found each other. Caitlin stored all this away for future gossip with her friends.

After their meal Kate served coffee as they relaxed in comfortable chairs, and Winston was able to show them his draft platform. He gave them each a copy and asked them to peruse it.

"I want to put a modified version of this on my campaign website and on leaflets to distribute when I door knock," explained Winston.

"Well you'd better take along a comedian for a bit of comic relief" Fiona said in her usual blunt way. "This is all so long and starchy I could stand a skirt up in it." Kate smiled and gave Winston one of those 'told you so' looks.

"What do you suggest then?" asked Winston, slightly miffed.

"I'd stick to three or four main points" Fiona tapped her pen on her teeth, "Yes, people had lost faith in the Government before the crises, but they responded well under pressure. The Opposition ceased their nitpicking criticisms and supported sensible Government decisions. So, pick up on those positives, and suggest some reform of the democratic system based on these experiences that lends itself to co-operation rather than point scoring. Suggest that a multi-party group look for common ground rather than prescribing your view of change."

"I agree" said Caitlin, emboldened by Fiona's bluntness to speak her own mind. "You could follow on with your views about a government with the courage to put National interest above the opinions of international lobby groups with their own social and political agendas, which could lead to a more co-operative system of government." She went on "also after seeing the havoc wreaked by groups of youths in the aftermath of the solar storm, I think people are even more fearful of the potential for disasters induced by home-grown terrorists. So your idea of a multinational society with British ideals, to replace a multicultural society where loyalties to other countries have led to non-integration, with racial and religious tensions, would go down well if you explain the difference between the two similar sounding words. The ethnic mix in your Cornish constituency is more likely to accept this than in other parts of the UK. You also don't have to worry about time-wasting debates on climate change. With the advent of real crises, this has been well and truly put on the backburner."

"Very sensible comments" agreed Fiona. "I like you young Caitlin, and I can see why Winston talked about your potential when we were happily marooned on the Scilly Isles, which seems such a long time ago now. Speaking of that, I also think your perception of a more self-sufficient society with home-grown necessities of life and its own industries, and less reliance on imported goods, would go down well after the debacle when it was impossible to access staples both during and after the solar storm."

"I also like the concepts of boundaries in that society" piped up Caitlin. "As I grew up there were few boundaries at home and at school. It's only since I've studied with you Winston that you've shown me the importance of clearer boundaries in life and work and I've benefitted enormously from them."

"So, change in the parliamentary system, but without prescription, and emphasis on National interests and a multinational, more values-based society with clearer behavioural boundaries all gain a tick," summarised Winston. "What about a new department to take a holistic view of the interrelationship between drugs, drink, crime, suicide and crises in the medical system and what can plausibly be done to prevent, cure and deal with them, perhaps replacing the many committees set up already. And more education on the benefits and dangers of the digital world, and the employment issues posed by the increasing dominance of multinational companies?"

"I think these are important concepts which you can raise if and when you're elected" interjected Fiona. "I think the four main points are enough for a platform. Perhaps also look for one or two more local issues that will directly benefit your constituents. The others are potentially contentious issues. You'll inevitably have drinkers, drug takers, digital fanatics, and supermarket and service station workers among the voters whom you can ill afford to alienate at this stage." Kate refilled their coffee cups and offered a bowl of chocolates.

"Thanks so much for coming tonight and giving your candid views. I felt Winston's platform had to be simplified and what I call 'humanised', but couldn't quite see how. His concepts all seemed so worthwhile and logically arranged to me, but it needed your more objective analysis." She said realising that Winston would have to be let down gently if he were to take notice. "Maybe you could get some of your friends to volunteer to help us out with our door knock campaign Caitlin. It would help to have some bright and enthusiastic young people working with us."

"Kate's right' agreed Winston. "This has been most useful for me. I have to learn the difference between the focussed logical world of the academic and the real world with all its vagaries if I'm to succeed as a politician. I hope I can draw on your wisdom when I need to be 'humanised' again." He laughed and Kate was relieved. She had done the right thing and hoped a new platform, revised in everyday terms, would be written and used with success.

After saying their goodbyes, Winston had driven Caitlin home, and Fiona and Kate had a self-congratulatory drink before Fiona retired. As Winston later joined Kate in bed, he had whispered, "You're a marvel, you always know how to bring me round." Lovemaking had naturally ensued with Kate warning to keep it quiet, as Fiona was next door.

64

Winston woke from his reverie as he was introduced to speak in the debate on parliamentary reform. He stood up, cleared his throat, and began:

"Like my namesake Winston Churchill, I bring a historical perspective to this House. In a world where history is often measured in the length of time an issue is discussed by the media, and where most of our schoolchildren don't know who Churchill, Roosevelt, Hitler and Stalin were, let alone Drake, Nelson and the Duke of Wellington, we need to bring history back to the table. That history tells us that the western world, as it was before the recent world crises, was in a state of accelerating decay as measured by criteria that define the demise of the Egyptian, Greek, Roman, Ottoman and, yes, even the British, Empires.

To me, as a staunch Englishman with traditional values, social, moral and economic decline has spread like a cancer over the western world through monosyllabic, sex and violence-filled TV, films and digital games. Traditional British culture has been eroded, the nuclear family is disintegrating, the barbarians are returning, and our economy is suffering. It all comes back to good leadership and good regulation. Adults, like children need to clearly know the boundaries over which they should not step for fear of repercussions. If there is no respect for, and no fear of, the 'Law', then lawlessness emerges, excuses are found for the perpetrators, and the public lose their faith in the justice system. The same can be said for our political system where disunity, negativity and lack of clear direction also erode public confidence." He then went on to detail his platform of reforms, stressing the leadership role that politicians should take and summing up with: "The press have termed the crisis of 2017 the 'Digital Apocalypse', signifying that it was nearly a cataclysmic end to our world. However, I was reading Dan Brown's novel, *The Lost Symbol* last year, and in it his two ancient historians point out in several places that the Apocalypse in the Book of Revelations in the *Bible*, actually means 'to unveil' or 'to reveal' and may not signal the end of the world but rather the end of the world as we know it. It could be interpreted as the appearance of a coming age of enlightenment. I sincerely hope that this is what the 'Digital Apocalypse' represents and that I am part of the process that will bring it to Britain."

There was silence for several seconds as the Members assimilated this anomalously frank speech, bordering on the politically incorrect.

This was followed by a smattering of applause that gradually increased in volume as several of the older more progressive, middle-ground Members stood up, followed, like sheep, by others. Only the extremists from all sections of the political spectrum stayed seated, concerned at this message of reform. It was almost a standing ovation, but not quite.

At home, Kate was extremely proud of Winston and thanked providence that she had received this second chance at a rewarding life in partnership with him. Although her children would not understand, she pointed to Daddy on the TV screen and told them they should remember this moment for the rest of their lives.

In the Chamber, the Prime Minister leaned over to his Deputy and whispered, "We'll have to keep a close eye on that one. Compares himself to Churchill, turns an apocalypse to his own advantage, and wants to change the Westminster System. We'll have to watch our backs."

The comments were prophetic particularly since he was about to collaborate with Maria yet again. Born out of a celestial disaster, his political career was to become a stellar one. The politicians of the old guard might not like their boat rocked nor dogmas broken down by the truth, but it resonated with the thinking public. In the end, it would be their votes which would count and determine the real significance of the 'Digital Apocalypse', and influence the future history of their Nation. Would Britain become 'Great' once again? Only time would tell.

This largely depended on whether the human race survived, and even thrived, in the next millennium or whether they were doomed to extinction as previous high-order occupants of the planet had been throughout Earth history. It required politicians like Winston to come together and admit publicly that the problems on which the world was fixated, the increasing scale of famine, pollution, natural disasters, extinctions and territorial disputes and concern over anthropogenic climate change, all had a common higher-order cause:

a rapidly increasing global population. Adam had realised it and given the world breathing space to reflect and act before it was too late through drastic, but well-intentioned action. Similarly, the solar storm had demonstrated the vulnerability of a technological society to disaster if back-up systems were not in place for the ultimate threat, a gigantic solar storm and reversal of the Earth's magnetic field. Winston clearly understood these issues and could have a pivotal role in instigating world action if his voice was heard. He just had to be one of the brave leaders to break through the political-correctness barrier, speak the truth and influence others to follow to ensure that humans continued to thrive on the planet for the foreseeable future.

****

About the Author

Born in Brighton, England, David Groves was educated at Varndean Grammar School before migrating to Tasmania with his family. He studied Earth Science at the University of Tasmania where he gained First Class BSc Honours and PhD degrees.

David joined the University of Western Australia (UWA) as a Lecturer in Economic Geology progressing rapidly to Professor and Director of successive Government-funded research centres in economic geology. Throughout his career, he published approximately 500 scientific papers and book chapters, including Nature and Scientific American, and served on editorial panels of several international journals. He has been awarded numerous medals for his scientific writings, multinational student supervision and other career achievements, plus an Honorary DSc and Emeritus Professorship from UWA and Fellowship of the Australian Academy of Science.

In his post-academic life, David has become an industry consultant and provided courses and workshops to geologists and investors world-wide. He has recently commenced writing fiction, using his extensive global experience from international travel and strong interest in natural science and history. *The Digital Apocalypse* is his first commercially published novel.

Lightning Source UK Ltd.
Milton Keynes UK
UKOW04f1331110315

247689UK00001B/115/P

9 781925 138504